AN IDIOT GOES EAST

A Vietnam Memoir

CHRIS SNELL

CHAPTER ONE

"Dear Fuckface..." *Lacks eloquence.*

"Dear Marcus..." *Too eloquent.*

"You prick..." *Might be considered offensive.*

With his private school education paid for by his rich daddy, he may well have a planet-sized brain, but he has the common sense and charisma of a cabbage. Marcus was one of those clowns with a big floppy head of private-school hair and oversized eyebrows which begged the question 'How come Daddy can afford everything apart from some decent grooming for his son?'

I hated him and waited for the inevitable day he got fired for gross wankerism. At our last Christmas party, I got a bit drunk and told him exactly what I thought of him. I called him every name I could think of and demanded he remove the large stick from his arse he had acquired since his promotion to team leader. I suspected that his wife, who happened to be standing next to him at the time, agreed with me but I could see that he didn't appreciate it when I asked for her confirmation of my assessment. It was inevitable from that moment that my career would follow the trajectory of a North Korean missile.

The time had come for me to get out of this mind-numbingly dead-end job, and do something with my life. That time had unexpectedly arrived the previous evening. The A4-sized brown envelope laying on the doormat stood out like a tramp at a dinner party. I ripped it open and removed the contents, experiencing unexpected shock as I realised what it was. It was in response to an application I'd made to do charity work with an organisation called BAFCWA—the British Association For Charity Workers Abroad. I'd forgotten that I'd even applied.

What began as a ploy to attract a girl I've been fond of since my teenage years had now resulted in a six-week charity mission in Vietnam. I hated my job and needed something different, and this was it. My sole task for the day was to find a way to resign and get out quickly as they wanted me to complete the necessary paperwork by the end of the week and leave for Vietnam the week after.

It transpired that I'd been selected because of an illness in the current team, and they were inviting me to join a group of three other people for the six-week trip. We were to teach English and assist in other projects involving underprivileged children. Although unpaid, they provided flights, accommodation, breakfast and lunch, and I would be required to work about thirty-five hours a week. They wanted me to leave the following Thursday, which was only eight days away. I sat there on my stairs in utter shock with a million questions flooding my tiny mind, like 'where the bloody hell is Vietnam?'

Working abroad was something I was very keen on, mostly because I'd never left the UK before except for a week in Majorca with my parents when I was fifteen. I hadn't ever worked outside of London except for a milk round when I was eleven. As for charity work experience, my few attempts were shameful.

"Dear Shithead..." *Maybe a little rude.*

Six years, three months, nine days and three hours working every other weekend, with one hour to get drunk, or 'lunch' as it's more commonly known. The harsh reality of tending to brain-dead tossers who find their computers *such* a challenge. Helpdesk? Bollocks! I didn't want to help anyone. I wished ill upon all of them: not something as mundane as the flu but a brute of an uber-virulent tropical disease which would cause their cock and balls to shrivel up and fall off, preferably down their trouser leg at one of their wanky social functions. *"Careful where you tread darling, there appears to be someone's genitals on the floor."*

At twenty-five, the timing of this opportunity was perfect. I had arrived straight from College following a useless BTEC National Diploma in Computer Studies. That was another two and a half years of my life wasted.

"You pumpkin-faced melon head..."

"Twat..."

"Hello Helpdesk, Harry speaking," I said to the bound-to-be idiot who had interrupted my creative flow.

"My stupid, crappy computer has broken itself again. Get yourself around here now," said the consistently stupid Barney Rodgers, Head of Innovation. This fucker couldn't innovate his way out of a paper bag.

"Can you be more specific please, Mr Rodgers?" I forced through gritted teeth.

"My screen has gone black, and I can't get in. I go to a meeting, come back, and this piece of shit has broken again," he blasted.

"Have you tried pressing any key on the keyboard?"

"And how will that fix my screen?" he shouted. "Oh," he whimpered. "Now it's asking me for my password, what's that?"

"The password you use to log in." *You fuckwit.*

"I don't remember what that is," he shouted. "How am I supposed to remember all this shit? I need to use my computer now, or innovation grinds to a halt."

"I've reset it to 'welcome' for you, all lower case. Can you type that in?"

"How are you spelling that?" *How do these fuckers make it out of the house in the morning?*

"w-e-l-c-o-m-e," I spelt in disbelief.

"That's it. Well done," he replied, hanging up the phone. *Twat.* I knew I'd have him back on the phone when his screensaver comes on again.

"Pub," Trev whispered as he walked by, offering momentary respite from the struggles of writing a simple resignation letter.

Trev and I had always been the outcasts, which is probably why we got on so well. He's a bit of an ugly fucker and so northern that a compass would point straight at him. He's a little on the short side and has a face so twitchy that I'm convinced it burns more calories than the rest of his body combined. He has a love of poor man's sports cars and is the overly proud owner of an Audi TT. One night I drunkenly—and I thought, very cleverly—vandalised it, and he's been driving around in an Audi TwaT ever since. He's recently single having broken up with his long-term girlfriend, because, in his words, "I told her that her family was a bunch of fucking rednecks!" She was a bit of a minger anyway, so he's better off—just him and his TwaT.

We ran to the Builders Arms, a pub we'd found years prior where no one else would go. It's one of those back-alley shit holes that has somehow survived thousands of years, which is likely when it was last decorated. Thankfully for us it wasn't up to the standards of the pretentious City tosserati. They prefer posh places where there's no piss on the toilet floor.

Four pints, six games of pool, and an hour and a half later it was time to resign.

"Where have you two been?" shouted Manky Marcus. "You've been gone for two hours."

"I was with the Sales team. They had a few problems," I slurred. We knew that he'd never check because that would involve 'customer interaction'.

"OK, phone Gavin, he rang for you an hour ago."

"Marcus,

After six years, three months and nine days, I've decided the time has come for me to hang up my headset and get out of this shithole.

You've been shit to work for, and I hope you lose all your good looks and hair through a tropical disease. You're a crap boss, especially as I spend half of my time fixing your computer because you are a techno-retard like all of the other pricks in this place.

I know 'those pricks pay my wages', you tell me every day, but I feel my time here is up and I want to leave while we are still on good terms.

Thank you for all of those opportunities you never passed my way.

Yours Sincerely,

Harry Fisher

P.S. A haircut would help you look less like a twat."

"SEND" before I changed my mind.

Quarter to three, I was being escorted from the premises. The big brute of a security guard was kind enough to let me 'gather my belongings' before helping me to leave. He did, however, stop me from taking my collection of stationery consisting of one box of pens, six packets of Post-it notes, and four reams of copier paper. In hindsight, my biggest mistake was asking him to carry the paper.

My invitation for everyone to stage a mutiny and come to the pub fell on deaf ears, but a few of the guys agreed to meet me for drinks after they'd finished work. The security guard declined my invitation.

"Carling please," I asked the world's most miserable barman.

"Four-eighty," he asked of his newly unemployed customer.

When I'd decided to resign that morning, I hadn't planned on it being quite that sudden.

Two hours and four pints of Carling later, the boys began to drift in. Trev drew a big 'L' on my forehead in thick, black marker, but in the absence of any remaining common sense, I didn't care.

To say I got drunk would be an understatement but after what seemed like twice my body weight in lager, I couldn't walk, or in fact, stop myself from throwing up.

I woke up at home, which in itself was quite remarkable. Less remarkable was the fact I was in the hallway with my face pillowed by a pile of my own sick. The headache was on a whole new level with pain of such epic proportions that I wished I was dead. My suit was soaked through with a mixture of alcohol, sweat, piss, and vomit—most of it mine. Even in my confused state, I was quite aware that I'd shit myself. I threw my clothes into the bin and went up to bed. I somehow had to make it into London to accept the charity role that afternoon and needed to be somewhat presentable.

As my head hit the pillow, a waft of Dorothy in the Wizard of Oz came over me. My house had taken off and was spinning around in circles. So violently, that not a thing moved except for the contents of my stomach.

Had it all been a drunken dream? Was I, in fact, still employed? I couldn't remember. That was, of course, until I looked in the mirror. My bloodshot eyes, dishevelled hair and the enormous 'L' on my forehead all told me that it had been no dream and I was now unemployed.

Six painkillers and a small lake of water later, I fell back to sleep, hoping that my house would soon touch down on the yellow brick road. Maybe the Wizard could fix my head if the painkillers didn't. 'I hope the wicked witch isn't around', I thought as I drifted to oblivion.

The phone interrupted my candlelit dinner with the Tinman.

"Hurrrlllloooowww"

"Harry. Trev. How's the head?"

"Broken." I got up to look out of the window, desperately trying to find the yellow brick road. Even the wicked witch would have been a welcome sight. All I found was that I was back, safely in Kansas upon Thames.

"Shit! What time is it?" I asked the idiot tattooist. I'd forgotten all over again about having to visit BAFCWA.

"It's eleven o'clock you fool. Everyone is talking about what a twat you are."

"Don't make me feel worse. And this bloody 'L' won't come off you fucking idiot!" I whimpered. "What are they saying?"

"Well, your letter has become pretty famous. Marcus made sure of that," he laughed.

"Bastard!" The shame sent further pain through my head. "I've got to go. I've got an appointment I can't be late for. I'll call you tomorrow."

"Good luck loser," he shouted before slamming the phone down.

CHAPTER TWO

By eleven-forty-five I was sitting on the train into London to visit the BAFCWA offices. My head was pounding, and I was convinced my breath was flammable. My quick pass through the shower had done little to mask my tramp-like aroma, and the baseball cap I was forced to wear due to the stupid 'L' on my forehead made my head feel like it was going to explode.

I thought back to how I'd made this trip every day for years, travelling to and from my crappy helpdesk job. I enjoyed the train journey for the first time, noticing things I'd never seen before along the way. There were big houses where the posh folk live, crappy derelict houses where crimes probably took place, and the woodland areas that always look so out of place nowadays because of the country's pathological need to ruin grassland with new building developments.

The long walk along Moorgate towards the Barbican was surreal. I felt like I was in one of those commercials where everything else is sped up, except for the person advertising something. I was surrounded by stressed-out people rushing around, each with a more critical task than the next person.

"Hello, I'm here to see Mr King," I told the friendly-looking receptionist, who, judging by her name badge, was Karen.

"OK, Sir," she replied, with a warming smile. "And your name is?"

"Harry. Harry Fisher," I replied, feeling strangely nervous.

She picked up her phone, obviously reaching Mr King immediately and told him I was there. On replacing the handset, she asked me to go up to the third floor where he would be waiting for me.

I walked up the stairs, trying to imagine working in an office like this. It would be strange working in an organisation where your focus is on other people's poverty instead of your own financial rewards—being part of a project team whose goal is to change not only one life but a village, a community, or even a country. They were raising money to help others, not for themselves or for some rich bloke with squillions to gamble.

"Hello Mr Fisher," Rob King said with a smile as I reached the third floor.

He was a smart-looking man, late forties maybe, well-groomed and nicely dressed in a white shirt and chinos.

"Hello Mr King," I replied, smiling as we shook hands. "Please call me Harry."

"Only if you call me Rob," he replied. "I hope the wall looks worse than you."

"Sorry?"

"Your head," he replied, laughing and raising his eyebrows, "I *assume* you walked into something?"

"Oh, yes," I replied, somewhat embarrassed and realising the baseball cap was of no use, "I… fell over." I was sure he could smell the stale alcohol on my breath and the bullshit in my words. The copious amounts of mints I'd eaten had done nothing.

He led me into an office and invited me to sit down. It was quite a large office, but not the kind I was used to. There was a table in the corner with a kettle, and the usual equipment for making tea and coffee, pictures and maps on the walls, and chairs randomly placed around the room. There was no pretentiousness here, no table to divide boss from worker. It was laid out in a way that was conducive to relaxed conversation. Rob walked over and put the kettle on, as I wandered around the room gazing in awe at the maps of places I'd never even heard of.

When I'd finished with the maps, I started looking at the pictures. The first one had "Cambodia 1997" in the bottom right hand corner, and in the photo was between fifty and seventy young children surrounding five adults wearing Charity T-shirts. The beaming faces of the children, crowding around the five adults, trying to touch them or hold their hands, sent a shiver down my spine. I felt a little overwhelmed trying to imagine myself being one of that team.

"That's incredible," I said to no one in particular.

"Which picture is that?" Rob asked from somewhere behind me.

"This picture of the children," I replied turning around, "Cambodia 1997. I have never seen such beautiful smiles." I felt my voice take on a new soft tone as I said those last words—one I hadn't heard for a long time. I was utterly in awe.

"They are," he replied, smiling. "That will be the most rewarding part of your work in Vietnam, Harry. When a kid approaches you to say thank you, then gives you a smile that comes from the very depth of her or his heart. It will remain with you forever." I was ready to get on the plane, and that was from one picture.

"Tea or coffee?" Rob asked, as I studied the other pictures. It was touching my heart in a way I had never experienced.

"A coffee would be great," I replied, "milk and two sugars. Thanks."

"Congo, 1999." This picture showed about twenty older children, probably between twelve and fifteen, all seated in a low roofed hut smaller than the room I was stood in. They were rested on their knees, each holding a pad and pencil watching the tall blond guy at the chalkboard, which was resting on a cardboard box. The entire classroom was so small that it had fit into a single frame. Again, the one thing that blew me away was the expression on each of their faces—admiration for the man at the chalkboard, the man who was offering hope.

I walked away from the photographs thinking how significant every little thing we do can be if someone needs it. I'd always felt that I couldn't make a difference to someone else's life, but these pictures had proven that I was wrong. The charity workers in these pictures had clearly made an impact to the lives of the people they were there to help.

"So how are you feeling, Harry?" Rob asked as I wandered towards a chair.

"Strange," I replied, trying to gather my thoughts, "very strange. I've heard the expression 'a picture can tell a thousand words', but I've never actually seen a picture that can." He nodded. He had probably seen many people before me going through similar emotions. People who had also spent their lives craving money and walking past homeless people as if they were invisible. I vowed never to do that again, even if I only handed over a few pennies.

"I'd always thought that one person couldn't make a difference, but seems I was wrong," I said.

"So do you still want to go to Vietnam?" he asked. "Do you think you can make a difference?"

"Yes," I replied almost too enthusiastically. "I want to help others. I knew that before I walked in here, and those pictures have confirmed my thoughts."

"I understand how you are feeling, Harry," Rob replied. "Three years ago, I walked into this office as you have today. It's people like you and me who *will* make a difference because if those pictures hadn't affected you, then you aren't the right person for this type of work. That is why I invited you here. I wanted to make sure you saw the photographs. They separate the people who *want* to help and the people who *can*." I nodded as I tried to relax. It was a cruel test but a good one for both of us.

"And do you think I can?" I asked, wanting to know whether he believed in me.

"Definitely, yes," he replied with a comforting smile. "I can tell that you have the determination and, more importantly, a big heart. You will be a valuable asset to our Organisation." I felt myself smiling like one of the children in the pictures.

We spent the next hour discussing everything I needed to know. Rob giving me the details and me questioning everything like a child with a new toy. I gave him my passport, which I had to collect on Wednesday, and signed a bunch of forms that I didn't even bother to read.

I left the BAFCWA offices shortly after four o'clock with a renewed vigour, the alcohol poisoning of the previous evening an almost distant memory. I was so excited at the thought of doing something useful, and I finally knew where Vietnam was.

"Spare some change for a cup of tea, mate?"

"Nope. Nothing is spare until I'm dead," I chuckled as I walked past a scruffy little homeless man.

I cursed myself at the sudden realisation that I'd made a vow to be a better person just moments before, and I walked back to the dishevelled bastard to make amends.

"Sorry Mate, how much do you need?"

"A fiver," he replied.

"A fiver for a cup of tea? It's only fifty pence where I come from," I replied, trying to be civil.

"Well, give me fifty pence then," he snapped.

"No 'please'?" I asked the shabby fucker who had obviously been thrown out of Charm School.

"Piss off," he shouted.

"What?"

"Piss off you twat, stop wasting my time."

"I'm sorry," I said, feeling angry. "I offer you money and you tell me to piss off? Who the fuck do you think you are you scruffy, smelly fucker?"

The last part was definitely a mistake as suddenly I experienced momentary blindness coupled with a sharp shooting pain deep inside my head. From my new vantage point, which unfortunately was on my arse on the pavement, I watched my attacker slowly walk away as I tried to control the blood spurting from my nose. My first foray into the charity world had been a failure. I hoped the bastard never got another cup of tea.

I made my way back to the station getting looks from people that weren't too dissimilar to those the scruffy violent tramp likely gets. My shirt was covered in blood, and the pain around my throbbing nose was extreme. All I wanted to do was get home.

"Hi Mum, how are you?" I asked as she answered the phone. I always ended up calling my mother when I was in self-pity mode.

"I'm fine thanks, stranger," she replied in her customarily sarcastic manner. "How are you?"

"Good thanks," I replied. "How's Dad?"

"Still attached to his armchair, love, but he's got a pulse."

"Can I come over on Sunday?"

"Bloody hell, is it Christmas already?" Only your mother can put you on a guilt trip so efficiently and succinctly.

"Ha. Ha. Is that a yes then?"

"Of course it is. Do you want to eat here?" she asked, knowing full well that I'd never decline her God-given right to 'feed me up' because 'I'm not looking after myself'.

"That'd be nice," I replied.

"OK love. Well, I'd better go. I need to vacuum around your father."

"OK, see you Sunday."

"Are you free tomorrow night?" Nicola was the reason I'd applied for the charity gig, and I hadn't even told her my news yet.

"Hi Harry, how are you?" Her voice always gave me tingles.

"I'm great thanks, how are you?" I lied through the throbbing pain in my face.

"I'm great too. Yes, I'm free tomorrow night. What do you have in mind?"

"Dinner. You owe me a date!" Plus she was technically responsible for the state of my face.

"Owe you how?"

"I'll explain tomorrow night over dinner."

"OK, Harry, I look forward to it."

"I'll pick you up at quarter to eight." There'd always been a chemistry between Nicola and me, but I'd always thought she was a bit out of my league. I was so excited. It would be my first date in ages, and with a girl I already knew to be gorgeous, fun and extremely shagable.

When I arrived home, my first task was to book a restaurant. I wanted things to be perfect, so I consulted Yellow Pages—which in itself demonstrated that I'd been out of the game for too long.

"Hello, Archibald's." Archibald's sounded date-worthy, and was the first entry in the 'Restaurant' section.

"Hello, do you do romantic meals for two?"

"That's generally the recommend number for romance, Sir." *Everyone's a comedian.*

"Oh, yes, of course. Have you got a table? For two obviously. For tomorrow. Eight o'clock."

"Eight o'clock," he mused. "Yes, I can do that. OK, Sir, that's booked."

"Thanks," I replied. "Eight o'clock. Table for two," I confirmed.

"Yes, Sir. The romance part is an additional twenty-five pounds for a bottle of house white," he laughed. Cock.

I looked in the mirror, and despite the fading 'L' on my forehead, I now had the early shadows of two black eyes. I decided to call it a night and hope that a good night sleep would magically mend me by morning.

CHAPTER THREE

I woke on Saturday feeling refreshed but looking like my face had been run over by a tractor. The 'L' was still visible, and the swelling underneath my eyes complimented the swelling in the bridge of my nose. In short, I looked a mess.

I decided to forget about my broken nose, as there was nothing I could do about that. Besides, I might gain some sympathy because it was the result of my attempted charity efforts to a psycho tramp bastard. However, the 'L' on my forehead was there to remind me of my stupidity and my very original 'resignation'. It *had* to go.

Soap was failing to remove it and in my infinite wisdom my thoughts turned to bleach. Bleach removes everything. Whiter than white! It's all over the commercials on TV, so surely it would be the perfect way to remove black marker.

I found a soft cloth and poured a teeny-tiny drop of bleach onto it and began to rub. The bleach-impregnated material slowly burned through the top layer of skin, and then felt like it was burning through my entire head. *What a fucking idiot.*

I think the screaming could be heard in the next village, as I jumped around hoping the senseless bouncing would ease the pain. Every swear word ever created was used in an almost rhythmic fashion in time with my jumping.

"Medical Centre," said the aloof female in a terminally bored voice.

"I need to see a DOCTOR! It's an EMERGENCY!" I screamed. The burning sensation was making me feel weak and hysterical.

"If it's a genuine emergency, Sir, I suggest you call an ambulance."

"Well, it's not an emergency to the point where I can't bloody walk!" I shouted, "I poured bleach on my forehead, and rubbed…"

"You did *what*?" she interrupted laughing.

"Bitch!" I screeched as I hung up the phone, feeling like a complete arse.

Cold water. I stuck my head under a cold shower and watched small pieces of my skin disappear down the plughole. Then I recalled seeing Rocky Balboa having a black eye treated with a lump of steak so I ran down to the fridge.

I didn't have any steak, only a frozen chicken breast. After about ten minutes, the frozen breast was stuck to my forehead, and I tried to peel it away but couldn't. I was convinced I was going to pass out.

Three hours later, I left the hospital with a confirmed broken nose, epidermal and dermal scarring and a massive plaster on my forehead. I also had a defrosted chicken breast in a small bag which I would probably never use.

My visit had thoroughly entertained the doctors and nurses, one even comparing it to a previous incident when a man came in with a broom stuck up his arse from an apparent accident. I wasn't sure how you accidentally get a broom handle inserted into your arse, but I'm sure he would be equally unsure as to how you can get a chicken breast stuck to your forehead.

They had been reluctant to discharge me but provided me with tablets and sent me on my way. I had to take two pills three times a day, and they advised me to avoid hot water and chicken breasts.

It was three o'clock by the time I got home, and my date started in four and a half hours.

Deciding what to wear was the next challenge. I thought that maybe I should wear something funny to avert the attention away from my comedy face. Or perhaps I should go for the 'dress to kill' option. Although with my recent luck, I probably *would* kill someone.

I ran the bath and collected the usual hidden extras from their hiding places. A nice relaxing bath with aromatherapy oils would calm me down and put me in the right frame of mind for my hot date. Black Levis, smart yet casual, with my white linen Hugo Boss shirt. 'That'll make me look great,' I thought before I caught a glimpse of myself in the mirror. *Perhaps I should wear a bag over my head.*

I climbed slowly into the steaming aromatic tub. As the sweat started to run down my forehead, the burning sensation under my bandage was excruciating. I leapt from the bath, screaming the well-worn mantra: 'Bugger! Bugger! Bugger!'

Two gallons of cold water later, I climbed back into the bath, lay back and allowed the scented oils to relax me and wash away all my troubles. I floated off to my 'special place' where women love me, and men are envious.

"Bugger, shit, bugger," I shouted at my rubber duck. "What time is it?" My yellow companion couldn't help me as ducks don't have wrists to put watches on. I found my watch under the cucumber and mango facemask and it was only quarter past six. I had seventy-five minutes and relaxed.

I sat there in my tepid bath wearing half a face mask and what looked like a sanitary towel on my forehead as I chatted to my duck about how I was going to seduce Nicola. I exfoliated my body with what smelled and felt like a raspberry smoothie and then, very carefully, washed and conditioned my hair.

Quarter to seven: Forty-five minutes to get beautiful. I knew precisely how Mr Potato Head felt except he had the luxury of changing the bits he wasn't happy with. In the absence of an entire Frankenstein-type transplant, I was buggered.

Twenty past seven: Dressed to kill. Nerves shot. Deep breathing exercises a complete failure. ten minutes to spare. Everything was going to plan. I looked great, and I was even having a good hair day.

Quarter to eight: I knocked on the door after it won the 'Do I beep the horn or knock on the door' debate, and nervously waited for her to answer.

"No questions," were my first words to a shocked looking Nicola as she answered the door.

"What the bloody hell have you done now?" She kissed both cheeks, the only accessible flesh on my face while shaking her head in a resigned sort of way.

"You ready then?" I asked, not allowing her to get the better of my nerves.

"Would you like a drink before we leave?" she asked.

"Well, the table is booked in," I said, looking at my watch, "thirteen minutes, and with the seven-minute drive, that only leaves six minutes." She looked at me and smiled. "A drink would be lovely," I said, smiling. "Whatever you're having will be great." *Get a grip!*

"There you go," she said, handing me a glass of wine. "Cheers."

"Cheers Nicola." As I took a sip my entire face shrank as the sharpness of the dry, white acid touched my tongue. *What the fuck is this shite?*

"Is that alright?" she asked, laughing at my gurning.

"A cheeky little number." I couldn't hardly tell her it tasted worse than the bleach I'd drank that morning.

"Table for Harry," I told the young face at the reception desk.

"Oh yes, the romantic table for two," he smiled, making no effort to ignore my forehead handiwork by staring straight at it.

"So, Harry, what's the story with your face?"

"I'll tell you after a couple of glasses of wine. It's too embarrassing to talk about sober." I stood more chance of inventing something believable given a bit of time.

The meal was excellent except for a couple of predictable incidents: A stray lava-hot garlic mushroom had narrowly missed Nicola's face as I spat it out, and a spare rib rolling down my white shirt resulting in a loud 'BOLLOCKS!' Then there was the "you're so gorgeous, you make the stars look shit" line. The enigmatic, James Bond-like charm was eluding me.

"That was delicious," Nicola said as she swallowed her last mouthful. "Did you enjoy yours, messy boy?"

"It was nice. I just didn't expect I'd be taking so much of it home with me," I laughed.

"So," Nicola prompted, "what did you walk into?"

"A wall," I lied rather predictably.

"Bollocks."

"OK. You remember that charity thing you said I should sign up for?" It was time to finally tell Nicola my news and reveal why it's her fault that I'm damaged.

"Yes," she answered excitedly. "You got beaten up by the man that runs the charity for being such a ludicrous applicant and wasting his time?"

"What? No! And what the does that even mean?"

"The thought of you doing anything for anyone else is hilarious, Harry."

"What the bloody fuck?" This conversation wasn't going to plan. Nicola sat there laughing at herself and shaking her head at me. The cute way she used her napkin to wipe the tears from her eyes softened my heart a little, but I still wished the mushroom had hit her. "Well, I'm going to Vietnam next week with that same charity. I quit my job, and I leave on Thursday." Nicola's face froze. The whole restaurant seemed to go silent, or perhaps that was only in my head.

"Ha. Ha. You're such a bullshitter, Harry. You're a liability to even yourself."

"I'm serious." I thought this was going to be the smoothest story ever, and Nicola would find me irresistible and pounce on me. Instead, she sat there, taking the piss.

"And your face exploded with the idea of charity work?" she asked. "Oh, and this is why I owe you a date?" I think it was at this point the penny dropped. "Oh shit, you're serious."

"Yes, Nicola." Watching her overly expressive face switching between emotions was amusing.

"Oh shit. You're going to Vietnam? Wow! How? Fuck! Oops!"

"I am. And I know where it is." It was the oddest response. "What the fuck was all that about me being a ludicrous applicant?" This set her off into hysterics again, snorting and all.

"I thought you were joking. You'll be great, I think. I don't know. I've never thought about you doing something sensible." I wish I hadn't asked. "Dessert," she said excitedly as the waiter arrived at the perfect time.

"You have to be joking. I'm stuffed." I replied as I rubbed my barbeque-coated stomach a bit too theatrically.

"I am. A girl has to fill her dessert compartment."

"What the bloody hell is a dessert compartment?"

"You must know," she laughed, "there's always room for dessert." *Women are weird*! "I'll have the special please," she asked. She didn't even know what it was. Why are women so trusting? It isn't like wine where you can send it back if it's crap. "So, how did you go from getting offered a chance to do a charity mission to your face exploding?"

I told Nicola everything that happened since I found the letter on my doormat. I covered the unexpected and immediate departure from the helpdesk, the corresponding shitfacedness of the following few hours, including the dickhead drawing a 'L' on my head. I omitted the parts where I woke up in my own sick having shit myself. Nicola got great amusement by the fact that a scruffy homeless twat broke my nose, and that I'd even called him that given my entry into the world of charity.

"I wanted the 'L' gone before our date, so I tried to rub it off."

"You what? How hard were you rubbing it?"

"Well, I, kind of added bleach to the cloth."

She laughed so hard that the wine in her mouth came flying out of her nose, extinguishing the candle on the table.

"Bleach? You bloody idiot!" she spluttered as she managed to calm herself down. With her eyes still streaming, she said, "I like you, Harry, you're different." I wasn't quite sure how to take that comment but she did, at the very least, say she liked me. I decided against telling her that I subsequently stuck a chicken breast to my forehead and had to go to the emergency ward.

"This looks lovely," she exclaimed when dessert arrived. "You must try some," she said as she launched a spoonful of it straight at my mouth giving me no other option but to eat it.

"That was lovely. I'm so full now," she said as she finished the last mouthful.

"I'm not surprised," I replied, laughing. "You've eaten enough to feed a small village."

"Are you calling me fat?" she replied inquisitively.

"Of course I'm not, silly," I replied. "I am just amazed at how much you can eat and still be so skinny." I was in a hole but still digging like an idiot.

"I'm *not* skinny," replied the size ten. What was I thinking? Why the hell did I mention anything 'eating' related to a woman? I needed to stop digging and recover but couldn't quite put the shovel down. "It's great to see a girl eating as much as a man."

"What?" she gasped. Bollocks. I wish there was a wine invented that paralysed vocal cords.

"Bugger." I replied, not knowing how to get myself out of the this, "I just meant…"

"Harry, I'm joking. Relax, I don't care about my weight and I love my food."

"Phew! I hate skinny women, anyway. I like them to have a bit of meat on 'em."

"Shut up, Harry."

"Fuck!" I replied as my head fell into my hands. "It's the wine, it makes me say stupid things."

"No, Harry, you make you say stupid things."

"Are you having a coffee?" Nicola asked.

"I don't think so," I whispered. "Caffeine keeps me up all night."

"We'll have *two* coffees, please." Rats and drainpipes sprang to mind. How could she *possibly* be attracted to a man that had two black eyes, a sanitary towel on his forehead, spat his starter at her, is wearing half of his main course, told her she ate like a man and liked women 'with a bit of meat on them'?

"You want me to stay awake?" I said rather lamely.

"Of course," she replied. "I can't have my date falling asleep on me, can I?" The 'house romance' was starting to work. The drunken feeling, together with the somersaulting butterflies, were making me feel ill. I took deep breaths to try and control my nerves.

"It's only ten o'clock," I replied, laughing nervously. "I wouldn't fall asleep yet anyway." She looked at me and rolled her eyes. There was only one solution to my nerves and I necked my glass of wine.

"Thirsty?" Nicola gasped.

"No," I hesitated, hoping she hadn't seen that. "I wanted to catch up with you."

"Oh right, so now you're saying I drink too much?" I let it go. She picked up the wine bottle and emptied it into our glasses.

"Do you want another bottle?" I asked.

"No, let's have a drink at my house," she smiled.

"I'll get the bill," I said, like a fifteen-year-old with his first erection.

"Shall we finish the wine first?"

"Yes, of course. Sorry." *Very cool. Well played. Twat.*

We arrived back at Nicola's place, and she went to get us drinks. I started feeling a little ropey from the wine, the food and the nervous tension, and there was an imminent possibility that I would shit myself. *I knew I should have gone in the restaurant.*

"Nicola" I shouted, "where's the toilet?"

"It's up the stairs, straight in front of you," came the voice from the kitchen. "Mind your head on the way down, Mr Bump."

I ran up the stairs like a man possessed, locked the door behind me, wrestled my jeans to the floor and sat, just in time for the horrific explosion. It was so violent that I could feel the water splashing straight back up. *Had she heard? Was my arse now covered in shit water?* My stomach continued like Niagara Falls, with the odd sputter of 'air', so noisy, that my attempts to disguise it with a cough were futile. I was begging my bowels to stop, but they wouldn't. I had shit a week's worth of shit.

"Is that better?" she asked with a beaming 'I heard you' smile.

"I don't want to talk about it," I replied, embarrassed to the core.

"OK, Mr Bump," she laughed. All remnants of dignity were gone.

"I hate you," I said laughing, feeling sorry for myself.

"No you don't," she replied in her silly voice, still laughing at my pathetic misfortune.

"I think it's something I ate," I said in my wimpiest feel-sorry-for-me voice, hoping to gain some sympathy, and wondering if I smelled of shit.

"Should we call it a night?" she smiled. "Not that there's much left of it."

"I suppose we should," I answered rather unconvincingly, still hoping that the night would never end. "I'll make a move," I said getting up, conscious that the chair had an imprint of my arse on it.

"You can stay here if you like," she smiled. "I have a spare room."

"It's OK," I replied. I wasn't sure if the alcohol had rendered me useless, causing further potential for embarrassment.

"*Please* stay," she begged. "I'll make you breakfast in the morning. It's the least I can do after you treated me to such a wonderful evening." I thought about it for about two nanoseconds and decided that any amount of embarrassment would be worth the chance of seeing her naked.

"OK then," I smiled. "What time is breakfast?"

"Lunchtime," she laughed as she stood up, walking towards the stairs.

Upstairs and she showed me to my room. I walked in while she stood in the doorway waiting silently. For the first time in the many hours, I felt uncomfortable and didn't know what to do. Do I kiss her? Do I shake her hand and thank her for a wonderful evening? I decided I would kiss her on the cheek. I leant forward towards her, turning my face so she knew I was aiming for her cheek when at the last minute, she turned her face and kissed me on the lips.

A frisson of excitement came over me as our lips finally touched, and my whole body became a mass of goosebumps. We held the kiss, our lips touching lightly for a few seconds, but to my tingling body, it was more like a lifetime. I pulled away, my heart pounding. I took a deep breath as I opened my eyes. My eyelids felt heavy, but I managed a smile.

"Come," she said, taking me by the hand. *I'd hoped I hadn't!*

"Really?" I replied. The invitation was very tempting, but what remained of my good sense was wary.

"Yes Harry" she laughed.

"Okayyyy."

Her room was all too familiar. On the windowsill were pictures of her parents, who I knew so well. Perfume on the dressing table that I could smell anytime I closed my eyes. But closest to my heart was her bed. The bed I'd always tried to imagine being in with her. She placed her hands on my cheeks and planted a big kiss on my lips. I can't say it was quite as passionate as the first one, but it was still a nice, cheeky kiss.

"Thank you for a wonderful, perfect evening," she said. "I had an amazing time." Despite all the mishaps when I thought I'd ruined it, we'd laughed off each catastrophe. That was what made her so perfect. She genuinely liked me and was so laid back that she was able to appreciate the real me, even with the cockups.

"I wish you knew how much of a pleasure it was for me," I replied, looking into her mesmerising eyes. She kissed me again and disappeared.

I took the opportunity to get shag-ready. I undressed down to my boxer shorts and climbed under the covers. I lay there feeling quite tired but excited at the thought of Nicola coming back all sexied-up. The alcohol was wearing off and the heavy head had moved in, but I was ready for action.

She returned a few minutes later wearing a thick, fluffy dressing gown. *Shit. Maybe the sexy stuff is under the dressing gown.* She lifted the covers, raised her eyebrows and lay next to my near-naked body. I felt ridiculous.

We lay there motionless. Eventually, she made the first move, again, by moving her hand across the duvet to touch mine. As my heart started to pound, I rolled over towards her. We instinctively put our arms around each other and I felt the breath being squeezed out of my body.

I lay knowing my boxer shorts were a thin veil for the momentum building behind them, but knew that nothing was going to penetrate that damn dressing gown.

We awoke shortly after eleven o'clock, still tangled in each other's arms. I studied her perfect face with those divine ocean coloured eyes while she looked back at my sanitary towel-covered forehead and black eyes. I definitely had the better view.

Now and again, I would catch her looking at the mess my face was in and smiling. She of all people knew what I looked like undamaged and was still happy to be where she was. The previous night had been the turning point in our friendship, and my only regret was that I hadn't asked her out years earlier.

"Kiss me," she said softly. I was instantly in heaven as our mouths joined, our lips perfect together as we slowly kissed, holding each other like we would never let go. It was the most perfect kiss in the history of all kisses ever kissed in the world, except for the fact that I probably tasted like a dog.

"Shall we have some breakfast then?" she asked, just as I was beginning to think I might penetrate the dressing gown.

"That would be nice," I replied. "I'm starving." My stomach was well again, and my nerves had calmed. I was ready to eat.

Nicola gave me a T-shirt, which despite being ill-fitting, I put on with my jeans. She remained in her Fort Knox dressing gown and looked more radiant than ever. I put the kettle on, my need for a cup of tea overwhelming anything else. Meanwhile, Nicola produced the frying pan, bacon, eggs and an array of other things she intended to cook. Not only was she beautiful, perfect company and great fun, but she also liked a fried breakfast. Was she real? Was I going to wake up from this perfect dream? She was real and she was perfect to the point of three rashers of bacon, three sausages and two perfectly runny eggs. *Should I propose now?*

"This is a long shot, but would you like to come for dinner at my mum and dad's tonight?" I asked, expecting her to decline.

She laughed, "you only want me there to stop them shouting at you when you tell them about Vietnam."

"No, of course it isn't," I lied. "You know they've always been a big fan of you."

"Liar," she laughed. "I will come with you to stop your dad from beating you up."

CHAPTER FOUR

Nicola was excited to see my parents, partly because she hadn't seen them for a while but also because she was looking forward to the imminent drama.

"Hi Alice," she shouted at my mother as she threw her arms around her.

"How are you, Nicola?" my mother asked as they hugged.

"Great thanks," she replied as she kissed her on the cheek. I was conveniently hidden behind Nicola so my mother couldn't see my face.

"Hi, Mum," I said, kissing her cheek and giving her what must have seemed a rather perfunctory hug by comparison.

"What happened to your face?" she asked. "Why have you got that big thing on your forehead? And your nose?"

"I'll tell you later, Mum," I replied, knowing that if I didn't, Nicola would.

"Did you fall out of a moving car? Or out of a plane? You have to start taking care of yourself."

"Yes, Mum," I replied rolling my eyes at Nicola as she stood there smiling.

We walked through to the lounge and for the first time in as long as I can remember, my father stood up. Sadly, it was to welcome Nicola, but it was good to see that his legs still worked.

"Hi Dad,"

"Alright kid," came the usual response. "What have you done to your head?"

"It's nothing Dad, I had another accident. Nothing to worry about. Looks worse than it is," I replied.

"Nice to see you two have finally got it together." My mum smiled approvingly.

"About time you did something constructive with your life," my dad added, smiling at Nicola and winking. *Miserable bastard.*

My mum walked out of the room and was back in under three minutes with a tray full of tea and biscuits. How do they do it? It takes longer than three minutes to boil a kettle.

"I have some news that you're not going to like," I began, "but hear me out before you get upset, Mum, or shout, Dad," I said, in a futile attempt to bring some humour to the inevitable. This was enough to start my mum crying, which caused my dad to show his disapproval at 'upsetting my mother again'. I put my arm around my mum and continued. "I've been invited to go and work in Vietnam," I started.

"Viet-bloody-nam," my dad interjected, shocked out of his slippers.

"Please, Dad, let me finish," I asked sternly. I was determined to get through this before the inevitable onslaught. "I've been invited to go to Vietnam to work with a charity teaching underprivileged kids English for six weeks, and I'm very excited about it."

"And what about your job? What about your house?" my dad asked as if nothing else mattered. *I'd forgotten about the house.* "You're twenty-five. You should be taking your career seriously? Charity begins at home, and that hedge down the back could do with a trim."

"We've talked about all of that," Nicola cut in before I could, "and I know how much Harry wants to do this. If he doesn't come back after the six weeks, I will be over there dragging him back by the hair," she laughed, trying to take the tension out of the conversation.

"If that is what you want to do Son, then we will support you," my mother said in a quiet voice.

"I think you're bloody mad," my father offered rather unhelpfully, "but if you have to do it, then off you go, but be bloody careful." *Was he being polite because Nicola was there?*

"Thank you, Dad. Thanks, Mum," I said. "That means a lot to me." I meant it. Their support meant more to me than the going itself.

"Vietnam. The most pointless and tragic war. Thirty years they were at it for you know? First, the French, then the Americans. Terrible shame." *I knew I'd heard of it somewhere.*

"So, when do you leave?" my mum asked.

"Thursday morning," I replied.

"Oh!" she replied. The shock on her face was enough to stop any further tears.

"Bloody idiot," my dad said, withdrawing all his previous support. "Still ample time to trim that hedge."

"That's about the reaction I expected," I replied, smiling.

"Are we going to see you before you go, Love?" my mum asked.

"Of course," I replied, "it's ages away yet."

"I know, Son," she replied, looking a little happier. "How about you and Nicola come over for dinner one night next week?"

"That would be lovely," Nicola answered for both of us.

For the next hour, we told them about our date. Nicola took great pleasure in telling them, in detail, about all my little disasters, causing the three of them to laugh at my misfortunes. I told them how I felt when I'd received the letter, and my decision to resign from my job, obviously without the detail. They seemed to mostly settle with the idea, despite my dad banging on about that bloody hedge, and the fact he'd have to trim it himself.

"So, what happened to your face?" My dad wasn't going to let it go, so I continued with the lies, saying that I'd fallen into a hedge after my leaving drinks. There was little chance they believed me, but it was the most plausible explanation I could come up with at the time.

"Can I stay with you tonight?" Nicola asked as we got in the car.

"Abso-fucking-lootely!" My over-eagerness was pretty bloody obvious, and that made Nicola smile. I was extra happy because it was a school night, and she had one of those job things to go to on Monday.

When we arrived at my place, we went straight to bed. It was my turn to give Nicola a T-shirt, which she gladly accepted. She came back from the bathroom wearing only the T-shirt. Her long, sexy legs caused involuntary changes to the musculature formation that ordinarily hangs limp between my legs, like a stray sausage hanging out of a butcher's bag. *Margaret Thatcher, Margaret Thatcher.*

I woke up about six o'clock, and lay there looking at Nicola for the next few minutes, partly because she looked so beautiful, but also because I had to get her off my arm so I could piss! I was inching towards a full biological disaster that would not only cause extreme child-like embarrassment but also mean that I'd have to wash the sheets again. I slowly pulled the arm that was underneath her neck out until I only had the wrist part to go. So far, so good, she was still in the land of dreams. With my other hand, I gently supported her head and whipped the remainder of my arm out, feeling like an accomplished magician.

The scream was enough to deafen the people all down the street. I couldn't work out what had happened. Had she had a nightmare? Had my movement had woken her?

"What happened?"

"My bloody hair," she shouted. "You pulled my bloody hair."

"What?" I asked. "Oh my God!" I said, staring at the small clump of hair lodged in my watch strap. "I'm so sorry." I felt awful and could see the tears in her eyes.

"What the fuck?" she asked, rubbing the back of her head.

"I'm sorry," I replied, kissing her head repeatedly. "I am literally about to piss myself, and had to figure out a way to escape." The involuntary dance moves provided adequate evidence.

"Well that didn't bloody work did it, Houdini?"

"I'm *so* sorry," I continued to kiss her head. "Go back to sleep. It's only twenty-past six. I'll buy you a wig later." She whipped her arm around and caught me straight on my forehead. It was my turn to wake the neighbours.

"What the bloody hell did you do that for?" I roared in pain.

"Shit, I'm *so* sorry," she replied, not meaning a word of it. "It was an accident! It was meant to be playful. Anyway, who the fuck bleaches their forehead?" *That sympathy was short-lived!*

Now she was feeling bad. I lay back on the bed, making the most of the attention she was giving me. After a few minutes of apologies and more kisses, my bladder reminded me of what had started this bizarre sequence of events. I climbed off the bed, kissed her on the cheek and threw back the clump of hair I'd removed from my watchstrap.

"You're such a tosser," was all I heard as I ran into the bathroom.

Shortly after seven o'clock, I decided to take Nicola a cup of tea. I walked in the room where she was still fast asleep and sat down on the bed beside her. She looked so gorgeous that I didn't want to wake her, so I gently stroked her hair until she came around, and then kissed her on the forehead. She opened her eyes, looked up at me and smiled.

"I've made you a cup of tea," I said, feeling quite overwhelmed by her morning beauty. I couldn't remember the last time I saw something on my pillow that didn't make me want to burn it after they'd left—the pitfalls of being a less than selective drunk.

"Where have you been?" she asked, her voice quiet and soft.

"I went downstairs because I knew I wouldn't be able to get back to sleep," I told her.

"How's your head? When you didn't come back I thought I'd killed you."

"Clearly you were deeply concerned given you went back to sleep," I replied. "That's why I left you and went downstairs."

"I missed you," she said, as she moved her head over and placed it in my lap.

"Yeah right," I laughed. "You were fast asleep before I'd finished in the bathroom and then you thought I was dead?" She lay there in my lap, her eyes closed and a big smile. I closed my eyes and realised that in three days, I would be gone. This angel who had lit up my life since we met, was now in my bed, and I still hadn't seen her naked. *Amateur!*

"Trev, It's Harry." Nicola had left, and I was putting off getting my shit together.

"Fuck off, I'm busy. Some of us have a job."

"No, hang on," I interrupted. "I'm going to Vietnam for six weeks on Thursday."

"What?" he asked. "Is there another war on?"

"Haha, smart arse," I replied. "I'm going out there to teach English."

"You? English?" he laughed. "You can't speak it properly yourself."

"I know," I sniggered. "Ironic, isn't it, but that's where I'm going. Just wanted to see if you fancied a beer before I leave."

"I'm not one to say no to beer, and I need to take the piss out of this Vietnam bollocks some more." Supportive as always.

"Yeah right," I said. "Oh and I finally got Nicola into bed."

"So, you finally get it together with the her after a decade, and you're leaving the country. With your track record, she'll have fucked off with the milkman before you get back."

"Bastard!" I shouted. "Anyway, I don't have a milkman. I reckon she will wait for me until I get back."

"Never believe them Mate," he replied. "They're all deviants and philanderers."

"And that my dear friend is why you are single," I laughed. "I'll give you a call tomorrow."

Trev had never been very lucky with the girls. I put it down to the fact that he had a face like a cow's arse and the charm of what came out of it. He was a man's man and didn't bother with girls too much. He split with his childhood sweetheart after being together for over ten years and had never been the same since.

Early afternoon, I decided some manscaping was in order, as I had a genital area like Bob Marley's head. Manscaping was something I'd only ever read about, and I wanted to be sure it was neat and tidy before Nicola got near it. Presumptuous as fuck, but better than her feeling like she's running her hand around a monkey's back.

I carefully straddled the toilet and went to work with my electric shaver. The amount of hair that was dropping kept me entertained for a few minutes until I managed to nick my sack, causing it to bleed more than it should have. It didn't hurt too badly, and I knew I wouldn't bleed to death, so I stuck a little bit of toilet paper on it like I do when I cut myself shaving, and continued.

After about fifteen minutes, the toilet bowl looked like a barber's floor, but the jungle had been reduced to something that resembled a pitch on match day. I'd lost count of the number of pieces of toilet paper stuck to my balls and when I removed them it looked like a teenager's pimply face. *Fuck it, she won't notice.*

Nicola arrived back shortly after six and went straight to the shower. I'd prepared a Michelin Star dinner of chicken kiev and chips, courtesy of Tesco's freezer section.

"Harry, can you come upstairs for a minute?" *Fuck, had I left a load of stray hairs around the toilet?*

I got to the top of the stairs. "Where are you?" Her voice led me to my bedroom where she was standing, draped only in a towel. Her skin was still damp and glistened against the sunlight streaming through the windows. I was nervous that the throbbing erection would cause the manscaping scars to burst like a garden sprinkler.

I pulled her towards me. She made no effort to stop the towel from falling as I locked her into my arms and held her close. I could feel the water from her skin soak through my T-shirt, and I felt erotic excitement take over. I pulled her onto the bed and she fell on top of me, her naked body against mine, and we started to kiss.

Approximately four minutes and forty-seven seconds later, the deed was done! It wasn't quite the romantic encounter I'd imagined, being more like a biology lesson on premature ejaculation. Thankfully Nicola didn't make fun of my new personal best, or my yelling "Who's your Daddy?" at the most inappropriate moment. However, she was a little shocked when I told her that I was going to "huff and puff and blow her brains out!"

"Was it worth the wait?" She smiled as she rolled off.

"Abso-fucking-lootely" was the best response I had. "How about you?"

"It was… efficient," she laughed. *Fuck it.*

We spent another hour in bed fooling around with my prowess being a little less embarrassing the second and third time. She was so sexy, and despite visualising that moment for years, it was better than I'd ever imagined. And I'd finally seen her naked.

After mediocre sex and a re-heated chicken kiev and chips, Nicola had to get home for a nine o'clock call she had to attend. Or at least that's what she told me.

CHAPTER FIVE

"Alright tosser! When you off to war?" No mistaking who this was.

"Trev," I laughed. "It's more of a peacekeeping mission."

"When do you want to go for that good riddance beer, loser?" How could I possibly reject an offer like that?

"It'll have to be tonight or tomorrow night mate."

"Tomorrow. Where do you want to meet?"

"Three Horseshoes."

"OK Colonel Fisher," he giggled. "See you at eight."

I decided it was time to get my shit together. I made piles of T-shirts, shorts, trousers, long-sleeved tops and everything else I thought I was going to need. I made a list of what I needed to buy, which were added to the list of things I had to do before I left.

By the time I'd finished trying to organise myself, it was time to go to the doctors. What a depressing place. I sat there looking around at all the different *sick* people. There were mothers with their sick children and children with their sick mothers. There were no men apart from me. I was desperate for someone to ask me what I was there for, especially as the sanitary towel on my forehead should have inspired at least *some* curiosity. I thought how much fun it would be to tell a stranger my story, just to see if they believed anyone could be so stupid.

"Hello Doctor," I said, as I walked into his room and sat on the chair he pointed at.

"Mr Fisher," he replied in a stern doctor-type voice. "What can I do for you today?" I assumed that the giant-sized billboard on my forehead would have been enough of a clue.

"I had a small accident last week, which resulted in this," I joked and pointed at my head.

"I see. How did that happen?" I told him the story, laughing at the stupid bits and watching him for even the slightest reaction. Nothing. The man was a robot. I told him about the bleach burning, and the hospital bandaging me up and telling me to visit the surgery after a few days. He climbed out of his chair, making those struggling old-man noises, and told me to sit on the examination table. Slowly he began to take off the bandage. The pain was excruciating and felt as if the skin was going with the bandage. When it was all off, he looked over his glasses at what was left, while I sat there wondering why doctors always look *over* their glasses, when surely they would see a lot more *through* them.

"Yes, that looks OK," he decided. "I'll give you some cream. Apply it three times a day. There shouldn't be any long-term scarring." *Scarring?*

"How can I be scarred?"

"You did administer bleach to your own face, Mr Fisher." *Patronising—yet accurate—twat.*

"The bleach did cause some quite nasty blistering, but it looks like it will heal."

He sat back at his desk and wrote out a prescription, informing me that if I didn't apply the cream, I was in danger of infection. I was relieved that the silly bandage had been removed but dying to see what I looked like. There was no mirror in the surgery, and I wasn't sure how stupid I looked walking through the waiting room.

Very stupid. When I was back in my car and looked in the mirror, I realised my forehead looked as if it had a slice of Parma ham stuck to it. I could do nothing but laugh and that's all I did. My black eyes looked like bags from lack of sleep, the swelling had gone down on my nose, and all I was left with was a Parma ham forehead. I could live with that.

"Hello," I said to the young lad behind the counter in McKenzies Outdoors. "I need a rucksack for travelling."

"OK, Sir," he replied, sounding slightly over-eager. "What sort of thing were you after?"

"I don't know," I replied, not expecting any questions. "Just a rucksack."

"We have a range of rucksacks, ranging from the smaller model that has a twenty-five litre capacity, up to the largest which has an eighty-litre capacity."

"Oh," I replied, not having a clue how big either of them was. "I'm going to Vietnam for six weeks if that helps."

"Vietnam," he replied. "Lovely place. Are you going to Hanoi or Saigon? or Ho Chi Minh as they call it now." He knew more than I did, which wasn't difficult. I'd only heard of Hanoi from the Internet.

"Ho Chi Minh," I replied, impressed. "I'm going there to teach English for six weeks."

"Very commendable. You'll have a great time. I travelled around Vietnam en route from Cambodia to China."

"Wow! How long were you travelling for?"

"Only a year," he replied, seemingly disappointed. "Took a year out of University and travelled through South-East Asia and China."

"You lucky thing. How did you find Vietnam?" I asked, needing insight.

"I loved it," he replied, only too pleased to reminisce. "I spent two months there, starting off in the South and finishing in the North, before crossing the border into China. The people are lovely, non-assuming and very gentle. The main cities, Saigon and Hanoi, have seen poverty, but it's not overwhelming like Cambodia. I taught

English a couple of times in Nha Trang in Kim's Café, where you get free breakfast for teaching the kids for an hour. I've never met such lovely kids. They have smiles that light up the room."

"I can imagine." I thought back to the pictures on the wall at the BAFCWA offices.

"Anyway, let's see if we can find you a rucksack, shall we?" he said, walking towards the back of the shop. "When I travelled that year, I had an eighty-litre rucksack, but it was far too big, and you never wear half of what you take. I would recommend something smaller, especially as you sound as though you will be based in one place. There are plenty of places you can get laundry done in Saigon. How about something like this?" He pulled down a fifty-litre rucksack.

"Why do they come in litres?" I asked, laughing. "Do they expect you to carry water?"

"I'm not sure why," he replied, smiling. "It would be equally as useless if they gave you the space in square inches, wouldn't it?"

"I suppose so," I smiled, as I put my arm through the right shoulder strap, with my little friend helping me. When the rucksack was on my back, he made a few adjustments, and it felt comfortable but huge. Wearing the rucksack gave me a sense of nervous excitement and brought a big smile to my face. *I'm going to Vietnam! I'm bloody going to Vietnam!*

"When do you leave?" he inquired.

"Thursday," I replied, taking a deep breath to settle my nerves. "I can't wait."

"You like to leave things until the last minute," he smiled, helping me off with the rucksack. He pulled down another. This was a forty-litre backpack with a ten-litre removable daypack. It looked good and had the advantage of a bag I could use when I went on my weekend adventures.

"I only found out about it late last week," I laughed. "It's all a bit of a rush to organise everything. How much is this one?" I asked.

"One hundred and sixty pounds," he replied, "but worth every penny. It's waterproof, has a lifetime guarantee and is made from a three-hundred denier polyester material." *Sounds like the tights my mum wears.*

"Wow, that's bloody expensive," I replied, shocked that it was going to cost me that much to buy a large bag.

"It is, but at least you've got peace of mind that it's going to last for your entire trip. There could be nothing worse than being stuck in Vietnam with a ripped rucksack."

"OK," I replied, allowing my little friend to win his sale. "I'll take it."

"A good choice, mate," he replied, smiling. "Do you need anything else?"

"You tell me," I replied, laughing. "You've been there. What do you think?" I was utterly naïve as to what I needed and would probably end up buying a load of shit that I would never use if left to my own devices.

"Well, the one thing I wouldn't leave home without is a good pair of walking boots. I bought a cheap pair of boots before I went, and they broke within about three weeks. I spent the next three or four months buying useless pairs that kept falling apart." I was only going to take a couple of pairs of trainers. I never even considered walking boots.

"OK," I replied. "Which ones should I buy?"

"That all depends on what we have in stock and how much you want to spend."

"How much does a decent pair cost?" I enquired. "A pair that will last forever."

"At least eighty quid," he replied. This was proving to be a costly trip, and I hadn't even made it as far as the airport.

I tried on a few pairs, not knowing which ones were good and which ones weren't. The very last pair I tried on were the ones I *had* to buy. They were like strapping a pillow to each foot. Another one hundred and twenty quid gone.

"The sooner I get to Vietnam, the better," I laughed as I chose the miracle boots. "You're costing me a fortune." My personal shopper laughed, probably busy working out his commission. I was so excited that he could have sold me a whole lot more. "Anything else I need?"

"A travel plug, sun cream, mosquito repellent," he replied, "but I'm sure you've already thought of those things." I admired his optimism. He smiled and led me to shelves full of things all travellers should apparently have. Neck pillows, hidden money belts, travel adaptors, currency converters and a million other useless things that people probably don't need.

"I'm not very organised, am I?" I laughed. "What do I need then?"

"If you buy nothing else, buy mosquito repellent. Those little buggers are everywhere. The higher the percentage of DEET, the better the repellent," he replied, pointing at a bunch of bottles, "but also, the higher the price! Considering parts of Vietnam have a problem with Malaria, it's worth spending a few extra quid." Malaria sounded scary. I chose a moderately sized can at the bargain price of twenty quid.

"That's three hundred pounds please," he announced. Three hundred quid on a bag, a pair of boots and a can of stuff to stop flies eating me. This shit ain't cheap.

"Hi, I need some tablets for an upset stomach, please." I was in Boots to get the remaining stuff on my list.

"What seems to be the problem?" asked the young lady behind the counter.

"Nothing yet, but I'm going away for a while and want to take some tablets as a precaution." She walked away and returned with a box of twenty-four tablets.

"Take two of these after a loose bowel movement, and then one following each further bowel movement until the stool firms." If I started shitting stools, I'd need a carpenter not a tablet!

I bought two hundred pens and a load of cheap exercise books in the *shit shop.* Rob had mentioned that the poverty in Vietnam even went so far as pens and exercise books not being readily available in schools. He said that if the kids didn't have a pen and notepad of their own, they couldn't attend school. This fact alone shocked me. I spent forty quid in the shit shop—the equivalent of a good hangover—and now had enough stuff for a whole school.

I got home and took everything upstairs. I sorted all of my new things into their correct piles and laughed at how anal my packing was. Nevertheless, I had to do it right given I was going to be stuck in Vietnam for the next six weeks, and from what I'd seen of third world countries, they don't even have Starbucks.

"Alright soldier. Get us a Foster's," Trev said, looking as if he'd been dragged through a hedge. He was possibly the scruffiest man I had ever known, taking more pride in his sarcasm than his appearance. "What's going on with your forehead?" he asked, noticing the remaining scars from the 'L' that nearly cost me my good looks. I told him the whole story trying to apportion blame to him given he started all this shit with the marker pen, but he took no responsibility whatsoever, and questioned how the bleach was anything to do with him. Apparently it was a whiteboard marker he had 'borrowed' from work that should have washed off with soap.

"So, when does England get rid of your silly arse?"

"Thursday." He had the memory of a goldfish.

"I can't believe you're going there to teach English."

"It'll be fun. When I went to the offices of the charity I'll be working for, I saw lots of pictures of past missions, and they nearly left me in tears."

"You fucking tart."

"You'd be the same," I laughed. "I've never seen pictures like that before. They touched my heart!"

"Shut up, or I will punch you." I gave up.

By ten o'clock, the beer was flowing at a ridiculous rate, and the expletives per sentence ratio was increasing.

"So, Trev, when are you going to get yourself a woman?"

"Never, it's a trap. A moment on the lips, a lifetime on the bank balance," he replied.

"So, you're going to stay single and rely on porn to get you through life?"

"Yes. Porn doesn't argue, porn doesn't get angry for days at a time, and porn is only nine quid a month. Real women are walking versions of the chaos monkey theory."

"True, but porn doesn't do the washing and the ironing."

"No, but my mother does," he laughed. He didn't give a toss about what life threw at him, whereas I spent all my time worrying about what *could* happen tomorrow. I hoped that my trip would change that and make me more laid back. I had noticed a change in my attitude since leaving my job but wasn't sure if that was the novelty of being unemployed.

"Is there really no-one you're interested in?" I asked, not wanting to think of him getting old alone.

"Saucy Sarah."

"Who?" I asked, not having heard her name before.

"Thursday night. *Sauce and the City*. I'd marry her but not for her brains or personality."

We were kindly asked to leave just before midnight, the extra pint and double vodka red bull proving unnecessary. As we headed to the kebab shop, everything started to spin. Within seconds the contents of my stomach were once again spraying out through my mouth and nose, I was so drunk that I didn't even feel it coming. Trev stood a few metres away, offering helpful commentary like "twat" and "idiot" every few seconds as my stomach continued to evacuate onto the pavement.

I woke up on the floor in the hallway at six o'clock. My head was pounding, and bits of kebab were stuck to various parts of me. I sat up and laughed, causing my head to remind me that laughing with a hangover is strictly forbidden. I climbed to my feet and went into the kitchen to find some much-needed fluid. I drank two pints with a handful of painkillers and took another pint up to bed with me. The bed was a lot more comfortable than the hallway floor, and my stomach felt like I'd swallowed a waterbed.

"Hi, Harry." The phone woke me at ten o'clock.

"Nic?" It was all that would come out of my moisture-starved mouth.

"Good night, was it?"

"Was quiet," I lied. "How are you?"

"I'm not too bad," she answered. "I hope I didn't wake you last night."

"Huh?"

"I came over to surprise you, but you never made it further than the hallway, so I got dressed and came home," she laughed. "You looked cute laying there smelling of sick and covered in kebab."

"Fuck my life!" *How embarrassing.* "Why didn't you wake me up?"

"Because I was afraid you might kiss me."

I felt as if I was going to die, the flashbacks reminding me of the time I'd lost since leaving the pub. The memories weren't pleasant. Lots of vomiting, repeating of slurred sentences and kebab-related incidents, the drunkard's food that's awkward enough to eat sober, let alone shitfaced. I also had vague recollections of my head hitting the kebab shop counter.

I felt a little more human as I exited the shower. Luckily the kebab shop headbutting didn't cause any new bruising, not that any further marks would have made even the slightest difference. I had to accept that, for some unknown reason, my forehead and I didn't get along. I hoped that alcohol was illegal in Vietnam—my body, my liver and especially my forehead could do with a break.

"Hi. Rob King, please," I said when a polite voice answered the phone. I was dressing when I remembered that I had to collect my passport.

"Hold on, I'll see if he is around." I was put on hold and made to listen to some music that resembled a crap mobile phone ringtone. *Who comes up with that nonsense?*

"Hi, Rob speaking," came the familiar voice.

"Hi Rob, it's Harry."

"Hi Harry, I was expecting to hear from you. Your passport is ready if you want to come and collect it?"

"Great, I'll be there in about an hour and a half," I replied.

"Excellent. I'll be here. There are a few more things I need to go over with you."

That worried me. I'd put Trev down as one of my references and prayed to all the Gods he hadn't contacted him.

"OK, I'll see you soon."

"I look forward to it, Harry. See you later."

Everything was starting to seem like it was actually going to happen. I'd spent the last few days feeling quite cynical and expecting something to go wrong. I arrived at the BAFCWA reception desk and threw in a load of chewing gum to mask the alcohol fumes.

"Hello Mr Fisher," she said with a smile.

"Hi Karen," I said, being over-familiar but assuming that's what her name badge was for.

"Rob is expecting you. Make your way up to the third floor, and I'll have him meet you."

"Thanks," I said with an excited smile as I made my way to the stairs.

"Hi, Harry," Rob greeted me. "Nice to see you again. How are you?"

"I'm great thank you, Rob. A little nervous," I replied. "How are you?"

"Never better thanks. I understand your nerves, you'll be fine. That's all part of the fun." That was one way to put it. We walked into his office, and Rob flicked the kettle on. "Coffee, white, two sugars, wasn't it?" he inquired. "You smell like you need one." *What is the point of chewing gum if it doesn't cover up the smell of booze?*

"You've got a good memory. And yes, I had a few drinks with a friend of mine last night, he wanted to give me a good send-off," I replied, slightly embarrassed.

He smiled. "There's your passport and some other things for you." He pointed to a pile on the table. "The most important is the curriculum we suggest our volunteers follow. Have a quick look through it and let me know if you have any questions." I walked over to the pile which contained a big lever arch file and an envelope containing my passport and the flight tickets. I picked up the folder and began flicking through it. I guessed it was going to be basic, but didn't realise I'd be starting with "Hello," "Goodbye," "Please" and "Thank You." I worked my way through the curriculum, only pausing to drink my coffee and chat to Rob.

Within half an hour, I had gone through it and unleashed a thousand questions at Rob. Rob took all the questions in his stride and never once seemed bothered by any of them.

"There are also some *lovely* T-shirts we provide you with," he said, smiling. "It's up to you whether or not you wear them, but it's nice to have everyone in a Charity shirt for the pictures." He handed me five T-shirts, which inside their packets, looked okay but from the way Rob handed them over, I guessed they weren't. I stood up and looked at the Cambodia picture that had caught my attention during my first visit. There they were, wearing the very same T-shirts. *That'll be me soon.*

I left the offices shortly after two o'clock and made my way home feeling exhilarated. In less than twenty-four hours I would be on my way to Vietnam! I still had to finish my packing, have dinner with my parents, and ensure Nicola got some less embarrassing Harry-loving.

"Hi, Mum."

"Hi, love. How are you?"

"I'm fine thanks, how are you both?"

"Oh, you know us, love, nothing changes here." We compromised on an eight o'clock dinner, my mum starting the bidding early and me bidding late, as near to my father's bedtime as possible. I was already dreading having to say goodbye to them, my mum more than my dad because he would just wave. In contrast, there was always guaranteed snot and tears from my mum.

"How are you getting to the airport Love?" she asked. *Bugger. I'd not even thought of that.*

"Taxi." I lied.

"Oh, you should have said. Your father and I could have come to see you off." This was never an option. I couldn't stand the thought of my mum standing there crying as I legged it through to departures.

"A cab is easier, and I've got to leave quite early, but thanks for the offer. So, I'll see you about eight then, Mum."

"Try not to be late this time Love. I want to spend as much time with you as I can before you leave." The phone went dead as she probably went straight for the Kleenex.

"Alright, Trev?" I had to ring him to lighten my mood.

"Alright, Chunder. How's the head?"

"It wasn't good at six o'clock when I woke up on the hallway floor." That sent the giggling idiot off again. "Anyway, I phoned to thank you for a good night. It was a laugh."

"*You* were a laugh, especially when you head butted the kebab shop counter." He carried on laughing, awaiting my response.

"I hadn't eaten all day." I felt the need to defend myself, although I knew it would only make him worse.

"That's a tart's excuse, and you know it," he replied.

"Anyway, sod off now, I've got stuff to do. Take care of yourself, mate. I think my email will work over there," I said, knowing I wouldn't hear from him.

"Have a good trip, mate. Fight them in the trenches and all that."

"See you soon." I laughed as I hung up the phone.

I rang the local taxi company and booked a car for half past seven in the morning. I'd be at Heathrow in plenty of time for the suggested quarter past eight check-in. Another thirty quid but I didn't care. I was at the point now where I was so excited that nothing else mattered.

I made one final check that everything was in order and ready for tomorrow. It was all neatly packed into my shiny new backpack. The jeans I'd been wearing all day and would wear for the journey were laid neatly on the bed next to my free T-shirt ready for me to jump straight into in the morning.

I put on the jeans I'd worn for my date with Nicola and used a cloth to remove the small remnant of barbeque sauce. I had little option other than the student look as everything was packed into the rucksack. I had never felt this nervous before, but I think most of those nerves could be attributed to having to face my parents later, specifically my mother.

At half past seven I couldn't delay any longer, and I didn't want to be late in case dinner got cremated again in those extra few minutes. I took a deep breath to control my nerves as I walked out the front door and drove to collect Nicola.

Nicola wasn't long home from work, and she looked super sexy in her black suit and heels. She walked with the usual spring in her step, radiating the sunshine that had attracted me to her all those years prior. I felt like ditching my dinner plans and taking her back to my place for another demonstration of my sexual inadequacy.

"Hiya," I said as my mum opened the door. I tried to pretend nothing was happening hoping she'd forget.

"Hello, Love," she replied as she kissed me on the cheek. Nicola literally launched herself at my mum which lightened the atmosphere.

"Hi Dad," I said as I walked into the front room, knowing where to find him.

"Alright, Kid," he replied, even managing to briefly look away from the television. As usual, he made a beeline for Nicola, pushing past me to get to her. "You got that thing off your head then?"

"Yeah, went to the doctor's Monday."

"That'll teach you, won't it?" I wondered how long it would take him.

"Probably not," I smiled. "I'm sure I'll do something equally as stupid again at some point."

"True." He almost broke a smile.

"You all packed, Love?" my mum asked, as she handed me the tray with that night's delight. Shepherd's Pie. My favourite.

"This looks lovely Mum, thanks. Yep, I'm all packed and ready to go. Taxi is picking me up at half past seven in the morning, check-in at quarter past eight, and in the air by quarter past ten."

"Taxi? Bloody waste of money. Your Mother could've dropped you," my dad said in his usual heart-touching way.

When I'd demolished dinner, my mum told me to go and get some more from the kitchen because 'there was plenty'. She probably didn't think I was going to eat for the next six weeks so planned on feeding me enough to last until I returned.

It was about eleven o'clock when my dad decided he'd had enough. He was a creature of habit, always rising at six o'clock and going to bed at eleven o'clock. You could set your watch by him. It was when he stood up from his chair that I realised the time had come.

"You take care of yourself, Kid," he said as he walked towards me. He held out his arms and put them around me for the first time I could remember. "Come back safe," he said as released the hug. I pulled him back, letting him know he wasn't getting away that easily. I fought back the tears as he said, "Love ya Kid," the words I could never recall my father saying to me, words I'd craved all my life. That acceptance meant the world to me, and as I released him, he walked away without looking back.

"See, you've upset my mother now!" I called out using his ever-familiar words. This brought a smile to our faces as my mum stood up and put her arms around me. We both held and savoured the moment, as even though the weeks would pass quickly, it was still a long time for us to be apart. We held each other for what seemed like eternity until we both accepted it was time for me to leave.

"I'll see you soon, OK?" I said to my mum as I walked towards the door, "I'll send you a postcard."

"OK Love, take care, we'll see you soon." She kissed me on the cheek and closed the door behind me. I immediately felt a massive weight lift from my shoulders but was also still in shock at my father's reaction. That was an evening I won't forget, and the sadness turned to euphoria as we sped back to my house for the main event.

We arrived back shortly after eleven-thirty and went straight to bed. My visuals had been on overdrive all evening, and I couldn't wait to get Nicola's naked again.

Not to brag, but forty-seven minutes wasn't my worst sober performance ever. The fact that forty-three of those were foreplay is inconsequential, and apparently enjoyable. Nicola had no complaints when I asked for feedback on my performance, which with hindsight is a pretty uncool thing to do.

Nicola left at about half past six with a kiss and a "see you later" as she literally ran out the door. It was a great relief to have said the last of my goodbyes, and Nicola's expedient departure was precisely how we both wanted it to be.

CHAPTER SIX

A nineteen-eighties shit heap pulled up outside at twenty past seven giving me ten minutes just to make sure, for the twelve millionth time that I had everything, and that everything was switched off.

The taxi driver took my rucksack and threw it into the boot as I once again checked that I had everything: passport, tickets, curriculum, clothes. I climbed into the car and prayed that this clapped out old banger would make the twenty-odd miles to the airport. He probably wished he'd never asked, "So where are you off to then?" He didn't interrupt until I'd been talking for about fifteen minutes. "I meant which terminal?"

"Oh, sorry. Terminal One please," I replied sheepishly. At two quid a mile, he probably didn't give a shit.

We arrived at Terminal One at eight o'clock, the roads being clear, and the car, surprisingly, not having broken down. The drivers behind us wouldn't have seen much due to the black cloud that enveloped the three carriageways every time he went near the accelerator. My rucksack was thrown at the pavement, and he left another black cloud as he accelerated away.

I stood outside the terminal with plenty of time to kill and lit a cigarette. I'd never been to Heathrow or in fact any other airport since flying out of Gatwick as a kid. What a crazy place. Families happy to be off on holiday with about forty suitcases each, and people in suits wearing their customary weekday frowns, probably there to catch commuter planes for their next business deal. Taxis, buses and cars pulling up all over the place to unload passengers who were all going to get on that strange thing that doesn't belong in the air.

After my fourth cigarette, and enough time to convince myself that I didn't have a phobia of flying, I entered the terminal. After much deliberation of how the whole thing works, I joined the check-in queue with another five-hundred passengers. I couldn't fathom how all of these people were going to fit on my plane. I'd seen planes before but never one big enough to house a small nation.

I eventually reached the check-in desk and the interrogation began.

"How many bags do you have?"

"Two."

"And how many are you checking in?"

"One."

"Did you pack the bags yourself?" How old did she think I was?

"I'm twenty-five. I did it all by myself," I smiled, feeling bizarrely proud. Not even a lip movement from po-faced Valerie.

"Do you have any sharp objects: razors, scissors, knives, in your hand luggage?" Did I look like a hairdresser?

"No." She played about with my tickets for a while, sticking something sticky onto it, and then sticking something of equal stickiness onto my rucksack as it disappeared onto a conveyer belt.

"OK, seat number 45K. The flight will be boarding at twenty to ten from gate sixty-nine." My incessant immaturity forced a smile that made Valerie almost roll her eyes. No wonder she thought my mother packed my bags.

"Thank you," I smiled as she handed me my passport and boarding card.

I walked over to the Departures area where someone else checked my passport and then joined another long queue where people put their bags into a tunnel. I wasn't sure what they were looking for, but it was probably something to do with hairdressing equipment. I hadn't been able to keep abreast of current affairs recently, but perhaps the latest terrorist groups are recruiting barbers. The fella that did my hair was pretty handy with a razor, so you never know.

After another ten minutes, I was emptying my pockets into a small basket and loading my bag onto the conveyor belt. The metal detector predictably went off as I walked through it, and I had to stand with my arms in the air like a scarecrow for another miserable bastard to scan me with a circle on a stick.

"Can you remove your shoes please, Sir." *Barefoot on a plane? How will they know where to send my boots? What if I stand in someone's piss?* I removed my brand-new boots which he examined. It was when I saw the state of his shoes that the penny dropped. *He's poor.*

"They're nice, aren't they? I bought them in a shop called McKenzies Outdoors. They're like walking on a cloud, but they are a bit expensive." I gave him a pitiful look as if to say 'you'll never be able to afford them' to show I had empathy.

"Do you mind if I look in your bag?" asked a chap holding my bag in the air at the other end of the tunnel. *This must be how they window shop before getting off their lazy arses to go shopping.*

"Sure," I replied, becoming a little frustrated. He emptied the contents of my neatly packed bag out onto a table. He was admiring my digital camera.

"It's a Fuji. Six million pixels." I informed him, pleased that he liked it.

"Could you take a picture for me please, Sir?"

"Of you?"

"Of *anything*, Sir. For security reasons we have to make sure it's a camera." I had to start questioning the education of these people. There is no door and no timer, so that ruled out the chances of it being a microwave, and it was clearly nothing to do with hairdressing.

"Say cheese." I pointed the camera straight at him, and the flash made him blink. "Do you want me to email you a copy?"

"No," he blinked, as he hastily stuffed everything back into my bag.

I collected my bag and walked through to the shopping centre. What a bizarre experience this was turning out to be. There were about twenty minutes to spare before I had to board the plane, so I wandered around looking at the vast amount of shit for sale. As I was being forced to smell the latest scent some woman sprayed at me, I recognised a T-shirt matching mine. A tall guy with long girly hair was dressed rather scruffily, except for his new T-shirt complete with packaging creases. *Maybe I should have brought some hairdressing equipment.*

"Hello, mate," I said as we caught each other's eye.

"Hey Dude," he replied. "You must be going to 'Nam too?" *Dude? I thought only crap American films used such words.*

"Yeah," was my excited reply. "I'm Harry. Harry Fisher."

"I'm Jude," he smiled, holding out his hand, "as in 'Hey Jude' or 'Jude the Dude'," he laughed. *Oh dear!*

Jude the Dude and I made our way to gate sixty-nine, which he didn't find amusing either. Clearly, stupid things that rhyme with his name are much funnier. Not a great deal rhymes with Harry, so I didn't stand much chance of getting this hippy to laugh.

At ten to ten, we started to board. Jude the Dude was in row thirty-eight, so would 'stand up and wave once in a while', which I thoroughly looked forward to. Jude seemed to know a lot about planes as he informed me that this was an Airbus.

"Hours of thinking must have gone into that name," I remarked.

"It's named after the Company," he replied, smiling at my ignorance.

"Oh right," I nodded lost for words. "It's a pity that someone with a sense of humour didn't name it 'Big Flying Thing'," I laughed, "the BFT." He looked at me like I'd forgotten my medication and I got the impression he pitied me. I tried to think of things that rhymed with Airbus but thankfully failed. I wasn't too desperate yet that I had to take on this hippy's sense of humour. I spotted another matching T-shirt in the queue behind us. A rather attractive young girl, maybe early twenties, was standing on her own engrossed in whatever the headphones were feeding her ears. I turned all the way around, pointing over-excitedly at my T-shirt and waved. She smiled back, probably wondering who the twat was.

"Hey Jude!" I felt like one of the Beatles. "She's one of us." I sounded like a child, and looked like one too when I motioned for her to come over.

"Hi, I'm Harry."

"Hi Harry, I'm Emily."

"I'm Jude, as in 'Hey Jude' and 'Jude the Dude.'" *Fuck me, that again!*

"I'm Emily," she smiled, "as in, nothing but Emily." I liked her already. Jude did one of those laughs that hippies do, which involves head nodding and no sound. Emily looked at me and raised her eyebrows. "No guesses where you boys are off to then."

Eventually, we boarded the plane and found our seats. Emily was sitting in the row across the aisle from me. To my surprise, she came over and asked the person next to me if he would mind swapping as I was her 'brother'. Upon seeing our T-shirts, he gladly accepted the trade.

"That's better," she said as she parked herself next to me.

"Who's that?"

"Jude?" I asked, wanting to be sure we were thinking of the same fool.

"Yeah."

"I met him in the smelly section. It was a T-shirt recognition thing."

"You often hang around perfumeries?"

"No. It was a coincidence. Jude the Dude is going to be *so* much fun." It was then, true to his word that I noticed Jude waving at us. We waved back, which sent the nodding dog off again.

Within a few minutes, the plane doors were closing, and the engines started making noise. I could feel my palms beginning to moisten as I began to panic about take-off. I could never understand how planes flew. These big metal bastards with hundreds of people and thousands of suitcases shouldn't be able to make it off the ground. I hoped this one would otherwise my adventure would be short lived.

The safety presentation, 'which everyone, including frequent flyers, must give their undivided attention to' was just silly. Even a never-flyer like me could work out how the seat belt worked, and I certainly knew how to put my head between my knees, I did it most Friday nights. Showing us the exit is pointless because when the plane hits the sea at a trillion miles an hour having your head between your legs isn't going to do shit! If the plane crashes into the sea, you die. If not, you drown. If not, you're a wizard made of magic, and you don't need a door.

The cabin crew took their seats, and we were ready to go. With the engines screaming, my palms sweating, my knuckles white from gripping the armrest and my eyes closed, I was ready.

"Are you OK?" Emily inquired.

"Of course." I lied, opening my eyes and loosening my grip on the armrests.

"Are you a nervous flyer?" she asked.

"I don't know. The last time I flew was ten years ago with my mum and dad."

"Excellent," she laughed. "At least if the in-flight entertainment is crap, I've got you to watch."

"Thanks. You want me to swap seats with Jude the Dude?"

"No!"

"You have to look after me because if I freak out, you're the one in the way."

Tea and biscuits were thrown at us, and the rubbish collected in the short hour we spent in the air. My first cup of tea of the day came in a half-filled plastic cup with a silly little handle. During the flight, Emily and I put the world to rights, and I could tell we were going to get on well. We still had one more person to find to make up the team, and I hoped the person would be more Emily than Jude, otherwise we'd have our work cut out taking the piss out of two of them.

The captain's voice came over the tannoy to let us know we would be landing shortly and that the local time was twenty-five past twelve. I adjusted my watch like a sad little tourist, knowing we were only going to be in Paris airport for an hour and a half. I sat back and assumed the scared-to-shit position for landing. Emily was having great fun watching me making a complete tit of myself asking things like: "What if we miss the runway?", "Is the runway bouncy like a kid's playground?" and "Should we assume the crash position just in case?"

The closer the ground became, the more terrified I got. Rather than being as caring as before Emily was being a knobette.

"Apparently the window seats are the first part of the plane to fall off if we have a bad landing."

"Fuck off," I demanded, "I'm praying." I closed my eyes, expecting to never open them again and braced for the impact. We hit the runway so gently, I was embarrassed.

"See, that wasn't so bad, was it?"

"I was being a bit of a girl wasn't I?"

"Girl's don't act like that." *Touché, smart arse.*

As the plane came to a standstill near the hallway on legs, everyone jumped up to disembark. Even I knew the doors weren't open yet. Why were they all so desperate to get off? Flying was fun. Jude stood up and did his nodding dog thing at us.

We left the plane and made our way to the 'Transfers' area. It was a good job I was with the other two otherwise I may have ended up on the same plane back home. We walked for what seemed like miles, with Emily telling Jude all the fun she'd had watching me. *Bloody traitor!* We arrived at the Air France transfer desk and were given three seats together for our onward journey, with me in the middle.

We found a coffee shop to waste away the next hour drinking coffee and smoking, me with my Marlboro Lights and Jude, predictably, with his roll-ups.

After a couple of coffees, half a dozen cigarettes and a crumbly pastry thing that only French people eat, it was time for us to make our way to the gate. This was going to be a painful ten hours. I hoped and prayed I would be able to sleep through most of it, but judging by the energy of the two on either side of me I doubted I would.

The journey from check-in to gate was much more straightforward in Paris. I didn't have to remove my shoes, be touched by men, empty my bag or take any pictures. I just had to walk there. Why was everything so much more complicated in England? Or is it perhaps that all French people are indeed a bit lazy?

We boarded the plane, which according to Jude was a Boeing 757, and took our seats in the central aisle. Ten seats across and about nine hundred rows—this one was definitely not going to get off the ground. I buckled my seat belt and made myself comfortable to watch the silly presentation with the seat belts and rubber rings. Suddenly, the engines began to scream!

"There's something wrong, isn't there?" I said, panic-stricken.

"Why do you think that, Dude?"

"The engines don't sound right. The last plane wasn't this noisy."

"Relax! You're safer in the sky than you are on the ground," Emily reassured me. "Fact."

"Yeah, but we've gotta get up there first," I replied, tensing every muscle in my face to ensure my eyes remained closed. The plane began to move, so I grabbed the armrests and squeezed as tightly as I could. The plane started to accelerate down the runway, and suddenly my seat flew backwards.

"What the bloody fucking fuck is going on?" I screamed. I opened my eyes and realised I was practically horizontal and on the lap of the passenger behind me. My surrogate parents informed me that I'd pressed the recline button. My body felt weightless as the plane took off, and my eyes remained firmly shut. "Are we up there yet?" I asked.

"Panic over Dude, we're off the ground." Worst part over, but we were yet to reach the clouds.

"That wasn't so bad," I lied, opening my eyes and trying to readjust myself into the seat. The other two idiots sat there laughing, apologising to the other passengers.

"Good afternoon Ladies and Gentlemen," came a squeaky little French voice over the tannoy, "my name is Marcel Legroin (or that's what it sounded like anyway) and I am your Captain today."

"He's a bit short to be a pilot, isn't he?" I asked.

"How did you figure out he's short, Dude?" Jude laughed, looking at me all weird.

"Did you not hear how high-pitched his voice is?" I replied, illogically. "He can't even be four-foot tall, which means he won't even be able to look out of the windscreen to see where we're going." Jude laughed his nodding dog laugh and went back to his magazine.

"We have reached our cruising altitude of thirty-eight-thousand feet," the groin continued squeakily. *That's over six miles high, we had zero hope of landing safely in the sea.* "We will be flying out over Europe, through Eastern Europe and then down over Thailand, Cambodia and finally into Vietnam. I'll get back to you as we make our approach into Ho Chi Minh but for now, please relax and enjoy the in-flight entertainment." *Relax? At least you're in control of this bloody great big bastard!* "Should you require anything, Marie Bernhard is your cabin crew manager and her, or one of her staff, will be only too glad to help."

I was starting to relax a little by the time the in-flight entertainment began. We were having a good laugh and had managed to avoid any talk of what we were on our way to do. We still hadn't found the final member of our team, even though we'd tried to in Paris.

I checked my watch and gradually became more and more restless. We'd been flying for a little over two hours and still had a long way to go. As I was about to go to the toilet and stretch my legs, the entertainment paused, and a bleeping sound informed us that we had to fasten our seat belts.

"Is that normal? Are we landing?"

"Ladies and Gentlemen," Captain Squeaky was back, "I have put the seat belt sign on because we expect to be going through some mild turbulence. Please remain seated until the seat belt sign has been turned off."

"What the bloody hell does that mean?"

"It's going to get a little bumpy, Dude," Jude smiled.

"How can it get bumpy?" I asked, mildly distressed. "We're six miles in the air with nothing around us." Jude went into scientific overdrive about jet streams this, and bollocks that. Then the plane began to wobble like a jelly.

"SHIT!" Jude was still banging on with his pointless explanation about thermals and wind speed or some other shit, when all I wanted to know was when it was going to stop. The plane continued to wobble from left to right as I tried to stop myself shitting in my underwear. Then we started falling. I felt the seat belt pushing into my stomach and my now-weightless testicles going airborne. "I told you the bloody plane was too heavy!" I did my best to get my head between my legs for the crash landing, but gravity was fucking everything up. "Put your seat forward!" I shouted, jabbing at the seat in front of me.

"It's just *mild* turbulence, Dude."

"How about I give you a *mild* kick in the bollocks?" When I finally got into the crash position, I glanced under my seat. "There's no lifejacket under my seat!" I panicked, my head swinging between Jude and Emily like a tennis spectator. "Of all the bloody seats they could have forgotten to put a lifejacket in, the bastards!" I pressed the call button to ask for a life jacket, and resumed the crash position. I tried to slow my breathing while my weightless body was being slowly strangled by the seat belt. The trolley dollies calmly continued collecting lunch remnants and other rubbish ignoring my call. *We're all going to die, and they're making the plane tidy.*

Within a few minutes, everything was smooth again. Slowly, I lifted my head out of my lap and looked around like a big stupid meerkat. I slowly resumed my upright position and nonchalantly pretended that nothing had happened. "I still can't find that bloody pen," I said loudly, shaking my head, trying to recover from my blatant dickheadism, "I don't know where it could have gone."

I thought I'd got away with it until Paul, the in-flight comedian, turned off the call light and told me my lifejacket was the yellow thing under my seat.

"Well, I don't think the pen landed in there," I replied with an obnoxious, smart-arse attitude. I wanted to jump out of the plane as free-falling six miles could never be as bad as this. Within moments the seat belt sign was turned off, and I went to hide in the toilet for the remainder of the flight.

After rinsing my face with cold water for the hundredth time and trying to resume some composure, there was a knock on the toilet door.

"Is everything alright in there?" I immediately recognised it to be trolley-dolly, Paul.

"Yes," I called out, "won't be a moment."

I slowly opened the door to find a queue of about eight people all waiting for me to come out.

"Did you find your pen in there?" he asked with a silly giggle. *Wanker!*

After a couple of hours and another shit movie, I was relaxed, falling in and out of sleep. I checked my watch again. Four hours gone, six to go. Time was going way too slowly. I did my best to sleep but couldn't manage any more than a few minutes at a time. Jude was engrossed in some music magazine, and Emily was still watching 'Friends'. I sat there looking around, bored out of my mind wishing I could fall asleep to make the time pass before I went mad. The fidgety little twat between his newly adopted parents.

I was woken by Captain Squeaky Groin on the Tannoy. "Ladies and Gentlemen, we have started our descent into Ho Chi Minh City and will be landing in about twenty minutes. The local time is ten to seven in the morning, and it's looking like a beautiful morning in Vietnam. The temperature is currently twenty-four degrees Celsius." This brought a resounding 'Ooohh' from around the cabin. "I hope you've enjoyed the flight and wish you a wonderful time in Vietnam." And he was gone. He sounded very calm for a man that could potentially kill us all if he misjudged the runway. Maybe he was sedated from inhaling too much helium.

As we came into land, I resumed my stiff upright position, determined to crush the armrests before leaving the plane. They were tougher than I'd expected, my grip not even making a dent in them. As we hit the runway, we bounced straight back off again. "Shitttttttt!" This happened a few more times, and each time I shouted "Shit!" thinking it would make the bouncing stop. All it did was make me sound like an idiot with Tourette's on a pogo stick.

We finally stopped bouncing, but then the plane started sounding unwell. The engines seemed to be under severe pressure and much louder than ever before. We were going to explode.

"What the bloody fuck is that noise?" I asked every person on the plane within earshot. This set Jude off into his nodding dog routine as he likely appreciated the educated nature of my vocabulary.

"It's the brakes, Dude. Don't worry. They put the engines in reverse-thrust to stop the plane."

"What if he forgets to turn them off again and we start reversing back down the runway?" I asked, all rational thinking gone. The armrests still wouldn't collapse, and it was starting to piss me off. “Oh, you two can laugh, but if I’m right, you’ll be sorry.”

“If you’re right,” Emily piped in, “then we’ll be taking off backwards, and will be back in Paris in ten hours. I’ve only heard of it happening once before.” I couldn’t face flying all the way back to Paris just because of some silly pilot error, especially as flying backwards was bound to be worse. The shock on my face made Emily realise I was panicking and a bit gullible. “I’m joking, silly. He’ll stop in time.”

“Oh, ha bloody ha Emily. It *could* happen.” The noise died down and we began travelling at a more reasonable speed. We weren’t going to die. We continued at this speed for about ten more minutes until we finally came to a complete standstill and the engine noise died. “We made it! We made it!” I shouted to reassure all my fellow passengers. I was predicting certain death right up until he’d turned the engines off and taken the keys out. The seatbelt sign was switched off, and the stampede began with everyone up and out of their seats with nowhere to go.

Funny-boy Paul opened the door allowing us to exit the plane, down some steps and onto the tarmac. The solid ground felt good and I felt like dropping to my knees to kiss it.

CHAPTER SEVEN

I followed the green cross code down to the letter as we made our way into the terminal building, checking left and right for aircraft coming towards me. We walked inside and joined the single file queue that had formed and waited. The three of us were like excitable children as we stood laughing at everything each other said, no matter how stupid it was. Jude and Emily seemed to be well-travelled but had never been to Asia, and my Majorca experience wasn't really anything to speak of. We reached the front of the queue and waited. They checked our passports and visas thoroughly and let us through. I was relieved as Jude was winding me up about being jailed and deported if things weren't right. After that, we went through a door and into the baggage collection area, which consisted of a small circular carousel, and a few small men taking the bags off when they had completed one lap. It took me a while to remember what my bag looked like, and anything shiny and new I checked and double-checked to make sure it wasn't mine. Jude and Emily had their bags, and after another ten minutes mine still hadn't appeared.

"Dude," I looked over to see Jude standing by the pile of bags the small men had built, "I've found it." I walked over, not recognising the bag he was holding, and checked the name badge.

"It's bloody brand new, look at the state of it," I said, disappointed that my shiny new bag was now covered in shit. I threw it over my back as we walked towards the 'Nothing to Declare' lane into the Arrivals area.

It was Emily who spotted the BAFCWA board. It was being held by a smiling Vietnamese man standing next to the last remaining member of our team. We walked over and introduced ourselves.

"Welcome to Vietnam," he said as he shook each of our hands. "My name is Lou." That didn't sound very foreign, but what did I know?

"Hi, I'm Angel," announced the fourth member of our team. She was, I guessed, in her late thirties and unmarried judging by her naked ring finger. She had long dark hair, brown eyes and travel-tanned skin. She was quite attractive but a little too much like a pretty version of Jude. She had decided against travelling in the Charity T-shirt, which was why we hadn't spotted her earlier.

As we stepped outside into the crazy heat, we were met by a wall of people blocking the path, offering various accommodation and transport. Boards were held in the air all claiming 'The Best Hotel in Saigon.' I was confused as to what the real name of this place was—Saigon or Ho Chi Minh? We battled our way through the crowd, politely declining accommodation while Lou aggressively spouted off to them in what I assumed to be Vietnamese. By the time we'd reached the small, white minibus, I felt as if I'd been in a brawl.

Lou put our rucksacks into the back of the minibus and we climbed aboard. The dust-filled air immediately hit me in the throat as I attempted to remove some of it from the seat. I sat down and took a swig of the warm water I had left in my bag. I inhaled more dust than if I'd stuck my face into a Hoover bag. Sweat poured down my back sticking my T-shirt to my overheating body, and the dust coated the sweat on my face.

"This is bloody disgusting," I whispered to Jude, "look how dusty it is in here." Jude raised his eyebrows and smiled.

"Are you all sitting comfortably?" Lou asked as he climbed back into the driver's seat. *NO!* "Yes."

As he drove, Lou told us that he was taking us to our accommodation which was on the City border, and that he would give us a full rundown of things once we arrived. He said that we would begin work on Monday morning, so had the weekend to settle in and familiarise ourselves with the new surroundings.

We relaxed into the bumpy, dusty transport completely taken aback by the sheer beauty of what was on the other side of the windows. It was unlike anything I had ever seen before, including on television. We were surrounded by hills and mountains covered in trees and bushes in a spectrum of green. Children waved as they looked up from whatever they were doing, and we excitedly waved back, amazed by how friendly they were.

"Look at him, look at him," I shrieked as I saw a man riding his bicycle along the road with at least one billion bananas balancing on the back! We all made a grab for our cameras, as Lou laughed at his over-excitable passengers. All the man on the bike could do was wave as we took his picture.

We saw a buffalo in a field less than twenty metres away from us, led by a man up to his knees in water, wearing a lampshade on his head. Lou explained that it was rice they were farming. I was almost naïve enough to believe that rice grew in the bags you found on supermarket shelves.

The only distraction from the mesmerising beauty was the sound of a car horn every five seconds. We eventually worked out that it was a signal to let other vehicles know we were overtaking them, but it still drove us mad. If you honk your horn in England, you are generally cursing someone and are likely to end up in a fight. Here, they waved.

It wasn't long before the beauty of the open roads started to fade, and we reached the city border: the traffic, crowds and built-up areas being the obvious clue, coupled with the hundreds of other car horns joining the orchestra. The streets and buildings looked like something out of an old movie, but the people that lined the streets all looked happy, going about their morning routines. I felt as if I had a permanent smile as I took everything in. I hadn't felt so happy and excited for as long as I could remember. We continued our collective observation of everything that was happening around us, twisting and turning to catch a glimpse of each other's new discovery.

Eventually, we pulled up outside a building which I guessed was our accommodation given that Lou had driven the minibus up onto the pavement. The building looked very thin, no wider than the minibus was long and I wondered if there would be enough room inside. Even as we walked into the building, we were still being approached with offers of accommodation.

We walked into what looked like a café and were greeted by two friendly faces.

"Hello, my name is Minh, and this is my wife, Linh. Welcome to Bhut Phom."

We introduced ourselves to Minh and Linh and took a seat at a table they had prepared, complete with an orange drink. Lou sat down with us, leaving the minibus taking up a quarter of the road.

"I'll show you to your room shortly. You'll be staying in a four-bed room with its own bathroom, so I hope you don't mind sharing." I hadn't brought any pyjamas! "On Monday morning at seven o'clock I will meet you here for breakfast and then take you to the building where you will meet the children." seven o'clock? I prayed he was joking. I also prayed for pyjamas. "You will each have a class of between ten and fifteen children, and all you need to do is stick to the curriculum you have been given. Lessons are very informal, so don't worry. Do you have any questions?" *Where can I buy pyjamas?*

"How old will the little loves be?" Angel asked. *Little loves?*

"Between six and fifteen." *Fifteen!*

"Do they ever beat up the staff?" I asked, welcoming back my brain-overriding vocal cords. This was met with much-unwanted laughter from the other three. "What?"

"No, Harry, they never beat anyone up. I understand your concern, but they are very docile children who want nothing more than to learn. They are children who until now have never been given a chance at anything. What you give them will be received as the greatest gift on earth. There's more chance of them trying to kiss you than hit you." I frowned. I didn't want any fifteen-year-old boy kissing me.

The questions continued for about half an hour, with Lou trying his best to ease our apprehensions. "Any more questions?" he asked as we fell silent. He didn't seem phased by any of our questions and remained calm and relaxed. He was a kind and gentle man, probably in his late fifties, although even my best guess differed from Jude's by over ten years. "OK. I'll take you up."

We grabbed our belongings and followed him up the winding stairs to the second floor. It was a surprisingly large room, with bunk beds at each end, and a bathroom to the left near the door. There was adequate drawer space along the walls, plus space under the bunks. The high ceiling had a solitary light hanging from it, with a switch on the wall by the door offering little protection from the live wires visible through the small crack above it.

"I want the top bunk," I shouted like a child at a holiday camp. Jude acknowledged with a smile as he threw his bag onto the one beneath. We were on the far side of the room, furthest from the bathroom, the girls' being on the bunk adjacent to it.

"I'll see you on Monday morning then. If you need anything, Minh and Linh will be glad to help." Lou handed the key to Angel and said his goodbyes. He walked out and closed the door behind him, leaving us alone for the first time. We all lay on our bunks, exhausted from the long day and chatted about nothing in particular.

After about five minutes, my heavy eyes slowly opened, and I launched myself across the room, petrified.

"Don't look now," I panicked, "but there's a crocodile on the ceiling." I stood behind Emily for protection from the dangerous reptile. "What? What are you laughing at? Can't you see it?"

"It's a gecko," Jude laughed, having come out from the lower bunk to see the upside-down croc. "They're harmless. It's more scared of you that you are of it."

"Does he look this bloody scared?" I shrieked like a child.

After some deliberation, Jude agreed to trade bunks with me due to my forgotten fear of heights making the top bunk an issue. I nervously lay on the lower bunk having first checked out the entire surroundings for any other jungle creatures. Eventually, I managed to close my eyes.

It was only when I heard the toilet flush that I woke up, checked my watch and realised that I'd been asleep for nearly two hours. It was after eleven o'clock, and I immediately checked to make sure I still had all my limbs. Thankfully, they were still there. I sat up and rubbed my filthy hands over my filthy face.

"Who fancies going for a wander?" I liked Jude's idea and offered my Lonely Planet guide to the others. "We don't need that," Jude replied, "it's more fun getting lost." I resigned myself to his plan as everyone else agreed that I was 'such a tourist'.

We took it in turns to use the bathroom to have a quick wash to wake ourselves up. It felt good to rinse my face and brush my teeth. The bathroom was very simple. There was a sink with a mirror above it, just big enough for men to shave and women to pluck, and a toilet. In the corner was a shower base with a shower above it, and a shower curtain that went across the width of the room. By my reckoning, you could pee into the toilet from the shower if you got a decent arc, but testing that theory would have to wait because if my theory was incorrect there would be piss everywhere, and an unhappy Angel, as she was in next.

We turned out onto the street and followed Jude. Men on bicycles with two-seater trailers on the back and motorbikes were everywhere. "Cyclo, cyclo" or "Motorbike" came the overwhelming chorus, all of which were politely declined.

We wandered around the streets observing all the strange things we encountered. Snake wine, street stalls selling what looked and smelled like fried maggots, but thankfully lots of normal looking places to eat and drink. The streets and air were filled with dust and flies, so I kept my mouth firmly closed for fear of swallowing something. The hot sun beat down on us as we covered street after street of shops, restaurants and hotels, continually beating away the flies, the cyclos and the motorbikes. Young, barefoot children would run, hold out their hands to shake or high five, and say "Hello Mister" before running away again, smiling. We were experiencing what it was like to be famous as people stopped, smiled and greeted us in their wonderfully friendly manner. It was good to be somewhere where everyone was so friendly to each other and especially friendly to us. As a committed cynic, I'd assumed that the locals only wanted to sell us something or were going to beg for money, but not once did any of this friendliness appear to have an agenda. They were nice, friendly people, pleased to see Westerners walking around their streets.

We eventually came across a bar called 'Apocalypse Now', apparently named after a film about the Vietnam War. Jude suggested we get a drink, which was his best idea since we'd met. We walked in and sat at a table by the door. The bar was full of Westerners with not a single local present. The bar was filled with pictures from the Francis Ford Coppola film, and was completely open-fronted except for small barriers to prevent drunken punters from falling out into the street.

"Four beers please," I shouted over the music to the only local in the bar. She returned with four glasses of lager and asked for sixty-thousand Dong. It took me a moment to remember that it was the equivalent of about two quid.

I placed the beers on the table and realised I could probably drink myself to death multiple times over before running out of money. "Two quid for four beers. Bargain!"

"It's Vietnam," Jude laughed, nodding, rolling a cigarette, "not England." I already liked this place and wanted to move here forever.

“You buy book?” asked a young girl who appeared out of nowhere carrying a pile of books. The pile stood taller than her when she set them onto the table in front of us. They were faded and I guessed second-hand. We all looked through the books that were all related to Vietnam. Not knowing anything about the place, I decided I should get one.

“How much are they?” I asked the adorable little salesgirl. She had long dark hair and a beautiful smile that radiated through her dust-coated face.

“Which one you wan’?” she asked, placing one hand on her hip, knowing she was getting money out of at least one of us.

“How about this one?” I pointed at a book called ‘The Ten Thousand Day War’.

“That one,” she said, pausing to inflate the price, “ten dollar.” I realised it was the equivalent of about forty beers, and I liked beer more than reading.

“I’ll give you three,” I said, trying out my best bartering skills.

“No!” she snapped.

She took the book out from the pile and explained that it was worth that much money due to its excellent quality. Apparently ‘excellent quality’ is something poorly photocopied to this cute little menace.

We chatted with our salesgirl for a while and I quickly warmed to her. She told us that she had to sell at least ten books a day for her family to eat. I had read in my Lonely Planet that these 'street kids' are sent out to work for long hours because their fathers are sometimes hooked on booze or gambling, and the kids have to make money to cover that and for their families to eat. I felt sorry for her and wanted to adopt her, but I knew this wasn't going to be an option. Eventually, she relaxed and offered me a challenge: rock, paper, scissors, best of nine. If she won, I had to buy five books for thirty dollars. If I won, I could have my chosen book for five. This was like taking sweets from a child, literally. How could I lose to a six-year-old?

I was, to the amusement of my friends, annihilated, losing eight games to one. She was a rock, paper, scissors master, and I was humiliated. I honoured the agreement and chose five books—which she pretty much selected for me—and handed over three featureless American tens. I knew I'd been completely conned, as the books probably sold for about a dollar each, but I was new to her country, and she was smarter at selling than I was at bargaining. She left with a shorter book tower and my money in her pocket, pleased as punch that her rock, paper, scissors expertise had once again gone unchallenged. I promised to keep an eye out for her when rock paper scissors becomes an Olympic event. I packed the books into my rucksack and tried to forget the embarrassingly bad challenge, but thankful that I had enough reading to last me the remainder of my life.

A few beers later, we decided to find some food as we hadn't eaten since the Air France microwave meals. Jude suggested we go and get 'Pho', which is apparently a noodle soup and the Vietnamese equivalent of fast food.

We walked deeper into town, each road-crossing becoming more of a life and death experience because of the thousands of motorbikes swerving to avoid each other. We stood and observed how this was done, knowing a gap in the traffic was never going to come. The art appeared to be to look to the other side and cross, allowing the motorbikes to perform the impossible and swerve around whatever they saw in their way.

"Ready?" I asked, predicting imminent death. "Go!" We walked into the road and crossed, hoping the noodle soup was worth it. Horns were blasting all around, as the motorbikes swerved to avoid us. "Halfway there." We carried on crossing, knowing that if we didn't lose our lives, we were going to lose our hearing. We somehow made it across, knowing we'd have to make the return journey later.

We walked into the smiles and stares of the locals and found a table. We looked around for something, anything written in English but found nothing. When we were joined by a young lady with a notepad, Emily pointed at a bowl on the table next to us, which was being devoured with over the top slurping noises, and held up four fingers. The woman nodded and left. "It's either that or we get nothing."

A few moments later four identical bowls arrived, together with a large jug of water. We all tried to work out what was in our bowls but were too hungry to care. I broke open some chopsticks and stirred the noodles and tried to work out what the other colourless things in the bowl were.

"Is that a bloody fly?" I asked in disbelief, pointing at a small, black thing with wings. I knew it was but didn't want to believe it. At that moment, another fly dived in to join his backstroking friend. "I can't eat this," I cursed as my soup slowly became a pond.

"Pick them out," Jude laughed, "before they eat it all." I looked around the table and noticed that Emily and Angel were doing the same.

"Why don't we send it back?" I asked. "I can't eat food with flies in it."

"If you can work out how to send it back, we will," Emily laughed.

"I will," I replied, not wanting to share my cuisine with these winged bastards. I motioned to the woman who had brought our food to come over and pointed at the two flies doing laps in my soup. She stood there and laughed. I shook my head to say "No" whilst again, pointing to the flies with my chopsticks. She retrieved some chopsticks from the centre of the table, split them apart and proceeded to extract the flies, flicking them onto the floor as she caught each of them. Then she was gone.

After I'd finished, a good twenty minutes after the rest, I felt ill. The noodle soup was nice, and the slices of unknown animal were tasty, but the thought of having eaten any flies made me feel sick. We paid our bill and left, knowing that worse than infested soup was crossing the road again.

We walked out, closed our eyes and made the hazardous crossing, this time with a little more confidence knowing we would probably make it. We did, and again congratulated ourselves for a crossing well done.

We wandered back in the direction of our beds with the night slowly closing in on us. The streets were noticeably busier as younger people emerged for their Friday night out. We decided to have the mythical one beer.

We found a small bar around the corner from the accommodation. Angel went to the bar as we found a table by the window. This bar was a lot quieter than the last place, and we didn't have to shout to be heard. This bar was also filled with Westerners, but they seemed to be couples rather than groups of backpackers.

It was ten o'clock by the time we left, one beer turning into about six and the conversation getting weirder as the beers met with our tired minds. We staggered back, all of us craving the proper sleep we'd missed since leaving England. As we arrived, we noticed a metal shutter down over the front of the accommodation, and the only key we had was to our room.

"Shit, we're locked out," I panicked. "What are we going to do?" Emily started pounding away at the shutter, the noise of her banging echoing down the street. "Shush," I said, "you'll wake them up."

"That's the idea," she laughed, "I'm not sleeping out here."

Within a few minutes, the shutter started to open, and we were greeted by Minh still smiling. We offered our apologies a few times over, for which he smiled and told us not to worry. We sheepishly said goodnight and made our way up the stairs to our room.

Once inside, my pyjama dilemma hit me again. What was I going to wear? How do we get changed? We sat on our beds, probably thinking the same thing but not wanting to voice our concerns.

"Right, how are we going to do this?" My only suggestion would have been for them to get changed in front of us while we promised not to look. I decided not to voice that idea.

"Easy," Emily replied, standing up clutching some clothing. "We'll take it in turns to use the bathroom." She walked into the bathroom while we made small talk. I looked through my backpack for a T-shirt that I could wear with my boxer shorts. Jude sat on the top bunk, removed the T-shirt he'd had on all day, climbed into bed and a few seconds later he threw his jeans over the end of the bed.

"Easy as that," he exclaimed, showing us his way of doing it. I wasn't ready to risk that, just in case I messed it up and accidentally hurled my underwear at one of the girls, especially as the chances of it sticking to them were quite high. Emily walked out of the bathroom in a T-shirt that just about covered the good stuff. She had gorgeous, long, thin legs and I knew the instant my eyes locked onto her and my chin hit the floor that she had caught me staring. I looked up at her face the second I realised what I was doing. She smiled back at me, one eyebrow raised. I soon realised that my eyes had doubled in size, and my entire face was burning with the embarrassment.

"I've done a preliminary check of the room for any unwanted reptiles," I smiled, hoping to divert the attention from my red face. I looked over to see Emily, still smiling and shaking her head in an 'I know you were looking at me' way. I felt a rush of nervous embarrassment and a flutter in my stomach, which I hoped wasn't the noodle soup. I suddenly felt attracted to Emily, and her flirtatious smile added to the excitement.

Angel came out of the bathroom, thankfully wearing pyjamas so I didn't make a fool of myself again and I ran in with my T-shirt.

In the bathroom, I took some deep breaths to calm myself. I noticed how attractive Emily was when I first met her, and we'd got on well. When she walked out of the bathroom, her hair neatly brushed, wearing nothing but a T-shirt, she looked hot. The way she seemed to almost enjoy me looking at her had turned me on, and her flirtatious acknowledgement of it was so sexy! I had to stop thinking like this because I had to walk across the room in only a T-shirt and boxer shorts, and didn't need anything else but my feet leading the way. I changed and splashed my face with cold water all the while trying to think of anything that could avert my mind away from Emily's legs. *Margaret Thatcher, Margaret Thatcher.*

I walked out after about ten minutes and made my way across the room, praying no one was looking at me and that nothing below my waist made any sudden movements. I sat on my bunk, crawled under the sheet and immediately checked to make sure Emily wasn't watching. She was lying on her side, also in the bottom bunk, facing me with that same knowing smile on her face. Was it the beer? I felt a stir of nervous excitement take hold of me again, as I could do nothing but smile back at her. I imagined that if the other two weren't in the room, something very bad could have happened and judging by the look on her face, she was thinking the same. I was safely under the covers now and Margaret Thatcher was no longer required, Russell-the-love-muscle could do whatever he wanted.

"Goodnight," Emily said as she reached up to turn the light off, all the while looking at me. Just as the light went out, she smiled and blew me a kiss. The last thing she would have seen was me, eyes and mouth wide open as if I'd seen a ghost. *Smooth!*

"Goodnight," resounded around the room like something out of The Waltons. I couldn't stop thinking about what had just happened, every now and again wondering about Nicola. I'd been there less than a day. Six weeks was a long way away, Nicola was a long way away. Emily was just across the room.

As soon as I closed my eyes I felt myself drifting to dreamland. It had been a long day, and not even the thought of crossing the room and jumping in with Emily was going to keep me awake, although Mr Winky was already reaching out.

CHAPTER EIGHT

At quarter to six, I began to stir with an annoying buzzing next to my ear. The first signs of daylight dimly lit the room, and I lay there wanting nothing more than to remove all the skin from my arms such was the itching sensation. It was driving me mad. Even in the absence of much light, I could feel that my arms were covered in small lumps. I tried to scratch them quietly but didn't have enough hands. Chickenpox? Measles? I tried to ignore them and go back to sleep but I couldn't, so I lay on my arms to stop myself scratching. In the distance, I could hear more scratching and knew that someone else must also have chickenpox. An epidemic? Were we all going to be quarantined and be made to leave the country? How could something like this happen so soon?

It was seven o'clock, and I couldn't lie there any longer. I was wide awake and wanted to get up. I crept out of bed and tried to put my jeans on. As is always the case, when you're trying to be your most quiet those normal everyday tasks always seem harder. As I put my second leg into my jeans, I lost my balance, and not even uncontrolled hopping could save me. I realised too late that my right foot was in a pocket and landed face first in the middle of the two sets of bunks with a resounding "Shit!" I lay there for a moment and tried to assess the damage. I heard quiet laughter amongst the sleepy drones. "Who's that?" I asked in a crap attempt at a whisper.

"Me," came the useless response. I knew from the pitch that it was a girl, so I proceeded with my apology. "Sorry I woke you, my foot went into my pocket."

"Don't worry clumsy boy I was awake. Jet lag and mosquito bites!" It was Emily. She was the one I'd heard scratching. Mosquito bites. Little fuckers!

I felt relieved at not having chickenpox but not relieved at the constant scratching my arms needed. I took my foot out of the pocket and put my jeans on properly before climbing to my feet.

"I'm covered in bites too," I said as I sat on the edge of Emily's bed. "They're driving me bloody crazy."

"I know. I could hear you about an hour ago."

"Jet lag." It all became clear, "I think I've got that too." I'd never seen five o'clock twice in one day before. "I'm going down to have some breakfast. I can't lie in bed anymore."

"Wait, I'll come down with you," she replied as she climbed out of bed, once again showing off her legs and enjoying me watching.

"Sorry," I said, realising she'd caught me looking again. *Bugger.*

"Get used to them," she smiled, "you're going to be seeing a lot more of them." I sat there wondering how much more I'd get to see, and hoping I'd have them around my neck at some point. *Margaret Thatcher, MARGARET THATCHER.*

"Come on then," she whispered as she threaded herself perfectly into her jeans.

We quietly went downstairs, hoping we could have breakfast so early on a Saturday. Minh was sitting in an armchair reading a newspaper when we arrived and stood up to greet us.

"Good morning," he smiled. "Would you like some coffee?" Never before was the offer of coffee so gratefully received. He wandered off and came back with a coffee pot big enough for a village.

"How would you like your eggs?"

"Poached," Emily asked.

"Me too."

Emily and I sat and chatted about nothing in particular, drinking coffee. There was a chemistry between us and I felt comfortable around her, except when she made flirtatious remarks that rendered me speechless. She was fun, intelligent and interesting to talk to. She was twenty-three, had recently finished an Economics degree and was looking half-heartedly for a job. She had done some charity work while in University but not for any longer than a weekend, and definitely nothing like this. She was single, her ex-boyfriend having finished things when they left University and "was better off without him because all men are bastards." I didn't deny that they probably are but, with a typical male response told her that I wasn't.

Our eggs eventually came and were quickly devoured. We were both starving having only had a bowl of insect noodles the day before. We discussed what we were going to do that day, neither of us having a clue as to what there was to do other than explore the city and avoid being killed by motorbikes. Jude and Angel joined us as we were finishing our breakfast looking even more alike, with their matching hair strewn across their faces.

They sat down and poured themselves coffee, both of them looking how we felt. Minh came over to take their egg orders, both of them choosing fried eggs claiming the grease would do them good. Not sure which scientific journal that was published in.

We discussed what we were going to do for the day: Go out for a walk, check out some of the sights and museums, have lunch somewhere (which I stipulated must be more hygienic than the previous day's attempt) and work through the curriculum in preparation for Monday.

The two girls made their way back to the room to shower whilst Jude and I sat drinking coffee and inhaling nicotine. The only rush we were in was caffeine-based, and we decided that we were going to relax and enjoy our couple of days of freedom before the work began.

Getting to know Jude was another lesson in not being so judgemental. He was twenty-seven and had a Mechanical Engineering degree. He'd recently been made redundant from an oil company, with whom he'd travelled a lot. He had been to Dubai, covered a lot of Europe and spent six months in South America working on various projects. He still lived with his family about twenty miles from me, finding 'no reason to move out and have to pay his own way!' He said he had never found the right girl and that his previous job hadn't helped as he was away from home a lot. We both ended up in Vietnam by accident, having been disillusioned by what our current lives had to offer. Jude also said he wanted to 'get to know himself a little better' and 'search within himself'. Not bad for someone I'd written off as a hippy who overused the word 'Dude' and made jokes that were shittier than mine.

Emily was the first to arrive back downstairs, looking radiant and refreshed wearing a white T-shirt and denim shorts that showed off her gorgeous legs. Her hair was still wet and fell nicely down her back, and her face had a healthy glow. She sat down with us and read through my Lonely Planet guide as Jude and I continued our bonding ritual.

Angel arrived shortly afterwards, also looking good for showering. She no longer looked like Jude, which I'm sure she would have been flattered to know. Jude and I ran up the stairs, buzzing from the ridiculous amount of caffeine we'd drunk. Jude managed to sprint into the bathroom, lock the door and shout loudly that he was the winner before I'd even located my towel. Child! I couldn't believe I'd lost. I sat on the bed and flicked through my guidebook, reading aloud anything I found interesting. I found the place we'd eaten last night, described as 'a nice little restaurant serving, Pho (noodle soup) which is a favourite of the locals. Good value for money'. I made a note to write to Lonely Planet on my return and tell them my version: 'A crappy little place, serving noodle soup with insects'. I threw the guide onto the bed and grabbed my towel as Jude finished in the bathroom. I felt perpetually dirty from all the sweat and dust that had formed on my body since we'd landed. I also didn't have nostrils anymore as a consequence of the shit that had found its way up my nose.

As the warm water hit my face, I was reminded of the scarring that everyone else had been too polite to mention, and that I'd nearly forgotten about. I also remembered the cream I was supposed to put on it that was still in England. The shower was heavenly and the water falling away from me was filthy. It took two washes to properly clean my hair, and I used nearly a quarter of the only bottle of shower gel I'd brought to last the six weeks. When the water started to get cold, I decided it was time to exit the shower. I felt so much better for being clean again but knew it wouldn't last.

I dried myself and blew my nose, the contents of which made me cringe. The feeling of being able to breathe again was heavenly. I examined my face in the mirror and realised that it was almost beginning to look normal again.

Emily walked into the room, as I walked out of the bathroom wearing only a towel. "Emily!" I gasped, feeling very naked. *Where the hell had Jude gone?*

"Sorry, Harry, I just wanted to borrow your Lonely Planet." There was that same smile as the previous night, looking me up and down.

"Oh, OK," I said, trying to tense the muscles in my chest to make me look like a real man. "It's over there," I motioned with my head. Emily continued looking me up and down as she brushed past me and grabbed the book from my bunk.

"I'll see you back downstairs," she said, smiling as she walked backwards towards the door, still checking me out. *Margaret Thatcher, Margaret Thatcher.* "Oh, and Harry, bring the guidebook," she smiled, throwing the book back onto my bed as she disappeared behind the door.

As I appeared downstairs, Emily was looking over at me, smiling, with her back against the wall. She was using her dark, sexy eyes to let me know she was still visualizing the towel while biting her lip. My John Thomas latched straight onto this, and not even Margaret Thatcher was going to stop him this time. I broke eye contact and took a deep breath as my butterflies awoke once more. Angel still had her back to me, but Jude saw the whole thing, and when I looked over at him, he smiled and nodded his head.

"Oh good, you brought the Lonely Planet." Emily was turning from a flirty girl into a game-playing little shit, and I was completely fucking hopeless.

At half past nine in the morning, the humidity and dust were an unpleasant change from the cool temperature we'd emerged from. We followed Jude who was guiding us from the Lonely Planet map and pointing out various things as we passed them. We were proper tourists, each with our camera at the ready.

While we were making our way to the War Remnants Museum, we passed a window with an advert for a day trip to the Cu Chi tunnels.

"Wow!" Jude exclaimed. "We have to go and do that. They're the tunnels they used to win the war. Miles of underground tunnels from where they hid and fought the Americans."

We walked into 'Sinh Café'—a café-cum-travel agent—and let Jude do all the talking. He arranged for us to make the trip the following day, which was our best option as we didn't know how much time we'd have once the work started. We were told to be back at the shop at eight o'clock the following morning.

As we were walking towards the museum, we passed Bến Thành Market, which is a huge building at one of the intersections we were waiting to cross. According to the girls, we had to have a look. Once again, we were attacked from every angle by people wanting to sell us all sorts of crap, from T-shirts to suits, and cutlery to saucepans. Did I look like someone who needed a pressure cooker?

As we approached the back of the market, we came across the food section. If I ever wanted to vomit from smells alone, it was then. We walked around looking at the variety of fish and shellfish that was for sale, all of it still alive. Then we reached the meat section. At the end of one of the stalls, lying there on the floor was a bulls head. My tether was broken. If I'd carried on walking around, I would either have thrown up or punched someone. As I headed for the nearest exit, someone bought a live chicken, put it into his shopping bag and walked out. Within a few seconds, the chicken's head popped out and was looking around wondering what the hell was going on. This made me smile, but I was like a man possessed. I needed the exit. As I reached the end of the meat section, I saw little puppies in a small cage, barking and yelping away. *Fancy having a pet stall next to the meat section.* As I was just thinking hygiene, a rat about nine inches long ran straight across my path, disappearing somewhere near the puppies. After I'd shrieked like a young child, I started to run.

"That was interesting," Emily said, as they finally reappeared.

"No, Emily. Documentaries are interesting. That was fucking disgusting!" The rat in my story was now about two-foot long.

As we crossed town, we passed the Notre Dame Cathedral. It looked absolutely beautiful with its red brick spires pointing towards the sky. It did look a little out of place though, being more or less in the middle of the road. I vowed to go back there and seek forgiveness for all my pornographic thoughts of Emily, and the cardinal sins I was keen to commit.

We eventually found the War Remnants Museum down Vo Van Tan Street. This was apparently once called the American War Crimes museum but had changed its name in recent years. As we walked through the museum, we were completely blown away. There were walls covered in pictures of the atrocities that had taken place. We saw pictures and evidence of the chemicals which had burned acres of land using 'Agent Orange'. The villages burned down by American soldiers, and civilians being shot as they tried to escape. There were 'before and after' pictures of years of history wiped off the face of the earth. There was wall upon wall of pictures of captured Vietnamese people, each with their own story to tell. You could see the terror and sadness in their eyes as they had their photographs taken. One picture that will remain in my mind forever was of two young boys lying in the road, having been shot in the back as they ran away. Amongst the pictures were two large glass containers with disfigured embryos of unborn babies as a result of napalm. There were other pictures of people being tortured as American troops stood nearby laughing.

Up ahead, I could hear the voice of a young boy talking about the way his life had been ruined, and as I turned the corner, I froze in sheer terror. The young man had an enlarged head—about twice the normal size—with regular-sized facial features. It was an image that would haunt you, especially as he was unborn during the war, and his disfigurements were as a result of his parents' exposure to chemicals—namely Agent Orange. After I'd watched the sequence and realised there would be more similar interviews, I left.

The walkway led us outside into a large yard, where there were tanks, planes, helicopters, and bombs captured during the war. We did our tourist bit and climbed all over them to have photos taken, wanting to do something fun to take our minds off the disgusting things we'd seen. I felt a deep sense of sadness for the Vietnamese who, for over thirty years tried to defend their country and their homes, whilst other rich and powerful nations who were supposed to set an example to the rest of the world, violated their human rights, bombed their villages to the ground, and murdered them.

After that depressing encounter, we decided it was time to go for lunch. We walked down Pham Ngu Lao, or

'Backpacker Street' as it's known, and settled upon Kim's Café because they sold burgers. We sat inside with the air conditioning providing a very welcome relief from the heat and dust and all ordered a cheeseburger and chips.

As we sat waiting and enjoying our cold drinks, we were still being asked if we wanted a cyclo. They never seemed to get it. If you are sitting inside, with a drink, waiting for food, you don't need any type of transportation. It is not a drive-thru.

Our cheeseburgers arrived, and the plates hardly hit the table before we all dived in.

"What the bloody hell is this?"

"All I can say for certain," Emily replied, "is that it's definitely not beef!"

"I blame Harry." Jude laughed while seemingly enjoying whatever it was.

"Cyclo."

"Sod off!" The other three looked horrified at my outburst.

"OK. You want cyclo now?"

"Sod off." They weren't so shocked this time.

When we'd finished what we could eat, with Jude eating whatever was left on our plates, we paid our bill and had a debate as to whether or not fly-infested food was any worse than fried dogshit. Insect soup won.

As we were making our way back to the hostel, we passed a place that did reflexology and massage.

"Reflex-what-ogy?" I couldn't understand why anyone would pay to have their knees hit with a hammer, as amusing as it is.

"It's a homoeopathic treatment," Angel explained.

"Is Vietnam very popular with the gay community then?"

"No, silly. It's an alternative treatment." Angel didn't appreciate the full extent of my ignorance.

"That's no treat, I'm a practising heterosexual."

"Idiot. They massage your feet, and it helps treat all the other parts of the body."

"And you believe all that shite?"

"Well try it and see," Emily challenged. I guessed by the fact we'd stopped outside that the others were keen, and a massage would be heaven after the flight and the walking we'd done.

"OK! But if any fella tries it on, there'll be trouble."

I was feeling a little apprehensive about the whole thing until I saw the little lady who would be treating me. She was about five foot four inches with the now-familiar long dark hair, dark brown eyes and perfect smile. She removed my trainers and placed my feet into one of those things women use that makes bubbles and cleans feet.

My feet were one-by-one removed from the hydrothingy and dried. My left foot was wrapped in a towel, making it look like something Egyptian and placed back on the floor. My right foot was placed into my little friend's lap, who was seated on a milking stool. She began to gently massage my foot, and it was absolute heaven, so I thanked my friends for making me come in. Then she started getting a little more violent and began some form of torture. First, she yanked at each of my toes until they cracked. I looked at her, eyes wide, begging for mercy, telling her I'd give her whatever information she required, but she didn't understand. For the next fifteen minutes, I switched between shrieking and laughing. The sensation alternated between pain and tickling as she pummelled away at my poor foot. The other three sat there amused and apparently feeling no pain.

"Would Sir like massage," asked the woman who I guessed ran the place. 'Now you're talking,' I giggled to myself, 'I've seen those movies!' Jude and Angel had already gone upstairs, so Emily and I followed, escorted by the same people who had tortured our feet.

It wasn't long before I discovered that this was an altogether different type of massage. What had started out as gentle massaging turned into contortion training. My arm was outstretched and forced back down towards my neck as I screamed for mercy.

"You're gonna bloody break it!" I shrieked, as it clicked and popped. I looked over at the others. "What is wrong with you freaks of nature?" as I continued my 'pain' noises.

After bending and twisting things in directions they aren't designed to go, she stood up. *Thank fuck for that. I survived.*

"What the bloody hell is going on?" I called out to anyone who was listening. "She's gonna crush me." The five foot four cutie was now walking up and down my back. "My back wasn't designed for walking on. If it was it'd be covered in bloody tarmac. OUCH!"

For about another thirty minutes, I was mistreated, punished and tortured, all apparently for my own good. How come you never see this type of massage on television? How come you only ever see the ones where you get all coated in aromatic oils by a sexy young lady and then taken out the back for some 'extras'? Lying, deceitful television bastards! Even if they had offered, there was no bloody way I was accepting any 'extras' in this place. She'd probably hang me up from the ceiling, stuff an orange in my mouth and suffocate me. There was no way I was going through all that again.

"Finished, Mister," she said, as she finally put an end to my misery. With no bones broken but guaranteed bruising for life, I stood up.

"That can't be bloody good for you," I said to the others, who were also finished and back on their feet. "I think she squashed one of my kidneys!"

We walked down the stairs and put our shoes back on and were charged fifteen dollars each for our 'treatments'.

"Please come again soon," said the friendly little manageress, smiling as we left.

"Not bloody likely!"

CHAPTER NINE

We made our way back to the hostel, me in pain, and the others banging on about how enjoyable the experience had been and how relaxed they felt. Bloody liars. It was physically impossible for them to be telling the truth. How can you possibly feel relaxed when your feet and body have been given such a horrendous pounding? And what was with the walking up and down my back? Didn't she know there are vital organs in there? Didn't she know that that is only acceptable when wearing stilettos? My complaints fell on deaf ears, and the more I argued, the more they ganged up on me. Apparently, I am ridiculous, and it was relaxing. Each to their own, I still preferred those television massages.

We arrived back at the hostel and spent the rest of the afternoon relaxing and working our way through the curriculum. It was so well laid out that even I could'nt mess it up, although according to Emily, I could. We worked through each day of the forthcoming week, discussing each step until we agreed on everything. We worked well together as a team, being able to be serious and have fun. Angel awarded me the status of 'group idiot' following my ridiculous questioning and alternative curriculum ideas, which included cockney rhyming slang and swearing. I admired the group of people I was with as they were good fun and so alike with a shared determination to do well at what we came here to do.

By about seven o'clock, we were all exhausted and starving. In the previous hours, we'd covered everything and weren't prepared to subject our brains to any more. By any English speaker's standard, the curriculum was very straightforward, and none of us would have any issues with it, but we wanted to be sure.

Emily found a place in Lonely Planet that apparently served an excellent green curry. As soon as she mentioned it, we were all on board. We changed into long trousers to prevent any more mosquito bites and left, having decided on an early night because of our eight o'clock trip the following morning.

We found the restaurant and seated ourselves in the corner, furthest away from the door. The waitress came over, and Angel ordered four green curries and four beers using her four fingers and the Lonely Planet translation page.

"I'm like a local," she exclaimed after the waitress had left, pleased she had used the local lingo.

"I hope you pronounced it right," observed Jude, "otherwise we might end up eating dog. Woof!"

"Yuck!" I gasped, screwing my face up. "Imagine eating dog."

"They do here." Jude said.

"Yeah right, I'm not that gullible!" I wasn't going to fall for this one. The streets of Ho Chi Minh seemed to be littered with stray dogs, mostly female due to the number of teats they had hanging from their undercarriage.

"Honestly, they do!" Jude defended. Now I was worried. "I didn't want to say anything at the time, but you know those puppies we saw in the market earlier?" Those poor, cute little puppies. "You could be eating one of those."

"Yuck, shut up, Jude!" Emily interrupted. "I did wonder what those puppies were doing in the market. I read somewhere that they eat dog, but apparently they farm them for that purpose."

"Farm them?" I tried to imagine how you would keep dogs on a farm. Do they use sheep to herd them? "Anyway, why the bloody hell would anyone want to eat dog?" I asked, confused. "Isn't chicken, beef, pork and lamb enough for people? Dogs are pets, not ingredients."

"Apparently not. They eat all sorts on this side of the world, mate. Rats, pigeons, bats," Jude explained, smiling. "But I think we'll be safe here." However much the others tried to reassure me, I was still listening out for barking noises from the kitchen.

"Rats, bats and pigeons? Now you're definitely winding me up. They're bloody vermin. Disgusting!"

"It's true!" Jude replied, shaking his head and looking disgusted. He picked up the menu and pointed at an English translation that was in brackets that read 'pigeon'.

"I think I'm going to be sick," I said, my appetite gone!

Our food arrived, and it looked and smelled delicious although until the first taste I was still slightly apprehensive as to whether or not it was chicken. I tipped the rice onto my plate and then carefully inspected the bowl of green curry for any sign of dog or flies. It was clean. I poured the curry over the rice, and my appetite was back.

"This is so nice," Emily said, her eyes closed savouring the food, "and it's definitely chicken, Harry!" she laughed. That was all I needed to hear. She wasn't wrong, it was delicious.

"We're coming here every night," I said, enjoying my first tasty meal. "This is heaven."

Not a single grain of rice was left across the four plates. I was tempted to order the same again but having already been called a pig I decided against it. We paid and left, telling the waitress we would see her again the following night.

Back at the hostel, the shutters were down again and it was only just after nine o'clock. Emily went through the same routine as the previous night waking the entire street up with her banging. Minh opened up and let us in, smiling as usual.

When we got to the room Emily went straight to the bathroom after grabbing her T-shirt. She smiled at me as I sat on my bunk like an anticipating spectator. Jude did his Houdini act in bed as Angel and I chatted waiting for Emily to finish. Within a few minutes, she pranced out of the bathroom like a catwalk model playing up to her perverted audience of one. She once again looked gorgeous and sat facing me on her bunk. She looked up at Jude and noticed that he had his back to her as Angel walked to the bathroom. She made small talk as she leaned back against the wall and crossed her legs, watching my eyes dart straight towards the fun zone. I realised what I was doing and shook my head in disbelief. I was acting like a dirty old man, but she seemed to like it.

The one-eyed-monster was trying to burst through my fly for a look, but the double stitching in my Levis was restraining him well. She looked so sexy, and if Jude hadn't been there, she would have ended up getting the big bad wolf treatment. She parted with the wall and slid herself forward, revealing her white underwear. There was a proper kerfuffle going on in my boxer shorts and I feared for the safety of the double stitching. She slowly covered herself up, continually watching me looking like a child wanting the candy, still making small talk. When Angel came out of the bathroom I stood up, turned my back to the girls and tried to adjust myself to avoid snapping the big fella. I grabbed my T-shirt and moved towards the bathroom with Emily watching me and looking straight in the direction of my under-pressure fly.

While changing I was calling out for Margaret Thatcher repeatedly in my head, knowing it softened my tallywhacker. I checked everything was in order and made my way back to bed. As I climbed into bed I blew Emily a kiss, trying to win a point back in this tease-off. She nodded her head and pointed at her lips challenging me. I hadn't expected that and lamely pointed at my own. She smiled, reached up and turned off the light to a chorus of "Goodnight!"

As I lay there in the pitch black trying to make the other two disappear with magic words, I felt a hand cover my mouth and it scared the shit out of me. Was it the crocodile?

"Shush," she whispered, as she removed her hand and kissed me straight on the lips. "Goodnight, sexy." And she was gone. I lay in shock, but wanted her to come back and do it again. As I closed my eyes Nicola's face appeared, but however bad I felt I still wanted the other two to disappear.

"Make that noise go away!" Emily shouted as Jude's phone alarm woke us at quarter to seven.

"Wakey wakey you lazy lot," Jude said, appearing from the bathroom brushing his teeth.

"Morning, You!" Emily mouthed in my direction. She looked gorgeous lying there half asleep, hair strewn across her face. She pulled the sheet back as she sat up. I pulled my sheet back after making sure my tallywhacker hadn't fallen out, and Emily looked straight down and bit her lip! I had to cover myself back up, feeling embarrassed. *Margaret Thatcher, Margaret Thatcher.*

"You're in there, mate," Jude whispered, as he smiled and winked.

"No shit, Sherlock," I replied in a state of shock.

"Did I hear you two kissing last night?" he whispered, so Angel wouldn't hear.

"Kind of," I said, unsure what to make of it. "She kissed me. Don't say anything, will you?"

"Of course not. None of my business Dude!"

Jude, Emily and I went downstairs, leaving Angel to shower. We ordered four lots of scrambled eggs when Minh brought out the usual jug of coffee. Emily poured us all a cup, hoping the caffeine would wake us up. Angel arrived shortly afterwards, as did the eggs.

As soon as I'd finished I went upstairs to shower. The shower cleaned off the previous day's shit, and I managed to find a few new mosquito bites from the previous night. Good job I bought that spray-on shit that supposed to keep those bastards away.

Once again, I was standing there in my towel as Emily walked in, this time without knocking.

"Sorry Harry, we're making a habit out of this," she said. She looked as shocked to see me as I was her. "I just need to shower. Don't worry, I won't look," she said, smiling and looking me up and down.

"You are a cheeky monkey!" It was a pitiful retort, but the best I could do given the circumstances.

"I know," she smiled, disappearing into the bathroom. I stood there shaking my head not knowing what she was playing at but loving the excitement of it all.

I dried myself and quickly dressed while Emily showered, knowing that I had at least until the water stopped before the devil woman would re-emerge.

As I was tying my laces, she walked out draped only in a towel. My heart was pounding as I looked up to see her putting a smaller towel in her hair—that strange skill women have where they can make a turban-style creation that never falls off. She looked good, and I knew I had to leave the room before she started playing her games.

"I'm going down now."

"No need." she smiled. We had thirty minutes until we needed to leave, which would leave twenty-nine after what I had in mind. She turned her back to me and unwrapped the towel, managing to dry her entire back without giving anything away. I was on the third attempt at tying the same lace. She wrapped herself back in the towel, pulled out a black thong, making sure I saw it, and put it on, followed by her shorts. I was still fumbling with my laces dying for a glimpse of anything. She removed the towel, dried her top half and put on a black lacy bra, with me only getting some idea of her profile. This was torture. It was as if I wasn't there, but she knew exactly what she was doing, and she had me under her spell. As she put on her T-shirt, she turned around, giving me only a microsecond to take-in what was left to see. She smiled as she saw I was still bent over trying to tie my laces, and she carried on towel-drying her hair in silence. She was incredible and had a body to die for. She had left me with enough to fantasise all day long.

"You having trouble, Harry?" she asked as she pointed at my trainers. "Do you need me to get down on my knees to help you?" This had the potential to be the first time I ever accidentally ejaculated while tying my laces.

"Go on then," I said challenging her. She moved slowly towards me and began to kneel.

"JUDE!" I shouted as the door opened. The hippy fucker's timing couldn't have been any worse. Knocking on the door was already a thing of the past.

"Alright Dude?" he replied, looking confused. "Gotta shower, we've only got twenty minutes."

"Next time," Emily winked while I tied my laces in under five seconds. Jude went into the bathroom as Emily and I got our stuff together for the day out. I sprayed myself and most of the room with mosquito repellent.

"Coming?" she grinned as she walked towards the door. She had no idea how close I was!

The coach arrived at eight o'clock, and we sat on the back seat, the coach less than half full. The drive to Cu Chi took about an hour, and we spent the time enjoying the beautiful countryside. People were already working in the fields, and according to our guide, had been since six o'clock. They stop for lunch between twelve o'clock and one o'clock to avoid the midday heat, and then work until about five o'clock. All that to put rice on our supermarket shelves, something I will never again take for granted.

We arrived at Cu Chi at half past nine and were handed a ticket that would give us entry into the tunnels. This place was an obvious tourist trap based on the seven other coaches I counted.

We were split into two groups, each with its own guide. Our guide was the thinnest man I had ever seen. He was about five foot two inches tall and a stiff breeze could have knocked him over. He took us back out and past the coaches to the other side of the road, and asked us if we could find a tunnel. After a few minutes of searching for what we previously imagined a tunnel looked like, our guide lifted up a small door in the ground, which was no more than eighteen inches by twelve. He pointed down at the tunnel—which to us was a covered hole—and then climbed down into it and replaced the cover. He was gone. After a couple of seconds, he popped back out again and held the cover above his head, smiling for us to take pictures. He asked if anyone wanted to try. Emily was the first one in, and even she found the opening to be tight. She crouched down but decided against replacing the cover. I decided to try, but only made it as far as my arse before it became too tight! Jude declined as his arse is marginally larger than mine.

The next stop was the main event: a fifty-metre tunnel that we could crawl through. Apparently the tunnel wasn't as small as the one we'd just seen and we would easily fit, even with our backpacks on. It had light the whole way through so we could see where we were going. We put our faith in our guide, crouched down and began to crawl. Jude followed by Angel then Emily, and me at the back. As we crawled down the steep entrance into the tunnel, the musty air hit us. As the tunnel levelled out we remained in good spirits and were laughing and joking, but that wasn't to last. As we continued to crawl, and lost all traces of daylight we had to rely on the tunnel's dim lighting. On my hands and knees, I had about four inches either side to spare, but the floor was a clay-type mud and was murder on the knees. I knew how far fifty metres was above ground but as we twisted and turned downwards and upwards it felt like a lot more. I started to feel mild panic from the heat, the musty air, the pain in my knees and the claustrophobic feeling that the tunnel was never going to end, but I had to remain strong as there was bugger all I could do about it. What started out as fun had become a silent fear with only the wish for it to be the fuck over.

"Shit!" Jude shouted, "a bat!" I prayed to every God from every religion to tell me this was his twisted humour in action. I hated those flying bastards sharing my world but to share the same narrow tunnel was too much. "It's OK," he continued, sounding calmer, "it's landed on the wall. Angel, stay to your left and you'll pass him. That's it, you're past it now."

"I can't do it," Emily said with a tremble in her voice. "Harry, we have to go back." Given the choice of crawling backwards through this tunnel when we were so near the end or passing a blood-sucking vampire bat was a tough call.

"Emily, there is more chance of me sticking my head up your arse and driving you the rest of the way than there is me going back again." I'd had enough of the tunnel and wanted to get out. I was struggling to hold it together and needed to be out, but fuck doing the whole thing backwards.

"I can't, Harry, we have to go back."

"Emily, stay to your left, I'll guide you. Jude said he can see the end of the tunnel up ahead," Angel said a little more tactfully. Emily started to crawl and I could just about make out her profile in the dim lighting as she stuck to the left-hand wall. "That's it, Emily, keep going. Keep going. That's it, you're past it." That was all very well, but now I had to do it. I'd rather have my neck bitten than go back, so I continued forward scaling the left wall to avoid being anywhere near the winged-vermin bastard. I carried on until I imagined I'd past it, Emily not being able to guide me because she had lost her shit. Within a few more minutes I could feel the floor begin to incline, so knew we were near the end. I could hear Jude and knew he was nearly out. The incline was very steep as we squeezed through a tight corner, which felt as if it was about forty-five degrees, and proceeded uphill until there was daylight. It was such a relief to be out of there and taste the fresh air. Our knees were grazed from the crawl, and we were covered in sweat and dust. Emily had her hands on her knees, doubled over and breathing heavily.

"You did really well," I said to her as I put my hand on her back, trying to offer her some support.

"Stick your head up my arse. What the fuck?" she asked, forcing a smile. She was getting a little colour back in her cheeks.

"I don't know where that came from. I got a little panicked and couldn't face doing the whole thing in reverse. I'm sorry."

"It's OK," she smiled, gradually standing upright. "I'm glad you did because I'm not sure I would have made it back again either," she mused. "Charmer!"

"Sorry," I said, mildly embarrassed at my ungentlemanly conduct.

Our guide explained that there were thousands of kilometres of similar tunnels used in the Vietnam war, stretching as far as the Cambodian border to the west, and halfway up the country to the North. The tunnels were built by hand using only hoes and rice baskets and began with villages of people making their own tunnels which were eventually linked. Armies would spend weeks down there—eating, sleeping and fighting—sometimes having to crawl for miles at a time to evade the Americans. Not to mention the ever-present danger of tunnel collapse. We'd crawled fifty metres in about ten minutes and barely made it.

"Jude," I whispered, "he said 'hoes' and not 'whores', right?"

"What the fuck, Dude?" he laughed.

"Just checking. That would be a bit wasteful."

We continued on to some replica areas that were built above ground for tourist purposes. There were kitchens, offices and living areas that matched what was below ground during the war. The whole thing was amazingly reconstructed in intricate detail. Huge kitchens deep below the ground use to funnel the steam and fumes many miles away using bamboo piping so the Americans couldn't find them. This was one of the innovative ways that kept the

Americans from pinpointing their location, hence the reason the Vietnamese so often outwitted the Americans.

The next area was set out to show the traps they used to capture their enemies. These traps lay covered up in the paths they knew the Americans would use. Six foot deep holes with a grid of sharp bamboo facing straight upwards, or side-by-side cylindrical barrels with bamboo spikes so the force of someone landing on them would cause a barrel to roll inwards both crushing and stabbing the victim. Disgraceful and inhumane, but they didn't have billions of dollars to waste on war so they needed to get creative.

The final part of the tour was the greatest tourist trap of all, but something everyone was queuing up to do—fire a machine gun. The bullets worked out to be about two dollars each with the choice being an M16 or AK47 machine gun, or a Browning hand pistol. I bought five bullets and chose the AK47. I put on protective goggles and ear protectors and was told to shoot at the targets, which were amusingly Coca-Cola cans, about thirty metres away. I lined up the first shot, my shoulder firmly cradling the butt of the rifle and as instructed, slowly squeezed the trigger. As I discharged the first shot, the gun's recoil nearly dislocated my shoulder, the weapon's power taking me completely by surprise. Somehow, I managed to hit a tin can! I think it was the one I was aiming for, but I'll never know and if ever asked will be sure it was. I fired off the other four of my bullets hitting another two cans, with the other two bullets missing everything. It reinforced my belief that the people you see in the movies, walking around shooting these things with one hand is ridiculous. They were much heavier than they looked and you'd lose your arm if you tried to fire one-handed. I walked away feeling like a bit of a tough guy having killed three Coke cans.

Jude had been firing an M16 and had only hit one can, and Emily had a go with the Browning pistol and had hit two. I was the winner and rather childishly made sure they knew it. Angel decided against shooting anything claiming she didn't believe in violence. I did point out the fact that no tin cans were hurt, but this didn't seem to help.

It was just after one o'clock when we were asked to make our way back to the coach as the afternoon tours had arrived. It was an excellent and very enlightening experience, except for the rather frightening fifty-metre crawl. Five metres would be about right, straight in and out.

We arrived at the hostel shortly after half past two feeling hungry but too exhausted to go out. We went up to the room and took it in turns to wash. My head had barely hit the pillow, and I was asleep.

I woke up shortly before four o'clock and realised that this time tomorrow we would have finished our first day of teaching. This made me feel a little nervous, as I still didn't know what to expect. I tried to imagine myself standing up in front of fifteen young kids being the only one able to speak English. How was I going to teach them what each word meant if I couldn't tell them the translation? It was Angel jumping down from her top bunk, wide-awake and ready to go that interrupted my train of thought.

"Food!" she said, waking up Emily and Jude.

"Green curry," I suggested.

"Pigeon," Jude answered, still sounding half asleep.

"Bat," I shouted, remembering the tunnel-dwelling vampire bastard.

"Shut up Harry!" Emily demanded. "I've been dreaming about that."

We decided to find somewhere by chance rather than planning it. We declined the usual entourage of cyclos and motorbikes as we paced the streets looking for something to keep us going until the evening.

As we walked, I spotted a KFC. It was such a shame seeing the city being exploited by American fast-food chains, but my ideals had to be put on hold. Nothing was going to come between me and a bucket of chicken.

"I don't know about you lot, but I'm heading over there," I said, pointing out the KFC sign.

"You're so bloody English Harry." Angel smiled.

"I know," I smiled back. "Anyone else?" I was quite prepared to risk losing my friends and probably my way home rather than risk losing the chance of fried chicken.

"I'm going to have to be typically English too, I'm afraid," Emily said. The other two declined and we agreed to meet back at the hostel.

Emily and I made our way over to the big building like excited kids discussing the imminent gluttony. We entered a massive department store that looked ridiculously out of place being too posh to be in a third world city, and confirmed our beliefs that this country would soon become a tourist trap and be ruined by modern development. The hypocrisy of two people headed to KFC.

We walked through the store and made our way up an escalator that led to a bowling alley. We found KFC and ordered more than we could ever eat! It was Emily's idea to get a Family Feast bucket, consisting of twelve pieces of chicken and four portions of chips, that cost more than all the food we'd eaten so far in Vietnam. We sat by the window surreally watching the busy streets from the clean, posh, air-conditioned building. We both got stuck into the chicken like we hadn't eaten for weeks, and only two pieces and one portion of chips remained when we had to admit defeat.

"I'm never eating again." Emily decided as she fell back in her chair.

"Nor me," I agreed, trying to remove the grease from my hands and face using the two-inch square lemon-fresh towel they expect to work miracles. We sat there regretting the family feast decision and fearing one wrong move would result in self-combustion.

"How do you feel about tomorrow Harry?" Emily asked. I told her about my trepidation of teaching English to non-English speakers. She sat and listened, agreeing with what I said. We sat and talked for about twenty minutes, both uncertain as to what to expect when we arrived at the school but knowing it would become easier as the days and weeks passed.

"At least if I can't do it, I'll have you to put your head up my arse!" she smiled, obviously still in shock at my earlier conduct.

"I'm sorry about that." I laughed, still surprised that I'd said such a thing.

When we'd finished chatting, we decided to make our way back to the hostel, trying to walk off the family of chickens we'd stuffed ourselves with. We walked down the escalators, through the out-of-place store and back into reality.

As we were about to turn down the street that would lead us back to familiar territory, we passed a cool looking bar that wouldn't look out of place in London. I noticed Emily looking at her watch, and as our eyes met, we smiled and walked in. The only thing better than allowing the natural digestive process of fried chicken is to throw alcohol at it, converse to the theory of throwing a kebab on top of a belly full of ale at the end of a night. Both theories are complete bollocks, but frequently used by idiots for convenience sake.

"Could I see the wine list?" Emily asked the waitress, as we found a table over-looking the street for an afternoon of people-watching.

"We're having wine, are we?" I asked, the decision already out of my hands.

"It's Sunday," she replied, "you have to have wine on Sunday." With the obvious exception of priests, I had no clue how Sunday and wine went together, but I'd long since given up making any sense of the female mind. "Red or white?"

"I don't mind, I'll drink either," I replied. "It is Sunday after all." *If you can't beat them, join them.*

"I fancy white, I think." She ordered a bottle from the wine list using the internationally accepted pointing method, which the waitress acknowledged. "Do you think the other two will be upset we didn't go straight back?" she asked.

"I can't see why they would," I replied, not having even thought about them. "We can't stay in each other's pockets for the whole six weeks, can we?"

"I suppose not." she agreed.

The wine arrived and was poured, then placed in an ice bucket. We clinked glasses, acting dead posh and said "Cheers."

"A cheeky little number," I observed. "Quite fruity, with a subtle hint of oak giving it a dryness to complement its medium qualities."

"Shut up you wanker!" I'd found my female version of Trev. "Where did that crap come from?"

"No idea," I replied, wondering the same myself. "Isn't it compulsory to talk like an idiot when drinking wine?"

As the wine was drunk and our brains became sedated, the thought of tomorrow couldn't have been more distant. We laughed at the fact that we had to meet Lou in twelve hours, but through our self-induced merry haze, we didn't care. We were going to be brilliant English teachers and would have all the kids in our class fluent within a month. It's incredible what wine can do for the soul.

As the second bottle of wine was slowly evaporating the conversation was becoming ridiculous. We were expected to teach English in less than ten hours, and had lost the ability to speak it ourselves.

"I quite fancy you, Harry," Emily said nonchalantly. I felt her bare leg touching mine, and my one-eyed snake getting firm. *Margaret Thatcher, Margaret Thatcher.*

"Shut up devil woman," I replied firmly. *Ah fuck it.* "You're not so bad yourself," I said, my flirting being entirely Chardonnay-driven.

"You can't keep your eyes off me," she laughed.

"You've given me plenty to look at," I replied, placing the blame squarely with her.

"And you like what you see?" *Dumbest question ever.*

"God, yes!" I replied, my eyes undressing her to the underwear I knew she had on.

"So what are you going to do about it then?" she asked. The big bad wolf analogy was on the tip of my tongue but I decided against it. I leant across the table as she leaned in towards me and our lips came together—in a bar on a Sunday afternoon. "I want more than that Harry," Emily said, her flirtatious pout driving me crazy. I looked around the bar wondering if I could get away with table-ending her there and then before realising that the street-facing windows made it unwise. My thoughts turned to taking her down one of the alleys and giving her one, but the rats made that a bad idea. She shifted in her seat towards me and we kissed again. And again.

"Sit the fuck back down," I smiled when she stood to come and sit next to me. I had to take charge before things got out of control, and the table-ending live-show kicked off.

After a lot more kissing, teasing and flirting we decided to head back. It was half past ten when we left, having spent thirty dollars on another hangover. We staggered back in the direction of the hostel laughing about how ridiculous it was having a hangover on our first day.

As we neared the hostel, Emily stopped walking and put her arms around me. She slowly pushed me up against a wall and kissed me. Our hands were quickly all over each other, and she wasted no time grabbing hold of the big fella. I failed miserably getting my hand up the leg of her shorts and ended up fumbling around like an idiot. It took every lesson I'd ever had in gentlemanly conduct to not nail her against the wall, but she was entirely in control. When she started playing with me through my shorts, I tried to stop her but failed. Then came the small explosion that immediately soaked through my shorts, leaving me feeling like a little boy who'd pissed himself. In retrospect, pissing myself might have been less embarrassing than the ejaculate that had soaked Emily's hand. She stood back and laughed, letting me know who was boss. I collapsed against the wall looking back at her.

She smiled as she stepped back. "Now, we'd better go."

When we got back Emily, once again, woken the entire street with her banging on the shutters, and we quietly (or so we imagined) made our way upstairs into the room. As we walked in, Jude and Angel were sitting up talking from their top bunks across the room. They took one look at us and laughed. Emily stood there wobbling, and I stood there covering up my little wet patch.

"Sorry, but we accidentally got a bit pissed," I giggled like a child.

"You speak for yourself young man," Emily smiled, trying to convince them she was sober.

"Bloody vino was your idea not mine." She was undoubtedly to blame for the whole incident. "I only wanted a Cola-Coca!" My speech was complete garbage. Jude and Angel were in hysterics as we staggered around the room blaming each other, wondering what to do with ourselves. Emily made the sudden and immediate decision that she had had enough and threw herself at her bed, shouting 'goodnight' mid-flight. I managed to wrestle off her shoes and proceeded to try and get her under the covers, but she was a dead weight. As I tried to whip the sheet out from under her—like a magician trying to get a tablecloth off a neatly set table—she spun into the air and hit the wall.

"What are you doing you fucking psycho?" she shouted, lifting her head. I was doubled over, giggling, holding the sheet as she shook her head and put it back on the pillow. I threw the sheet over her, took my trainers off and climbed into my own bed, still laughing as I passed out.

"Stop the noise! STOP THE NOISE!" I shouted as Jude's alarm clock went off way too early. I tried to lift my head off the pillow but it was fused to it and my eyes wouldn't open. "Check my pulse. I might be dead." Jude and Angel were way too full of energy, and were raring to go. I eventually opened my eyes and looked over at Emily enjoying the flashbacks from our drunken encounter. "Oh shit!" I said as I remember ejaculating in my own underwear. I also got a momentary visual of Nicola which made me feel like shit. What had I done? Fuck it, it was the wine's fault!

"Come on you lazy sods!" Jude shouted, enjoying the state Emily and I were in.

"Jude," I said, annoyed, "I shot three coke cans and won't hesitate to shoot you!" He carried on trying to get us up while laughing at my empty threats. It was half past six before I finally realised I had to get up. Angel and Jude were already downstairs for breakfast while Emily and I lay there wondering how we were going to survive the day.

"Do you fancy a quick one?" I asked for fun.

"Fuck you, Harry. Your 'quick one' is even too quick for you." I closed my eyes and wanted to die while she giggled at her own brilliant humour. "Why have I still got my clothes on?" she asked when she pulled the sheet back. I laughed at my failed magic that nearly sent her through the wall.

"You collapsed. I took your trainers off."

"Smoothie!" she laughed as she managed to sit up cradling her head in her hands. "We've gotta be downstairs in half an hour," she said as she made her way to the bathroom. "I can't believe you took advantage of me."

"You started it," I smiled, "now go and shower."

"I can't. The water might hurt my head."

Somehow we made it downstairs shortly after seven o'clock to find Lou and the other two sitting at a table with two plates of scrambled eggs waiting for us. I immediately went for the coffee, knowing that I needed to drink at least one gallon of it before I could go anywhere. Lou took one look at both of us and shook his head smiling. The eggs were cold and had to be forced down, and the cold sweat told me I might be seeing them again before the day was out. I drank about four cups of coffee before half past seven when Lou said we had to leave. We all looked very professional in our matching T-shirts, curriculum under our arm and a rucksack full of the pens and notebooks.

We boarded the same dusty minibus that had collected us from the airport. I was too tired and too ill to care about the dirty bus. I needed sleep, lots more sleep.

We arrived at about quarter to eight. When we filed out of the minibus, I was unsure if this was the place we would be working in. The building looked derelict, with barbed wire topping the six-foot wire fence that was broken in places. The grounds outside the building had areas that were dug up and looked hazardous, and there was shit everywhere. There was a field over to the right, with a single set of old wooden goalposts. The building was quite big but had some broken windows and a few staircases that looked like they had been blocked off. It was a concrete eyesore and I struggled to believe that this could be a school.

"Here we are," Lou said, removing my doubts. "The children are due here in about half an hour so I'll take you inside and show you around. Then we'll go over any last-minute concerns." My bloody hangover was something that was a last-minute concern, but I was quite sure there was nothing Lou could do about that.

We walked into the school grounds and felt quite sad at what we were seeing. Schools are supposed to be places kids can come to have some fun and play, as well as learn. The uneven playing surfaces together with the randomly dug holes were like nothing I'd seen before. I thought back to my school with its vast open spaces: rugby fields, running track, football pitches and gyms. One set of goalposts was all this place had to offer and a shitty old dirt field with the occasional patch of grass. We walked over towards the main building and Lou led us up a flight of stairs. There was rubbish scattered everywhere and dust that you could feel yourself inhaling with every breath. If there ever was an effective hangover cure this was it; dirt, dust and unthinkable poverty makes headaches and lethargy seem so irrelevant.

At the top of the stairs was a corridor that looked like a jail in a movie. Nothing but grey concrete, with a four-foot wall overlooking the grounds on one side, and four doors on the other side leading to some rooms. We walked into the first room. It was featureless except for a small window about eight feet from the ground, and a section of wall with chalk marks on it. The emptiness of the room together with the dim light from window gave it an eerie feeling. The cold, musty air made me feel like I was stuck inside a bad dream, not standing in a classroom where the kids would shortly be coming to learn.

Lou showed us the other three rooms. “You can fight amongst yourselves as to which room you have,” he said. “Now, do you have any questions? The kids will be here very soon.” I had plenty of questions, but had to accept the school for what it was and decided against asking them. Lou explained that the hours were generally half past eight until about half past two, and they could have a half hour to an hour to play at lunchtime depending on how that day’s work was progressing. The whole thing seemed very informal and more work-based than time-based. He said that the kids would be making their own way to school, so the time aspect wasn’t so important. I shuddered to think of a six-year-old making his or her own way to school but had to remember that I wasn’t back with all the creature comforts I was used to. I was in a very different country with a very different culture. I had to forget everything I understood to be ‘normal’.

CHAPTER TEN

We started to hear children's voices and walked over to the wall that overlooked the playground to find about thirty children gathered. I lost all memory of a hangover as sheer terror took hold of me. For some reason, I never believed this moment was going to come, so seeing the children was a huge wake-up call. I could tell by the others' faces that they too had become nervous, Emily being the worst. I hoped that her hangover had been blown away with mine and that she didn't still feel ill. She looked around, caught my eye and tensed her face to indicate her anxiety.

Lou led us downstairs where we were met with a playground full of smiles. There were about forty kids now, each one of them smiling, trying to excitedly touch or hold our hand. They came barefoot from every direction, as we stood frozen at how beautiful these little kids were. "Hello Mister!" and "Hello Miss!" rang from every direction as we became engulfed in children.

Lou clapped his hands together and shouted something in Vietnamese. Within seconds four lines had formed, all about the same length and silence fell upon the playground. He told us to go upstairs and each choose a room and he would send up one group at a time. This group would be the same for the next six weeks.

We made our way up the stairs and each chose a room at random. I was in the second room, furthest away from the stairs. We wished each other luck and suddenly I was alone in my desolate classroom for the first time.

I leaned against the wall and opened the curriculum in the right place for the day, and waited. I prepared the pads and pens ready to hand out and tried to compose myself, the previous night's activities playing heavily on my mind and the alcohol still clouding my head. I watched as the first group passed my door en route to Jude's class and could hear him excitedly greet each of them. Within a few minutes, I could hear another group approaching and took a deep breath. I saw a head poking around the doorway and motioned for him to come in, which he did, followed by a stampede of the remaining kids. When they were all inside they fell silent, standing with their hands by their sides waiting for my instruction. The groups had been split randomly and contained a mixture of ages. I walked from right to left handing them each a pen and a pad, and marvelled at the excitement on their faces as they received them. It was so humbling to see how grateful they were for something I always had taken for granted. I asked them to sit down employing an arm-waving technique at sign language, not knowing if they would have a clue what I was asking. They lined themselves against the surrounding walls and sat using it for support. *That was easy enough!*

"My name is Mr Fisher," I announced slowly. We were told to use our names in that format to save confusion. "Fisher."

"Mister Fishy," one boy replied.

"No, Fisher," I repeated slowly.

"Fishy," he laughed. Little bugger.

"OK, Mister Fish," I smiled. The rest of the room altogether said "Mister Fishy!" And in that instant, twenty-five years of 'Fisher' was gone.

I worked through the curriculum and was surprised how easily they picked things up. Most of them knew the easier words: "Hello," "Goodbye," "Please" and "Thank you," but some of the younger ones became so confused I couldn't help but laugh. "Hello Mister Fishy. My name is please goodbye" and "My name is hello Mister Fishy, hello please." Every time I laughed, the rest of the class joined in, probably not knowing why.

"Hello, my name is Mister Fishy," one girl tried.

"No, use your name. Say 'Hello my name is', and then your name."

"Hello my name is your name." She wasn't getting the hang of this.

"Hello, my name is Mai mate." In hindsight, my mistake was to call them 'mate' rather than try to remember their names. I decided that was close enough and congratulated her, one of the older kids would sort her out. I imagined the whole class next door would be proficient in the word 'dude' before long anyway.

I loved every minute of it and didn't want to break for lunch. It was eleven-forty-five when I saw that Jude had released his class. I motioned towards the door for my class to go and play and then went to find Jude. I still feared for them running around the dangerous play area, especially with no shoes on. However, I was quickly learning that all the locals have feet made of leather.

After another few minutes the girls had also dismissed their classes, and we all stood outside the rooms talking excitedly and reciting the events of the day. Emily and I explained to the other two how nervous we'd been the previous night, talking about our unfounded anxieties and blaming them for our accidental intoxication. We all walked down to the playground and watched the children playing or chatting as we ate the sandwiches Minh had kindly prepared. Such simple things amused them: running around, chasing each other oblivious to the dangerous holes around them, chatting and laughing. Their smiles gave me inspiration and I made a mental note to focus more on what I had, rather than always wanting more.

At about half past twelve, we made the collective decision to call them all back in, and Jude was the one appointed to do this.

"Hello," he shouted, knowing they should all at least know that word by now. Within about thirty seconds the same four lines were formed as they were that morning. Jude was pleased and used his nodding dog routine to show it. We looked at each other and laughed, wondering how and why they were so obedient. *Aren't kids supposed to be disobedient and annoying?*

We led our groups back to the classrooms—Jude first, then I, followed by the girls. I was pleased that lunch was over because I was looking forward to the afternoon session. I felt that it was benefitting me just as much as the children.

I continued the curriculum, having little difficulty teaching them the simpler words and the afternoon mostly went without incident, except when I accidentally taught them the word 'bugger' when I dropped my folder. Them being the obedient kids they were, repeated it out loud.

"No, no. Don't say that word," I panicked.

"Bugger," came the chorus of young voices.

"No, I said DON'T say it again," emphasizing a word that I hadn't even taught them yet. Why was it they had no trouble picking up this word? Why couldn't they understand when to use 'please' and 'thank you' instead? I turned my back as I started to laugh—they didn't need any further encouragement. What would the others think if they heard my class shouting 'Bugger'? I decided to carry on hoping they would forget it.

At three o'clock, I felt that we'd done enough and was also becoming a little tired. I'd been on my feet all day and although I'd enjoyed every minute of it, I didn't want to overdo it. We'd completed the required work for that day an hour early and were just repeating what we'd covered. Some of the English conversations they were having when I paired them off were good, and some of them were plain comical. As long as they could pronounce the word, when and where to use it would come in time. *Rome wasn't built in a day.*

When I was by the door motioning them out, they all stood smiling and left, some of them saying "Thank you Mister Fishy" and some shaking my hand or high fiving me as they left. Each was guarding their pen and notepad as if it was their greatest possession. They were all so endearing, and I tried to imagine what sort of home life each of them was returning to. Would they be going home to a loving family? Would they be going out on the streets tonight to beat some sucker with rock, paper, scissors? I knew I could never imagine their home lives, but their lovely, warming smiles gave me a great sense of hope.

When the last one had left I walked back into the classroom and experienced the quietness I hadn't heard since that morning. It was amazing how ugly the room looked without them; its shitty décor had become so irrelevant when they were there. They had brightened up the dreary room, and I missed them already. I smiled in satisfaction as I walked out into the corridor waiting for the others to finish.

I was only alone for a few minutes when the other three classrooms emptied. Jude's class ran past me, giggling and chatting, with the occasional "Goodbye Mister" coming my way. Jude walked out of his room rolling a cigarette, with the widest grin I'd seen so far.

"What a great day," he said as he came over and leant against the wall. "I can't believe how much fun I've had. I didn't want them to go but knew I had to when I heard your lot coming out." Emily and Angel came over as Jude and I stood smoking, both with the same big smiles.

"I taught them 'bugger' by accident," I said laughing when the two girls had reached us. I couldn't wait to tell them my story, and explained what had happened. We all stood there laughing, the euphoria of the day making us giddy.

"I did have a few saying 'dude' by the end, but I did that on purpose," Jude said, smiling. This set my mind racing as to what other words we could teach them for fun.

"You boys are bad," Angel laughed, trying to chastise us but probably thinking along the same lines.

We walked down the stairs past the playground and out of the gate where Lou was waiting for us. We climbed into the minibus laughing and joking and taking it in turns to tell a story.

"Good day?" he asked when there was a gap in conversation. We knew he was probably used to this kind of excitement from the previous people that had done this work, but he seemed to enjoy hearing our tales.

When we arrived back at the hostel Lou came in with us and carried on chatting and drinking coffee. Every one of us at some point mentioned adopting at least one of the children, if not all of them. It would be nearly impossible not to fall for such adorable children, but the reality of adopting them was a little far-fetched.

"So, after your first day do you have any questions?" he asked, probably guessing the response. Silence. We were too happy and excited that everything had gone so well. From our conversations it seemed we were all initially nervous, but as the day progressed the apprehension had disappeared. "Good," he continued after allowing us ample time to reply. "I'll see you at quarter to eight tomorrow. You can have a lay-in."

We went upstairs exhausted and lay on our bunks. Emily and I were experiencing our second hangover phase, the day's events having put them on hold. We needed sleep. I kicked off my boots and warned the others that waking me would result in their immediate death.

It was a little before seven when I awoke, the others still fast asleep. I lay thinking about Nicola and feeling guilty about what had happened with Emily. I had to make sure it was a one-off and didn't happen again but knew the likelihood of being able to restrain myself was slim. I turned around to watch her sleep. She did look bloody sexy and somehow innocent, but she was the devil. I giggled as I recalled the unwanted ejaculation, and wondered if the shorts could be worn again. *Skank!*

Moments later, Jude seemed to be bouncing up and down on his bed. I lay there thinking how uncool it was to be knocking one out with girls in the room. This bouncing continued for another minute or so and I climbed off my bunk fearing he was going to land on me when the springs gave way. He appeared to be in pain but was still asleep, his eyes squeezed shut, bouncing himself up and down like some eighties break-dancer. As I stood there watching, he sat bolt upright, his eyes open wide, and looking scared.

"Dude! What the hell are you doing?" he asked, looking stunned to see me. *What was I doing?*

"You were… bouncing a lot," I replied, understanding his shock at finding me watching him sleep.

"Bad dream, man. Dreamt the school was burning down."

"And bouncing helped that how?" I asked, trying to stop myself from laughing. By now the girls were awake and trying to figure out what was going on.

"I was trying to get away from the fire," he laughed, "and in my dream, bouncing was quicker than walking. Weird, man."

"Thank God for that," I whispered, checking to make sure the girls couldn't hear, "I thought you were, err, doing the five-knuckle shuffle," I smiled.

"And you thought you'd watch?" This stopped me smiling but made him laugh.

He climbed down from his bunk and went into the bathroom as I lay back down on my bunk. We were all quite tired and none of us could be bothered to get up but we knew we had to eat. It was Angel that suggested we tried the café downstairs because it was cheap and it was close. We had to start being a little less reckless with our money as we'd spent a lot already and were all on a limited budget.

We made our way downstairs and Linh brought over some menus. I ordered a Coke as soon as she arrived because I was severely in need of a drink, and the others copied. We concluded Minh must either get cheap eggs or can only cook eggs given the majority of the menu was different kinds of omelette. I decided on a cheese and ham omelette, given the limited choice and in need of something safe to fill me up.

Jude spotted a flyer about coach trips to Nha Trang. I remembered Nha Trang from the guy who had sold me my backpack and was intrigued as he made it sound like a fun place. We looked it up in the Lonely Planet and found that it had beautiful-looking beaches, plenty of nightlife and an Indian restaurant. That was the deal-breaker. The coach trip was eight dollars each way and we discussed making the trip that weekend. We could travel up either on Friday night or Saturday morning and return on Sunday. The downside was that the coach would take about twelve hours, but if we were going to see anywhere outside Ho Chi Minh we'd have to suffer the travelling. Angel found a cool looking place called the Sailing Club in Nha Trang that had all-night beach parties every Saturday night. An Indian followed by an all-night beach party. The flyer was from the same place we'd booked the trip to the Cu Chi tunnels, so we agreed to go and book it after school the following day.

We eventually made our way up to the room, and were in bed within minutes: reading, chatting or in Jude case, 'going to sleep for another nightmare.' I made a start on one of the photocopied books I'd bought from the rock, paper, scissors menace, 'The Ten Thousand Day War'. After reading only a few pages, I awoke to the sound of the book hitting the floor. I left it there and drifted back to sleep.

The next morning began with the array of cursing at Jude's alarm making annoying wake-up noises, today being quarter to seven.

"I've had enough of these early starts," shouted Angel.

"Only about another thirty to go," Jude laughed, his early morning energy starting to piss me off. People shouldn't be allowed to have energy first thing in the morning; it serves no other purpose than to annoy people.

"I am going to break your phone Jude, and then I'm going to feed it to you," Emily joined in.

Emily was next in the bathroom after Jude's record-breaking four minutes. I was in awe of how he managed that, as he always came out showered, shaven and shampooed. I needed at least ten minutes, and that was a rush. I needed to up my game, as six minutes extra sleep would always be welcome. The additional six minutes might even give me a glimpse of Angel half-dressed. *Shut up, shut up, shut up!*

Downstairs, I ate cold scrambled eggs and drank as much coffee as I could and was ready when Lou arrived. The kids turned up one-by-one with their big smiles and "Good Morning!" greetings, with a few of my lot giving it the "Mr Fishy!" routine, which the others enjoyed.

"Good morning!" Jude shouted. It was half past eight and time to go in. Jude turned to us and did his hippy laugh, pleased with himself that they had all stopped in their tracks and immediately formed their queues. We watched him enjoying the weird power he possessed over a yard full of young children.

The morning went well and was even more enjoyable without a hangover. I managed to avoid any slip-ups that could result in bad language, but had resigned myself to calling them 'mate' as their names were impossible to remember. I managed to pick up a few of them: Phuc, Dong, Thang, Binh, Hung and Dung, but that was only because they made me giggle. The one other I couldn't forget is 'Lan', which one of the other boys tried to explain by making a fist and moving it back and forth from his forehead. I struggled to believe that his name was 'dickhead', but Lou told me, much to my relief, that it meant something like 'Unicorn'. The rest of their names sounded like doorbells or vegetables, and it was easier to call them 'mate'. Jude and I had discussed this the previous evening and had given in to the fact that by the end of the six weeks there would be a playground full of 'dudes' and 'mates'. I was on my own when I likened this to the gangs in West Side Story.

Lunchtime arrived when I saw Jude's class running past my doorway and I let my lot go too. I was pleased with the morning's lessons, amazed at how quickly they were learning. Every time I heard them picking up and using a word I'd taught them it gave me more confidence in myself and in what I was doing.

We all met up outside our rooms and made our way down to the playground to eat our sandwiches. Jude told us the new word he had taught them today, for his own amusement, was 'pants'. I laughed as I remembered Jude's game and decided I too would teach my class 'pants'. The girls said we were childish, and I said Emily's ponytail was childish, which was even more childish than anything else.

Jude called them back in and we went through the same procedure as the morning until we were back in our rooms. I immediately set about teaching the kids their new word. I asked them to repeat it out loud hoping the others would hear, just for the sake of annoying the girls and making Jude laugh. They performed the exercise very well and added it to their repertoire. I looked forward to hearing it in the playground.

I continued the curriculum for the remainder of the afternoon trying to get back on track on the maturity front. As I saw Jude's class leave I once again slipped back into juvenile mode and asked the class, once more, to say 'pants' out loud. They did it masterfully so I allowed them to leave.

When they had all gone I walked outside to find Jude giggling like a child. He said that just as he'd achieved a good rhythm after lunch all he could hear was "pants" being shouted from the room next door. As he started to laugh so did the rest of the class and they too shouted "pants" but I hadn't heard them. It was a good job as I would have happily spent the rest of the afternoon trading words with Jude's class and no work would have got done. Emily was the first to walk out, shaking her head, as Jude and I tried to keep a straight face. She walked over to us and started laughing. She told us that her class had all looked at each other when they'd heard the outburst from my lot and seemed to be whispering "pants" to each other trying to work out what it meant. She had tried to stop herself laughing while trying to take their minds off it, but even at the end of the lesson, she could still hear a few of them whispering it to each other. Angel arrived not having heard a thing but wanted to know why we were all laughing. She didn't find it at all amusing.

We made our way down to the minibus. We told Lou that we were planning on going away for the weekend to Nha Trang and he was excited for us saying Nha Trang was a lovely place with beautiful beaches. This added to our excitement and Lou kindly dropped us off at 'Sinh Café' so we could book the coach.

Within ten minutes we were on our way to the hostel, deal done. We would leave on Friday evening after school for an overnight coach to Nha Trang, and return at stupid o'clock on Sunday morning. We walked back, excited about our first weekend adventure but not looking forward to being on a coach so early on a Sunday morning. Once again Jude came to the rescue saying he had 'melatonin' tablets. I thought it was some sort of party drug, but turns out it is quite the opposite.

When we got back to the room, it was time for a rest. I tried to read while others chatted ruining any concentration I thought I had. I knew Jude would be asleep in seconds. He was a man of many of the skills I wanted to possess, and

I knew that at some point I had to ask him for lessons. In return, I could offer to teach him how to ask for a proper haircut and laugh without looking like a clown. I went through my usual routine of reading until the book hit the ground signifying unconsciousness. Good job I wasn't on the top bunk.

I had a very restless couple of hours, a mixture of strange dreams and mosquitoes buzzing around me. Finally, I gave up the idea of proper sleep shortly after six. I carried on reading while Emily and Jude slept and Angel wrote what I guessed to be her journal, reminding me that mine wouldn't write itself.

Emily had begun the most magnificent snoring. We sat and listened to her, hearing Jude stirring from above and whispering, "what the hell is that?" She sounded like a pig when she inhaled, and a whistling kettle when she exhaled. We sat and watched in awe as she created a noise way too big for the little thing she was. After about two minutes, she woke herself up with a grunt to find three spectators laughing at her performance.

"Where the hell did you learn to snore like that?" I asked, wanting to be able to do it myself.

"I don't snore, shut up," she said. We looked at her inquisitively.

"I beg to differ, sweetie," Angel said, smiling.

"I don't snore," she repeated, "and if I did make any noise it must have been a one-off. You're all mean!" she said, taking offence, a technique masterfully employed by women to get their own way and shut down unwanted conversation.

The next few days passed pretty much the same way as the previous two, with the only exception being the 'word of the day' as Jude and I had named it. Wednesday was 'knickers', Thursday was 'boxers' and Friday, being my favourite, was 'bosom'. The whole thing was acted out each day after lunch with Jude and me, much to the disapproval of the girls, taking it in turns to coach our class to say aloud the word of the day.

Each evening after school was the same routine: returning to the hostel, a couple of hours reading, writing our journals or resting, and then out for a quick bite to eat.

After we bid the children goodbye on Friday, we rushed back to the hostel to pack for our weekend in Nha Trang.

Shortly after eight o'clock, we boarded the coach outside the Sinh Café, still with mad cyclo men after us, and were lucky enough to find a seat each in two rows next to each other. We made our way out of the City, hoping that the driver wouldn't need to blast his horn every ten-seconds throughout the journey.

After about an hour we were starting to become frustrated at our maniac driver. He was overtaking cars, motorbikes and anything else unfortunate to share the road with us, blasting his horn the whole time. He was a bloody lunatic and we had another eight hours to go. At one point Jude went to the toilet and came back looking as if he'd been in a fight.

The next couple of hours were a little better as there was less traffic on the road to beep the horn at. Maybe they had put out a warning to motorists about being on the same road as this idiot. As night fell and we couldn't see anything on either side of us, sleep came a-calling. Jude gave me two melatonin tablets—twice the recommended dose—and I gulped them down. It was going to take a miracle to sleep on this coach and these tablets were my only chance.

It was midnight before I started to feel drowsy from the tablets. The other three seemed to have passed out a half-hour before but I couldn't make myself comfortable however hard I tried. I ended up with my head on my rucksack and my legs sharing Emily's seats across the aisle. She stirred slightly when my legs hit her seat and put hers across into the space left on mine. I was finally comfortable and felt myself drifting off, the annoying driver blasting his horn became less frequent.

I was the last one to wake up and only did so as I was hurled into the seats in front of me when the maniac braked suddenly. It was a good job the seat in front of me was padded or my forehead would have got another battering. With my head and shoulders somewhere down the gap between the seats, and my torso and legs parked somewhere over towards Emily's seat, I wearily picked myself back up again. If it hadn't been for Emily holding onto my legs the whole lot of me would have ended up on the floor.

"He hit a cyclist!" she gasped. I sat up to see what she was talking about and trying to make my eyes work. I checked my watch and saw it was twenty to five and we were supposed to be there at about five. We watched a brief commotion, and we were moving again within about ten minutes. The cyclist seemed to be unhurt, having shaken the maniac driver's hand before he left, and he even waved as we passed. He looked as if he was apologising for being in the way. These people never ceased to amaze me.

Just as I was starting to feel human again, we reached the coastal road and got to see the sun rising over the sea. The view was amazing, like something you only ever see in a movie. The sea stretching as far as the eyes can see, and the shades of deep orange breaking the darkness as the sun woke up for the day.

"Welcome to Nha Trang," said the voice over the tannoy. We were finally here, and the bloody driver was happily finding new things to blast his horn at. "In a short while, we will be stopping at our first hotel." That was good news because we had nowhere to stay and Jude was the only one who liked the idea of sleeping on the beach. The idea of getting sand in my arse, in my mouth and every other place had zero appeal. "This one has twin rooms for fifteen dollars." What does a man have to do to get some privacy out here? Emily looked over at me and winked, which as usual, made me smile.

"That'll do," Jude said. "You and I will have to share Dude if that's OK with you." Damn him. Emily smiled as her and Angel also agreed that sharing was fine.

When the coach finally stopped, about ten of us climbed off. Most of the others had their big rucksacks and were stuck by the coach waiting for them, so we were the first inside. We got two twin rooms next to each other and made our way up the stairs, agreeing to wake at about ten o'clock. We were in desperate need of some proper sleep in a bed before we did anything else.

We walked into our room which was like a ward in a hospital. The wall against the corridor was made only of glass covered with curtains, the floor was covered in white ceramic tiles, and the walls were painted bright white. The two beds were up against the curtained windows and had a table between them. I walked over to the bathroom which was between the girls' room and ours. The bathroom had a large shower, toilet and sink with a huge mirror. It was better than our room at the hostel but was a little too white and bright. None of this detail mattered as I hit the bed and was dead to the world within seconds.

Mr wakey-wakey-hippy-bastard woke us all at ten o'clock with his usual annoying alarm and we laughed when we heard Angel and Emily shouting at Jude to make it stop—the walls being obviously quite thin. It was only when I looked above me that I realised why they had heard it—the window above my head which led into the corridor was wide-open. Anything could have crawled in and got me. No matter how many of them small crocodiles I'd seen since being in Vietnam I still didn't like them. I certainly wouldn't want one landing on my face however 'Crocodile Dundee' it would make me feel.

Jude was up and straight into the shower. I swore I would kill him before leaving Vietnam, and any rational policeman would understand my motives. Anyone who wakes up that quickly should be shot through all of their vital organs in quick succession so they feel the pain of each. He was in a room with a man who sets his alarm one hour before he wants to get up because repeated use of the snooze button is a necessity otherwise it wouldn't be there.

As he came out of the bathroom I realised I had no other option but to get up. I walked in swearing with each footstep and went into the shower. I swore at the water, I swore at the soap, and the shampoo received a good tongue lashing too. All of these things shouldn't be near a man that is so tired—he should still be at one with his pillow.

After about fifteen minutes of verbal abuse, I turned off the shower and dried myself. When I walked into the room I found Jude lying back on his bed. Bastard! He had caused this waking up bullshit. He was in his beach clothes and told me that it was gorgeous outside. Nowhere could be gorgeous this morning because I was grumpy. I put on my trunks and a T-shirt.

"Bollocks!" I shouted as I realised I had no flip-flops and had only brought my boots. Jude lay there laughing as I put them on with my shorts looking like an idiot. "I've got no other choice, laughing boy." I was now a giggling, grumpy man because I did look stupid. My little white skinny legs with big boots on the end made me look like I had two golf clubs hanging out of my shorts. There was a knock at the door and I walked over to answer it.

"Hello boys," Emily said as she and Angel walked in.

"What do you think?" I asked, looking down at my feet. They joined laughing boy, giggling and making childish fun. "What else am I supposed to do? I didn't bring any flip-flops!"

"Go barefoot," Emily suggested, "everyone else in this country seems to be doing alright."

"Yes, but that's because they have feet made of leather. Jude told me."

"Dude, that was a figure of speech!" *The lying little shit.* He told me that they had evolved differently to us and that's why they could walk around barefoot. He took great pleasure in explaining to the girls why Harry 'the gullible idiot' Fisher thought this.

"I hate you all," I announced as I threw off my boots, deciding barefoot was the only option.

I hadn't even made it down the stairs when I was screaming like a girl, having picked up a small stone in my heel. Luckily the hotel lobby shop had some for sale, but unluckily they only had a pink pair which were two sizes too small. I had no other option knowing I would only be wearing them to the beach and back and could throw them away that evening. I handed over three dollars and put them on having to squeeze my feet through the end bits and walk nearly on tiptoe to avoid losing my heel. Emily took out her camera but quickly put it away as I threatened to beat her to death with them if she took a picture. We made a deal that I would never video her snoring if she never pictured me in these women's beach shoes.

"See, they've all got them on," I said, as we passed a few local men also wearing pink flip-flops, "I'm so trendy!"

"Except they're not walking like a drag queen." Angel's observation wasn't unfounded.

"You have no style," I laughed as I teetered along, my stride length impaired.

We arrived at a section of beach that was the only area with sun loungers and headed straight for them. As we pulled over other loungers so we could sit together we were told we had to buy a drink or we couldn't use them. We ordered four cokes and made ourselves comfortable, ready to be baked by the already hot sun. My flip-flops were hidden out of sight under my lounger and I lay back demanding a good bronzing.

I'd only been lying there a few minutes when Emily spotted the 'big donuts.' They looked like enormous inner tubes with a perfectly sized hole in the middle for my generously-sized arse. The sea already looked inviting and this would surely be a fun way to be in it.

After paying three dollars each for the day Emily and I set out to sea. I followed her lead as I didn't have a clue what to do, but the idea is to catch the crest of a wave and be carried back in sat inside the tyre. How hard can that be?

"Ready," she said. She jumped into her tyre and I followed. Or I tried to. As I jumped onto it I must have got my weight distribution wrong as I went flying over the other side of it and was hit on the head by the tyre as I went. As I regained some composure I could see Emily coasting in towards the beach, and the other two sat laughing at me. Fluke, I'll get it next time.

Within a minute she was back trying to explain where I'd gone wrong. My overly analytical mind had already worked out that my weight distribution had to be met with the precise balance of the tyre. She called me boring and told me to shut up. I had a few practices at jumping onto the tyre whilst my cocky, smart-arse teacher observed until I'd perfected it.

"Right, are you ready? When I say go, jump in and follow me." There was a pause as she seemed to know when the right time would come, wave after wave passing us by. "Go." I jumped into the tyre and was carried all the way back to the beach. As I reached the beach it became too shallow and before I'd realised what Emily was shouting at me, my tyre was grounded, and I was flipped straight over onto my face and into the very coarse shingle. As I bashed my head on the floor I couldn't work out where I was. My tyre was gone and I was left drowning. I eventually found the floor and worked my knees onto it and pulled my head into the air. I turned around and saw Emily standing with one hand on her hip with the other holding her tyre.

"Didn't you hear me shouting for you to get out?" she laughed.

"Does it bloody look like I heard you?" I replied, still trying to recover from my latest head injury. I stood up and joined her on the beach. "When am I supposed to get out then?" I asked my failing teacher.

"When it gets shallow numb-nuts. You'll know because the wave will lose energy, and as you start slowing down, you jump out."

"You make it sound so easy."

"That's because it is, Mr Fishy," she said, sarcastically.

We walked out to try again and eventually I got the hang of it, and after doing that for a while we went further out and just floated, chatting and sunbathing. After half an hour or so, we decided that we should put on some sun cream as the sun was starting to get stupid hot. I was completely opposed to the idea of sun cream, but with my history of stupidity and pointless injuries, Emily forced me to put it on.

CHAPTER ELEVEN

"Do you think we could move the kids up here?" I said, unable to take my eyes off my lunchtime feast and enjoying the beach. The thick beefburger had cheese oozing down the sides of the bun, and there were proper chips like the ones you'd get in a chippy back home.

"We could ask," said Jude, equally impressed with his burger. I hadn't realised until the food had arrived that we'd all ordered the same thing. We sat, staring at our food as if it were the Holy Grail.

The burgers were heaven. Proper beef and proper cheddar cheese like a burger should be. The chips were also cooked to perfection and were delicious. Even though I was completely stuffed when I'd finished, I still wanted to order a hundred more to take away so I could eat them every day for the remainder of the trip. Fortunately, I didn't have five-hundred dollars with me or I would likely have caved to the temptation.

By four o'clock we decided we should call it a day. We'd been in the sun for nearly six hours and regardless of how good the sun cream was, we'd had enough. I was still full from lunch but had already started thinking about the Indian we had to find later on.

We walked back slowly towards the hotel—my drag queen footwear slowing my momentum—opting to meet up at six o'clock ready for our night out. By the time we'd returned we had an hour and a half: an hour to sleep and thirty minutes to dress. It was going to be a long night and we needed adequate rest in advance.

I walked into the room and kicked off the pink fashion disasters straight into the bin. I flopped onto the bed and fell asleep dreaming of that perfect cheeseburger.

At six o'clock, the girls came in as I was tying my laces. We made our way out onto the streets of Nha Trang to do some exploring before we went for a curry. After half an hour we came across Kim's Café which I recalled being the place the rucksack guy had told me about, where he taught English in exchange for a free breakfast. Curiosity and the need for an evening refresher led us in, and the pool table kept us there.

After two more beers Jude and I had had enough of annihilating the girls and we settled on six games to one—the one coming from Jude potting the black off the break. We knew we were onto a winner from the outset when we overheard Emily telling Angel the rules.

After our fourth beer we decided to leave and try to find 'Bombay', the restaurant we'd read about in the Lonely

Planet that apparently serves 'authentic Indian cuisine'. I didn't care how authentic it was as long as they had madras, rice, naan bread and poppadum. We knew from the map that it was close but as we walked out of the door there it was, straight across the road. As soon as my eyes locked onto it my stomach guided my legs across the street and through the front door. As I walked in the smell reminded me of home, although I'd rarely been this sober arriving at an Indian restaurant before.

I ordered the same as I always have at home: chicken madras, mushroom pilau rice and naan bread. The poppadum was brought with the menus, so I didn't even have to ask for them. We also ordered beer to wash it all down with. Spirits were high as a result of the beer we'd drunk and the excitement of the forthcoming beach party. The others had been to similar parties before, but the nearest I'd been to a beach party was drinking a can of Coke in a sandpit.

The food was perfect, and joined the still undigested perfect cheeseburger from lunch. It's a good job we were only in Nha Trang for one night otherwise I'd likely double my weight inside a week.

We left shortly before ten and made our way down to the beachfront to find the Sailing Club. We passed the place we'd spent the day, and many other bars that looked empty. Cyclo and motorbike drivers were stopping to offer us a ride, with one even offering us something to 'smoke'.

Jude became intrigued but decided against it after being 'talked to' by Angel.

As we approached the Sailing Club, we could hear that the party was already in full swing. The bar area wasn't all that big but as we walked through to the beach outside, there were people everywhere. They were drinking and dancing and this was obviously why the other bars were so quiet. Over to the left was a crazy girl eating fire, and others were dotted along the beach probably smoking the stuff the motorbike driver was selling. We went back in and ordered a beer each and then went back out and found a table. The party was well underway with people already falling all over the place, drunk and stoned. The place was rocking.

A few beers in and we were into the atmosphere a little more, dancing on the beach bottles in hand, me with my shoes and socks off and jeans rolled up. We noticed that Jude and Angel were paying more attention to each other, which must have been like dancing in front of a mirror. I was too full of beer and burger and Indian food, so I made the unwise decision to switch to gin and tonic. I very rarely drank anything other than beer, but on this occasion I couldn't drink any more. We went back to our table with the three beers and my Bombay Sapphire and tonic and left the other two dancing. Emily and I sat laughing as we watched them dance the perfect hippy dance. Flailing arms in weird directions, hippie head-nodding facing downwards for maximum hair wobble, and feet moving as little as possible. It was bizarre, almost tribal, but they did it well together.

I was hammering down the gin and tonics like a man possessed but developed an annoying cough which I assumed had been caused by the thousands of cigarettes I'd smoked. The result was violent vomiting, which instantly trebled my drunkenness and convinced my legs to not walk in a straight line anymore. I was all over the place, banging into tables, falling into people, and even landing face down in the sand when I tried to imitate the hippy dance. After vomiting on the beach, in the sea and numerous other places, the last thing I remember was looking at my watch at three o'clock.

"Shit, quick, we've got twenty minutes. Wake up!" Jude's voice hit me like a steam train. I opened my eyes and thought I was dreaming. Wrapped in my arms was long brown hair, and I momentarily thought I'd woken up next to Jude.

Emily was starting to wake and she turned with her face inches from mine. *Phew, it's Emily!* I didn't even remember getting back so surely there was no pissed shagging? She kissed me on the forehead and stood up wearing only the shirt she had on the night before. It was quarter past seven and the coach was picking us up in fifteen minutes. I crawled out of bed, still trying to remember how Emily and I ended up in the same bed.

"Emily," I said, not wanting to open my eyes because of the extreme pain in my head. "Did we?" She laughed as she walked over and put her arms around me, my head finding respite on her shoulder.

"You were so pissed you were of zero use to me. Plus you were puking a lot," she smiled.

"So how did we end up in bed together?" I asked, relieved but curious.

"Jude and Angel were all over each other at the end of the night, and when we got back hippy sex was imminent so I came in here with you," she said. "Oh, and in case you've forgotten, I think all of Nha Trang is covered in your puke!"

"Fuck."

"When I came in here with you and managed to get you into bed, you were begging me to look after you," she smiled. She kissed me on the forehead again. "Now stop worrying and get dressed. You have nothing to worry about." I felt completely shit as I ran my head under the cold tap hoping it would make my headache go away.

Somehow we made it onto the coach shortly after half past seven and were again lucky enough to find seats together. We all lay down desperate for sleep, and Emily and I arranged ourselves the way we'd previously and tried to sleep. I felt a lovely closeness with Emily after she'd taken care of me, and respected her all the more for not taking advantage of my wasted state and making me prematurely ejaculate in the only underwear I'd brought with me.

I lay trying to sleep but my stomach felt very empty and the coach journey was making me feel ill. I was pretty sure there was nothing left inside me to come out, and the cold sweats weren't helping. I looked over at Emily, fast asleep, our legs intertwined and noticed how lovely she looked. The hangover hormones ignited my determination to nail her properly once the alcohol was out of my system. No premature ejaculation, no vomiting and no falling asleep.

I awoke feeling a little better at about one o'clock knowing we still had at least another four hours to go. The feeling of sickness had subsided but my head was pounding. I lay back down desperate for more sleep. The other three were sleeping like babies and I noticed the extra closeness between Jude and Angel by the way they had interlocked their legs across the seats. They made a cute couple, and I was pleased they had hooked up.

It was half past three when we started to enter the familiar built-up area of the city, the sound of annoying horns blasting all around us. We cursed them all. We were nearly back and I couldn't wait to get into my own bed. We'd had a fantastic time and were glad we'd made the painful journey but wished it could have been for a few days longer. Within another half-hour, we were back at the

Sinh Café and more or less ran back to the hostel desperate for more sleep.

I woke up shortly after seven o'clock and the others were still sleeping. I was feeling mostly back to normal but was starving. I knew the others would want to eat as we hadn't eaten since the Indian the previous night. I was also at a further disadvantage having sprayed my previous day's meals across Nha Trang. I went into the shower knowing that If this didn't wake them nothing would. I stayed in there for about fifteen minutes, washing all the previous day's crap off me.

When I'd finished and came back out into the room, the others were awake and chatting. I overheard the words 'Captain Vomit' as I walked out and was met with laughter as they saw me.

"You lot wouldn't happen to be talking about me, would you?" I asked, knowing full-well that they were.

"No!" Angel lied sarcastically. The fact they had waited for me to come out of the bathroom before saying it was a bit of a giveaway. "We were saying you must be starving after showering Nha Trang with Indian and Gin." It was only then that I realised we hadn't spoken all day, hungover and tired as we were.

"Oh, OK. Shall we talk about last night then?" I said, first looking at Angel and then Jude. Jude smiled and left for the bathroom before anything more could be said.

I sat on my bunk wrapped only in my towel trying to work out how I was going to dress in the presence of the two girls. I remembered Emily's trick from the other morning where she dressed in front of me without giving anything away and decided to give that a go. It would be a lot easier for me as I didn't have any knockers.

What I imagined would be relatively straightforward was a lot harder than I thought. Thoroughly drying the General and his living quarters proved to be a mission I was ill-prepared for. I turned away from the girls, Angel not taking any notice but Emily enjoying the show. I tried to do it without making any strange movements. However, parting one's legs and shoving a towel in between cannot be done eloquently, so I gave up. They'd dry themselves in my boxer shorts. I slowly fed my legs into them, knowing any loss of balance could result in embarrassing consequences. I pulled them up slowly so as not to catch the towel inside them, and pulled them up to just below the crown jewels. I fed the General and his two Colonels slowly in, and eased the boxers over my backside. Mission accomplished! I was so pleased with myself I felt like taking a bow but as I was still, for the most part naked, I decided against it. I turned around to see Emily looking amused but disappointed. I quickly threw on a pair of linen trousers and a T-shirt and sat back on my bed. That hadn't been so hard after all.

When Emily and Angel were finally showered and ready, we made our way out. We planned on a quick bite to eat so we could have an early night ready for school the next day. We were all exhausted and although we'd slept on the coach, it was a shitty sleep as a result of the constant swerving and horn-blasting.

We made our way over to the backpacker area, Pham Ngu Lao, with Jude and Angel having taken up hand-holding. We settled upon the Luca Bar & Café for Italian food. As we walked in we realised it was happy hour. I wasn't the only one who cringed at the thought of any more alcohol. We had a feast of Italian wonderfulness and three large bottles of water, and then made our way back to the hostel to half-heartedly review the next week's curriculum.

Within an hour we'd covered everything we wanted to cover and put the folders away. The work for the following week was a little more advanced but still comparatively simple stuff. It was also good knowing the children's ability which we hadn't known the previous week.

By ten o'clock we were all in bed reading our books and looking forward to school. It was great that everyone was enjoying themselves as one unenthusiastic person would have made it a lot harder for the rest. I could see why some people would find it hard to do such a job but we were all strong-willed with a genuine desire to do something good. The children made the job so much easier by being so adorable. They absorbed everything we taught them because of their overwhelming desire to learn anything and everything, even the nonsense words Jude and I were adding in.

CHAPTER TWELVE

Amusingly, Angel's threats towards Jude weren't as violent when the alarm went off at quarter to seven. I was still determined to murder the fucker, his bouncing off the bunk above me was getting on my nerves. This time he wasn't so pleased with himself when he took six minutes to shower. Two minutes off his personal best, but six minutes was still pretty remarkable for a dude with girl's hair.

I was determined to beat his record. I ran the shower and made sure it was warm before I jumped in, hitting the start button as I went. I wet my hair, squeezed shower gel into it and while trying to massage it into my head put shaving gel onto my face. The shower gel and shaving gel combination sent them both to shit. Nonetheless, I worked fast and was massaging with the left and shaving with the right. All was going well, a minute forty-five gone and two minutes fifteen remaining. When my hair was good and soapy, I worked quickly with both hands on the remaining parts of my face, razoring like a man possessed. I was amazed that I hadn't cut myself as I was whipped the razor up and down and side to side. One and a half minutes left to wash the rest of my body with the soap from my hair. I dipped my head under the shower, not wanting to lose too many suds and began to wash like I'd never washed before. My hands were moving so quickly I thought I'd grown two new ones. Thirty seconds to go. I was going to beat him on my first attempt. I turned off the shower, threw the towel around me and stopped the watch. Three minutes, fifty-two seconds. I ran out of the bathroom cheering and showed Emily the watch. She called me a sad fucker but nevertheless agreed to be my witness.

I was dressed and ready to go at the same time as Emily. I couldn't wait to tell Jude that I was the new shower king. I charged ahead nearly falling down the stairs.

"I did it! Three fifty-two!" I said excitedly as I threw my arms into the air.

"Bastard!" He was genuinely disappointed. I looked at his hair but wasn't prepared to penalise myself for his floppylocks. "Three fifty-two?"

"Yep, and Emily is my witness." She walked towards us shaking her head.

"Yes, he did it," she said without enthusiasm.

"I'll regain gold tomorrow," he said, already trying to think of ways to shave valuable seconds off his personal best.

"And I'll regain it the following day. I'm only going to get better Jude, and you know it. Today was my first time don't forget." I'd turned into a smug idiot for the most ridiculous of reasons, but didn't care because I was now a record holder.

"Beginner's luck. Try not to choke on your eggs." I'd forgotten how bad cold scrambled eggs tasted.

Lou arrived at quarter to eight and we jumped aboard the minibus. We were becoming used to the dusty old thing now and were past caring about being dirty. We told Lou all about our weekend in Nha Trang omitting the parts he didn't need to know. He recognised most of the places we referred to as he and his family had been there on holiday, although never to the Sailing Club.

We arrived at school shortly after eight o'clock and waited in our usual spot to greet the kids. Was it really only a week since we stood nervous and scared not knowing what to expect? One week since we'd seen the building and wondered how we were going to work in it? It was amazing how long ago it seemed as we stood there waiting. It was also a week since the needless hangover and the unnecessary ejaculation.

Class began by briefly going through what they had learned the previous week, and I was amazed they didn't need any reminders. I paired them off and wandered around the room listening in. It was fun to hear the way some of them started to speak a little louder as I approached and I couldn't help but smile at their enthusiasm.

Lunchtime came and went, as did the rest of the afternoon. I was enjoying the fact that we'd settled into a routine and the kids knew when to expect lunch and home time. We were working from eight-thirty until eleven-forty-five, breaking for lunch, and then working again from twelve-thirty until three. Lou had also worked out our routine as he was always there at three o'clock waiting to collect us. He was such a wonderful man, always supportive and fun, and always there if we had questions or concerns—an all-round great guy to have there to look after us. He didn't probe or question anything we did and we forgot he was effectively our boss. Such a remarkable contrast to that prick I worked for in London.

When we were back to the hostel Jude stopped me outside and asked me if he could have a word. I was a little worried at first.

"Would you mind if I took Angel out tonight?" he asked, making me feel like her guardian.

"Of course not. Why are you asking me?" I asked inquisitively.

"I wanted to make sure you didn't mind us not going out as a group, or mind being left alone with Emily." His smile said it all.

"Mate, do whatever you want. We can't stay in each other's pockets the whole trip, and you and Angel should have some time alone," I replied, putting my hand on his shoulder. "Emily and I are pleased for you two."

"Emily and you, eh?" I let it pass.

"Have a good time tonight. You gotta be on form for the morning, three fifty-two to beat, sunshine."

"Piece of cake," he smiled as we walked up to the room together.

"Fancy going for a wander Harry?" Emily asked as my arse hit my bed.

"No," I could think of nothing worse and wanted to lay down for a while.

"Come on Harry." She motioned her head towards the door and reluctantly I stood up. "See ya later, you two."

"They'd better not use my bed," I said, letting Emily know that she would be held accountable for any wet patches.

"They want some time alone. Why do men always have to think like that?"

"Because time alone is code for rampant banging!" Emily shook her head. "What are we supposed to do around here for the next...," I looked at my watch, "seven minutes?"

"Men!"

We wandered around arm-in-arm exploring, and looking for something to do other than find a bar. With the museums closing at four o'clock we didn't have time to visit any of them. As we reached Sinh Café, the source of everything we'd done so far, we walked in and asked them whether they could suggest anything. Emily 'treated me' to tickets for the 'Water Puppet Theatre'. At two dollars each she should have guessed how crap it was going to be. We were given a map to where it was and had an hour before it started. Enough time to become sufficiently intoxicated so I could sleep through it.

As we neared the theatre with forty-five minutes to go I begged Emily to take me to a bar. So being the kind-hearted girl she is, she took me shopping. There was a hundred-metre strip of nothing but shoe shops.

"You've got shoes," I protested as I was dragged into the third shop.

"No harm in looking. I might find a pair I need." What sort of logic was that? How do you suddenly discover you *need* shoes when you *find* them? I could never remember walking into a shop, seeing a pair of Wellington boots and thinking, 'Oh thank God for that. I was completely unaware of how much I need a pair of wellies until now.'

Half an hour later—and it shames me to admit this—I had bought a pair of flip-flops, which in my defenceless-defence I did need. The female mind never ceased to amaze me. What sounds like complete bollocks when they are saying it, nine out of ten times turns out to be right. We made our way back to the theatre with me swearing that I would kill her if she said I told you so one more time.

In the theatre we sat in the second row of what looked like an old-fashioned cinema. It must have sat about four hundred people and the stage had a small, shallow looking pool in the middle with lots of different coloured scenes behind it. I sat there waiting to be bored.

At quarter to five the lights dimmed, my cue to sleep. The music started and a four-foot dragon came out of nowhere and started dancing across the water. *How are they doing that? Is there a man in full scuba gear down there, or is he snorkelling?* I became hooked as the two-foot-tall people had to be somehow real because of the way they were chasing the dragons with their axes. For the next twenty minutes, I sat in awe as puppets careered around the stage performing things that made them look like real little people. Dogs chased things across the water, people harvested rice, and the most bizarre thing was some sort of football that the dragons were playing with. The whole thing was brilliant and we said we would bring Jude and Angel back so we could see it again.

"That was bloody excellent," I said as we walked out, the bright sunlight making us squint after the darkened theatre.

"I told you so," she laughed.

As we walked back towards the hostel Emily said she wanted to check her email. I'd forgotten all about email and had promised to send Nicola and my family regular updates. I was so caught up in my adventure that I'd completely forgotten about them. We agreed to limit it to one hour as we didn't want to spend all night in an Internet café.

We found a place on the corner of one of the main streets that had email for a dollar an hour. We sat at computers next to each other and I logged in to find I had one-hundred-and-thirty new emails, mostly junk. I had three emails from Nicola, two from Trev and two from my parents, or rather, my mum. I opened the earliest one from my mum.

'Hello Son, hope you are well. We had the Kingsley's around for dinner on Saturday. Their youngest, Rebecca (I don't think you have met her) has been to Vietnam, but it was a long time ago. John Kingsley said he used to work with a Vietnamese man but can't remember his name. We are both well. Love Mum x'

My mother was alien to the idea of using carriage-return. Did she want me to ask everyone in Vietnam if they used to work with an English man named John? I opened the second one.

'Hello Son, I left you an email, but you didn't answer it. Love Mum x'

'Left me an email'? I typed her a quick reply letting her know what I'd been doing and that I was well and having fun. I kept it short to avoid any further confusion. I opened the first one from Trev.

'Tosser. I thought about you the other day when I was playing on my PlayStation. I was shooting things. Trev.'

It's great to have friends like Trev. I opened the second one.

'You obviously haven't got email in the trenches, silly me.'

I composed a reply that contained many expletives and sent it, hoping it wouldn't be blocked because of its industrial-strength vocabulary. Last but not least, I worked my way through Nicola's emails. I wanted to do them last so I could spend more time on them. I opened the first one.

'Hello stranger,

I'm a little worried I haven't heard from you. Are you OK?

I went around to your house today, everything was fine but I was a little confused by the baking potato I found by the door.

Love Nic xxx'

Shit! I meant to throw that potato out.

'Dear Nic,

Sorry I haven't been in touch but email access is hard to find here. I miss you and not a day goes by when I haven't thought of you.

I am OK. I'm having a good time and want to bring all the kids home with me. Will you help me look after them?

The baking potato. It's a long story that I'll tell you about at another time. I hope you've thrown it out, ha! I meant to do it before I left which is why it's by the front door.

Will email soon.

Love Harry x'

I continued onto her second email.

'Harry!

Where are you? You said you would stay in touch.'

That one made me feel bad. I opened the most recent one that had arrived only yesterday.

'Harry,

Have you forgotten about me already? I have sent you a few text messages and emails and you haven't replied to any of them.

Your mum also said she had sent you a couple of emails and hasn't heard back.

Please at least let me know you are OK, I miss you!

Love Nic xxxxxxxxxx'

I hadn't even turned my phone on. I felt a bit guilty for forgetting about everyone back home.

'Hi Nicola,

Sorry for not being in touch sooner, but as you'll read from my earlier mail this is the first time I've found somewhere I can access my email. Now that I have found it I'll check more frequently.

As for my mobile, I haven't been able to get a signal so I gave up on that.

I miss you and will see you very soon. I look at your picture every day.

Love Harry xxx'

If email had a bullshit filter they would have been blocked. I hadn't looked once at her picture, my mobile had been switched off since I left London, and there were internet cafes everywhere. In fact, the only truthful thing in either email was about the baking potato. I'd been more preoccupied figuring out how I was going to get into Emily's knickers than I had about replying to email. I had to start keeping in touch with her and my parents. This was a fun adventure but in less than five weeks I'd be going back to reality. I paid my dollar and went outside for a cigarette while Emily finished her emails.

When Emily had finished we decided to find somewhere to eat and maybe have a few games of pool. I remembered the Guns & Roses bar in backpacker street and the argument was won given I'd compromised on the Water Puppet Theatre. I went to the bar to buy our beers, already enjoying the sound of Guns & Roses 'Paradise City', one of my favourites. Emily went straight for the pool table convinced she could beat me without the handicap of Angel. A toss of some strange coin with a square hole in the middle decided that she was going to break.

After winning the second game in a row, with her still banging on about me not giving her a chance, she started to blame her hunger. An excuse for all occasions. Nevertheless: Two games to nil.

We ordered burgers and went straight back to the pool table, with me having to give her a chance. She broke and potted the black. Apparently, this was OK because all we had to do was take the black ball out and place it somewhere randomly on the table. A rule I hadn't come across before in all of my years as a hustler.

Three games to nil. Four games to nil. For the fifth game she insisted I play the whole game with the cue the other way around. Five games to nil. Our burgers arrived and we sat down at a table to eat. Emily reminded me of the relationship Nicola and I had before we got together. She was kind, caring, sweet and extremely attractive, both inside and out. I enjoyed being with her and was, selfishly, happy that Jude and Angel were now together so that Emily and I could hang out more.

The burgers were great, not as good as the ones in Nha Trang, but close enough. Despite multiple warnings Emily was back at the pool table racking them up. We were on our fourth beer and I always improved with beer on board. It was my turn to break and somehow I potted the black, which according to Emily was five games to one. I recalled her earlier rule but that rule only seems to apply if the person breaking is female.

Somehow through a combination of shameless cheating and point-in-time rule updates, she won the next three games which made it five four. I was starting to become a little nervous, wondering if her excuse about being hungry was true. I quickly blanked this thought and blamed the six beers I'd consumed as I went to the bar to buy the seventh. We knew we had to be up the following morning, but once again the alcohol convinced our silly brains that everything would be fine.

By midnight we were tied at eleven games each, the first time we'd been level all evening. We were now quite drunk having lost count of the number of beers we'd had, so the last game became a winner-takes-all single-game shootout.

It was my break and I was at the point where it was easier with one eye closed. Never a good sign. I managed to pocket one of the stripes, and potted two more before I missed and handed the table over to her. As I stood there wondering who had stolen Emily and replaced her with a pool demon she cleared the table right down to the black. I had four balls left and that didn't include the black. I missed them all. She potted the black and made sure the entire bar knew it. Twelve games to eleven. How the fuck did I lose that?

"I let you win," I slurred as she hooked her arm through mine and led me out the door.

"Whatever!" We staggered out laughing at the fact we were going to be a mess again in the morning.

"You…" this seemed to take an entire lung full of air, "are trouble." Then, another lung full of air, "Every time we go out alone you get me drunk."

"It was your fault," she slurred, equally as drunk. "You should have let me win earlier."

Emily beat the door until Minh answered it, and he smiled as he saw we were a little worse for wear, again. When we were outside the bedroom door Emily threw her arms around and squeezed me tight thanking me for a great time. She kissed me on the cheek and told me we had to be quiet so we didn't wake up the other two. We crept in, Emily every now and again turning around and saying "Sshhh" louder than if she had shouted it. I tiptoed over to my bunk and sat on it checking for wet patches. I eventually managed to get my boots off, and threw my shorts on top of them. Emily and I whispered goodnight to each other and I could feel myself already falling asleep as I lay down.

No sooner had I closed my eyes Jude's alarm clock went off. My head hurt and my eyes kept failing to stay open when I tried. I had to stop drinking on school nights.

"Three fifty-two!" he shouted at me as he made his way into the bathroom. "That record is mine." Not a single fuck could be given about my record, and all of my brain power was instead willing him to slip and hurt himself for repeatedly waking me up. Not a life-threatening injury, just something to stop him being such an irritating prick first thing in the morning.

"Water!" Emily pleaded from across the room, breaking my face into a smile. "Water!" It was her fault, so I had no sympathy.

"Late night?" Angel asked from above her.

"I beat Harry at pool. Don't know what time we got back here but you two were asleep."

"*Were*, yes. You trying to be as quiet as a mouse can be likened to an elephant tap dancing." Would he only use his two back legs or would he have tap shoes on all four of his elephant feet? What are elephant feet called? The best I could muster up was Dumbo using his ears to keep him airborne while tapping along next to Michael Flatley. Michael looked scared.

"Sorry," Emily said. "I tried to tell Harry to stay quiet but you know what he's like."

"All I could hear was you," Angel replied, laughing, "telling him to be quiet."

"Sorry! Water! WATER!"

Jude walked out of the bathroom looking very disheartened having only managed four minutes and five seconds. That thankfully took the spring out of his step. I surmised that he must have got some action last night and was giving his cock and balls an extra rinse. I rolled out of bed and headed towards the bathroom with no intention of trying to better my record even though Jude was egging me on. I did like Jude but because I had a bad hangover, I was still hoping he'd slip. I climbed into the shower, turned it on and supported myself against the wall allowing the water to cascade over me. I tried as hard as I could to wash the hangover off but everything was causing a child-like whimper. I felt like shit and made a pact with myself that I was to do no more school-night drinking for the rest of the trip. I eventually decided the shower tactic wasn't working and went for Plan B—copious amounts of coffee. I threw some painkillers at Emily and went downstairs with Jude. We ordered the eggs as I set about trying to drink the entire jug of coffee Minh had prepared.

CHAPTER THIRTEEN

"How was last night then, Romeo?" I asked Jude, who had a big smile on his hippy face.

"It was lovely thanks. We went for a walk down by the river and then went for dinner."

"You get the room to yourselves and you go for a walk? I expected her to be walking like a cowgirl this morning!" I hadn't yet taken much notice of the Saigon River that was only about a ten-minute walk away, something else for my to-do list. "We also saw a trip we were thinking of doing if you and Emily fancy it." He told me about the Mekong Delta which is apparently off the Southwest coast and something we could do as a day trip. It sounded like a fun day out and I was pretty sure Emily would be up for it too.

When Lou arrived we all climbed onto the minibus. Emily lay down across the back seat hoping the fifteen-minute journey would give her enough sleep to revive herself. When we arrived at the school I woke her and she looked even worse, her half-closed eyelids covered in dust.

She told Lou she was coming down with something as she passed him to which he smiled, probably smelling the booze on her.

The day went well with me keeping one eye on the time willing three o'clock to come. I couldn't wait to return to the hostel for some much-needed sleep. Emily had looked a little chirpier at lunchtime but was looking forward to the same thing. By the time three o'clock arrived we literally threw the kids out and ran over to the minibus.

Lou dropped us off, with him and Jude talking about the Mekong Delta the whole way back. Lou agreed that it would be a fantastic day out and that we would enjoy it. Jude and Angel were very excited about it and wanted to make the booking immediately. Emily and I were feeling too weak to put up a fight and handed over twenty dollars each. As we left the minibus they went to book it and Emily and I were up the stairs and in bed within seconds.

The rest of the week was spent taking it easy with Angel and Jude spending a lot more time on their own leaving Emily and me to our own devices. We were happy for them to do this as it gave us all some much-needed breathing space away from each other. Spending time together as a group was good fun but every now and again it was good to be apart. I have always enjoyed my own company and it was good to finally have some 'me' time as well. I would sometimes disappear for an hour or two to check email or go for a walk, but I spent most of my evenings with Emily going for something to eat or relaxing in the room. We avoided alcohol which made the mornings a little easier, and every morning Jude continued in his mission to beat my record failing every time. I beat his personal best of four minutes by one second on Thursday morning which annoyed him even more.

The kids were progressing in leaps and bounds. As they left on Friday a few said "Goodbye Mr Fishy, have a nice weekend," which I enjoyed hearing because it was something I'd taught them. I still hadn't bothered to teach them to say my real name properly.

After a quiet Friday night at the Guns & Roses bar for drinks and pool—which Emily and I of course won—we were up at seven o'clock on Saturday for our trip to the Mekong Delta. I still despised Jude for making us get up this early on the weekend but was looking forward to the trip.

We boarded the coach outside the Sinh Café at eight o'clock for the hour and a half journey down to where we would take the boat. We had the same guide who had taken us to the Cu Chi Tunnels, Quang. I was actually starting to remember names instead of just hearing jumbled-up letters.

No matter how many times you are on a coach in Vietnam you never become used to the noise they make but at the same time you never get used to the outstanding beauty. Apart from the city, everywhere I'd been so far had been incredible and so picturesque. It was almost as if you were travelling within a dream. If you tried to imagine the most beautiful shades of green you had ever seen you still wouldn't come close to the exceptional beauty of the Vietnam countryside. If by chance you could imagine such beauty, and you stuck a windy road through the middle of it with an orchestra of horns, you'd be even closer.

We arrived at Mỹ Hiệp and boarded the boat which was to take us downriver. We sailed down the Mekong Delta—the twelfth longest river in the world running for three-thousand miles through China, Burma, Laos, Cambodia and along South Vietnam—to the infamous Cai Be floating market. The Vietnamese call it Cuu Long which means 'The River of Nine Dragons' Quang continued with his fascinating facts as we reached the market. There must have been a couple of hundred boats there selling a multitude of goods, and even a floating petrol station. We saw one boat selling snake wine which Quang told us is made using snake blood, herbs and wine. It apparently boosts your sex drive and cures you of many illnesses. I still wouldn't drink it even if they promised it would cure my premature ejaculation. It was fascinating to see the various things being sold from vessels that didn't look as if they should float, looking like they were made from scraps of wood and thrown together in someone's shed.

After we have been up and down river through the market, we were dropped off at Mỹ Tho. We were guided through some woodland and arrived at a teashop where we were served tea. It wasn't proper tea as it tasted flowery and had no milk in it but it was still drinkable. While we sat there the owner, his wife and their daughter sang for us. I didn't have a clue what they were singing about, but even without instruments they sounded great.

After listening to them singing for about twenty minutes and drinking flower flavoured tea, Quang led us to where they made coconut candy. As we approached the hut the smell was gorgeous and we were all given a piece to try. It was so delicious that I joined the back of the queue to have another. Here they take the milk from gazillions of coconuts, judging by the pile that was in the corner, add sugar and boil the shit out of it until it becomes a thick and gooey mess. Then they pour it out, shape it and allow it to cool, producing a lovely toffee-type sweet. I tasted all the different flavoured samples—nut, chocolate and banana—and then bought five boxes.

We left, with me feeling sick, and were led around to where they made different types of pottery the 'old-fashioned' way. Their kiln was a hut they had built using bricks, with clay for cement. Underneath the hut they build gigantic fires, and the pottery is placed inside the hut and the door sealed for twenty-four hours. It's a long and arduous process, taking about three days from clay to finished product, but it's awe-inspiring to see how things can be done using only natural resources.

Next Quang led us around to another teashop for some honey tea. Little did we know that there was a bee's nest there from which they extracted the honey. The tea was gorgeous but there were bees around our heads, around our cups and the occasional one flying straight into our tea. The whole thing made me quite nervous, especially extracting drowning bees from my tea with a spoon. The art is apparently to sit still and drink the tea as they would soon fly away from the cup as it reached our mouths. Bugger that for a game. After we'd drunk the tea, Quang—who fancied himself as a bit of a comedian—asked who wanted to stick their finger into the honeycomb. I was somehow talked into it, and the bees created a path as my hand approached their honeycomb. What came out on my finger was well worth it. I have never been a lover of honey but this tasted different to what comes out of a jar. It may have been that I was happy to see my finger again.

Then I turned around and Quang had a snake around his neck. What's wrong with this guy? He held out the snake and tried to persuade me to put it around my neck. As predicted I was talked into it, but only for the sake of getting my photo taken with it. He put the giant python around my neck as I leant forward to receive it and then stood back upright, stiff as a board while Jude used my camera to take pictures. With one eye on the snake's head I told Quang, without moving my lips, that the minute the snake moved a muscle he was to take it back. The snake barely moved as we posed for pictures together, but when it did suddenly move—at least one full inch—I demanded Quang take it back before it ate me. I was so macho when the snake was gone. Quang put the snake back into its cage with two other smaller snakes, and then started to prod at it with a stick. After the stick had made contact with the snake the second time it flattened its neck and head, opened its mouth and launched itself throwing us all backwards in shock. The cage protected us but it was still quite scary especially as I'd had the docile bastard around my neck moments earlier. Clearly snakes don't have memories because he probably pissed them off on a daily basis for the tourists. He threw the stick away and took us over to a restaurant where lunch was provided. Then we were free to wander around the island or buy gifts and return for the afternoon tour. Lunch consisted of copious amounts of fruit which I didn't eat much of as I consider fruit to be dessert and not lunch. My thinking was obviously not shared by the other three as they devoured enough for a village.

We walked around the island, heading out as far as we could to see the various houses and farmland. We came across four houses that were floating on the water held up by oil drums—regular looking homes 'moored' on the river. I'd heard of waterbeds but this was a whole new concept.

"Look, a monkey!" Jude shouted, up to his old tricks. Monkeys don't live in Vietnam, they live in zoos and documentaries.

"You're a fucking monkey," I said, "I'm not falling for that… Wow, a monkey!" There it was sitting in the tree above us eating a handful of leaves. The monkey climbed down from the tree and made its way towards us. I ran and stood about ten metres away, shouting "Ebola" at the others, who told me to "shut up or I'd scare the monkey." I'd seen a documentary that said all monkeys have Ebola so if they didn't want the benefit of my wildlife expertise, on their heads—or corpses—be it.

As the monkey came closer to the other three I noticed Jude holding out a piece of bread. The monkey walked over, took it and sat eating it as the other three took pictures. I slowly walked back until I was about five metres away and took a picture, feeling like a bit of a pansy for having run away. Plus I wanted to have something to show their families and the coroner when they all caught Ebola and died. When Jude had finished feeding the monkey, it went back up the tree.

We wandered back with the rest of them making fun of me for running away and correcting me on my knowledge gaps. They would soon regret taking the piss out of me when they got Ebola-like symptoms and were flying home in a box.

When we regrouped after lunch we were led towards the other side of the island for another boat trip. We had to cross a 'bridge' over a small canal which Quang promised me wasn't infested with crocodiles. The aptly named 'monkey bridge' was about fifteen metres long, and was a three-inch diameter length of bamboo supported with lengths of bamboo on either side for balance. As to how much support they actually provided I didn't want to know especially if Quang was lying about the crocodiles. I went first with my eyes looking straight ahead, feeling the bamboo bounce beneath my feet as I crossed. When I reached the far side I felt a great sense of relief knowing that if anyone was going to mess it up it would have been me. The rest of the group eventually joined us on the other side without anyone falling in.

As we continued through the jungle-type forest we were led out to boats, much like large canoes, that held four people and a driver. We all climbed into one with me at the front behind our lady driver. Using only one small oar, she navigated us through narrow waterways no wider than three metres, with vast, dense jungle on either side. It was amazing. I felt as if I was in one of those places where hippos and alligators would be watching us. *Maybe this is where they grow those mini crocodiles like the one we had on the ceiling.* We carried on for about half an hour avoiding the overhanging trees and vines, weaving around a myriad of waterways. We saw the most amazingly coloured birds in-flight, and other animals darting into the water as we approached. Eventually we arrived at the end of the waterways, completed a U-turn and paddled back using a different route. The scenery was breathtaking and I didn't want the trip to end. The water was so calm as we floated along looking left and right, up and down trying to absorb everything around us. It was like a hidden world with trees growing downwards and across the water to form an arch above us, and amazing wildlife all around.

When we were back on dry land our last stop of the day was a visit to a house that contained a fishery, which Jude asked if I was related to. His sense of humour hadn't improved. We were led into one of the floating houses we'd seen earlier. The houses are built over the river and a large flap in one of the rooms revealed a bamboo cage-like structure which hung down into the river. Within the segregated cage they breed and grow fish until they are big enough to be sold. It's incredible how many different uses there are for something I previously thought was a stick.

It was disappointing that shortly after five o'clock the trip came to an end and we had to return to our coach. With hindsight we would have taken the two-day option but we couldn't change it at the last minute. We bid farewell to the Mekong Delta and made the short trip across the water, boarded the coach and made our way back to Ho Chi Minh. That would probably be my favourite trip in Vietnam—such a beautiful array of sights and experiences that I will likely never have the pleasure to repeat.

We were back in Saigon a little after seven o'clock and made our way back to the hostel to change. When we finally reached the hostel Jude asked us rather shyly if we would mind waiting downstairs for ten minutes. I assumed the jungle air had peaked the hippy's hormones, and he wanted to empty his load into Angel. Turned out he had a potentially volatile arse, and didn't want us to hear him shit.

After about fifteen minutes Angel was becoming a little concerned and asked me to check he was alright. Obviously being a man in the presence of two other females it was my duty to see if he had picked up any life-threatening shitting injuries. I walked up the stairs, held my breath and opened the door. I called out to Jude.

"I'm dying," he strained. "I should have listened to you. Fruit is the devil!" He told me to "fuck off" when I said it could be symptomatic of Ebola, so I left him to it and told him we'd wait downstairs, which after all, was his original request.

After half an hour we heard Jude calling us up from the top of the stairs. I feared for the state of the bathroom. As we walked into the room we could smell burning and I knew he had burned toilet paper to dispose of the unwanted methane he had produced.

"You OK, mate?" I asked as I walked into the room, smiling. These things have to be seen humorously because that is precisely why we have an arse. Girls pretend bottoms don't exist, or that they produce flowery smelling odours instead of shitty shit smells. Toilet humour is a gift that shouldn't be dismissed.

"Yeah, I'm fine thanks Dude. Had an issue I had to deal with." His politeness deserved an award on account of the girls. There was still an infinite number of gags flooding my tiny mind that would have to wait.

"Poor baby," Angel said as she put her arms around him. *Oh, get fucked.* Did she not realise that all the fruit he ate had resulted in a shit that was not of the preferred consistency? He would survive this ordeal.

"I'll be OK," he whimpered. Stop, please! I was aware he had girl's hair but that was no excuse to play up and gain sympathy for having an arse like a fireman's hose. If this didn't stop soon I was going to have to step in. He had been telepathically warned. I wanted to go into the bathroom but was afraid to, so like the gentleman I am, I let Emily go first. What I had expected to be the aftermath of war was not so. Within seconds, Jude was banging on the door.

Once again, we were made to wait downstairs while Jude dealt with another *issue.* I was quietly glad he was the first one to get the shits, but I did feel for him a little teeny-tiny bit despite the bastard waking me each morning.

Nevertheless, He and Angel were still new and I knew how embarrassing it could be, like when I shit a week's worth of shit at Nicola's house.

After being given the all-clear to return to the room for the second time Jude was looking a little off-colour. I left him alone in case he was genuinely ill, as calling him 'firework arse' would have been ill-timed. I changed into long trousers and a long-sleeved top as the nights felt cooler and I was sick of being a snack for the bastard mosquitoes. When we'd changed Jude decided he wasn't feeling well enough to come out with us and would stay in. Angel felt torn but after a little push from Jude decided to come out with us. Jude said he was too drained and needed to sleep. I don't know which medical dictionary reports sleep to be a cure for the shits but I let him off as he was too ill to fight back. As we left the other two said that they wanted something wholesome to eat, as they too were suffering a little from eating too much fruit. I was still quietly convinced it was Ebola, but they wouldn't listen.

We made our way to Allez Boo in backpacker street for some good old-fashioned English food. Emily and I had noticed it when we were down there playing pool and had wanted to try it. The entire front was open onto the street and the rest of the place was decorated with bamboo, by way of a change. I grabbed the beers and a few menus and walked over to the girls who were sitting at a table overlooking the street. Angel was saying how guilty she felt about leaving Jude on his own but after my opinion was shared—that men need to be left alone after their exit wound has taken a battering—she felt a little better. She even called me charming although I think I detected an element of sarcasm in the delivery.

After we'd eaten and had a few drinks Angel mentioned something she and Jude had discussed. Their idea was to do something special with the kids at the end of our six weeks to show how well their English had come on. Her idea was to organise for each to do something for anyone who would like to come along and watch. We knew Lou would be keen and hopefully some of their parents would too. It was a great idea. We discussed various options and my idea of nursery rhymes was the one we settled on. I was put in charge of researching some good rhymes as I was the one who used the Internet café more than the others. We became quite excited about doing this because it was something different and it would be good marketing for the charity.

By eleven o'clock we decided to call it a night. We were all completely exhausted and Angel wanted to check on Jude's arse. We were a little tipsy as we made our way back but that was a mixture of tiredness as well as alcohol. Emily went through her usual routine of trying to break down the steel shutters before Minh could get there but failed once again as he opened them before she could.

We crept upstairs and into the room to find Jude still awake reading. He was feeling a lot better having rested his arse, which was a relief because I was below him, and gravity takes no prisoners. I sat on my bed took off my boots and top and slid under the covers, trying to remove my trousers from under the duvet as Jude did so well. It took too much time and energy but I was getting better. I don't recall completing one full sentence before the book hit the floor.

It felt like a long time since we'd slept until we woke without an annoying alarm clock, but that was our Sunday treat from Jude. I woke shortly after ten o'clock finally feeling rested after a good lay-in. The others were still asleep so I lay there reading enjoying the rest. It didn't take long before Jude was bouncing off his bed and into the bathroom, causing the springs and entire bed structure to dance around. I preferred him when he was ill.

When Jude had finished in the bathroom I was ready for my turn. I moved swiftly across the room to avoid spectators, my skinny legs looking like a couple of pipe cleaners hanging out of a lampshade. After flushing I ran back across the room and was soon under the covers. It seemed quite cold in the room and in the absence of anyone else to keep me warm, I had to rely on the duvet. It was always when I was under a duvet in a cold room that I fancied having someone in bed to cuddle up with. Someone nice though, not one of those mingers you accidentally bring home drunk. I loved the idea of cuddling up to a cutie and having little chats, and a bit of canoodling when energy levels peaked.

My ex-girlfriend Rebecca always found a pathetic excuse not to stay in bed for a cuddle. She would never spare time for that one thing I craved, and we needed. It's a shame because perhaps if she had made an effort she might not have had the need to look elsewhere. I thought of Nicola, wondering if one day she would want that closeness with me. I recalled a quote I'd previously ignored: "Find true happiness and hold onto it because everything else in life is background noise." I've spent my life focused on the background noise and the material things in life. True happiness had always been about having fun and not worrying about what happens tomorrow, which I now realise was a bit selfish.

Maybe Rebecca wanted me to think about tomorrow. Maybe Nicola will be my tomorrow. I think Vietnam—the people, the experience, the school, the kids—has taught me that I don't need 'things' to be happy. I came here with a backpack and have needed nothing more to make the experience so amazing. I thought about the kids at school—they have nothing, and everything they receive is treated with humility, adoration and excitement. People who have everything always want more and aren't happy until they get it. Then when they do get it, they realise that it wasn't what they wanted to begin with, and so the cycle continues.

It's a sad existence and something I am guilty of. I couldn't think of one person I had ever met who was truly happy. I made a mental note to never take that attitude once I return home. I want to live for the moment and be satisfied with what I have. Everything else I obtain or achieve will be a bonus.

Emily woke, and I looked across at her and smiled. She always looked so adorable first thing in the morning—so sweet, so innocent and so lovely. I was tempted to ask her to come over for a little cuddle but decided against it. My close-proximity-with-Emily odds for soaking my own underwear was currently running at one-to-two, and no one would take that bet.

When we eventually arrived downstairs we'd missed breakfast by over three hours but didn't care as we had enjoyed the restful morning. We decided to have an early lunch after doing something touristy. We all had an extra spring in our step with the extra sleep and were in good humour. We decided upon the Reunification Palace which was the South's last stand before the North Vietnamese—or Viet-Cong—took over Saigon. It was the Presidential palace before the Communists took control of it forcing the President to stand down in 1975. We walked across the city and found it with ease, having passed it once before on the way to the War Remnants museum.

We were given a guided tour around the building which has been restored to its pre-invasion condition. We were shown conference rooms, the Presidential receiving room where the President met with the leaders of other Nations, and the living quarters. We were led down some stairs to a series of underground tunnels where we saw the telecommunications room, the war room and various other rooms used for the well-being of key staff. It was what I imagined the White House or Downing Street to be like. As we left the underground area, we were brought up two flights of stairs to the top floor of the building which had sadly been turned into a shop. At the back of the building was a helipad and massive gardens surrounded by a high wall. We were led back down some stairs to another part of the building where we watched a video on the history of Vietnam. The whole tour lasted just under two hours and was fascinating.

By the time we'd left and eaten it was quarter past three. Our touristy day came to an end because all of the museums closed at four o'clock, and we didn't have enough time to visit another. We were making our way back to the hostel not knowing what to do when Emily spotted a sign for bicycles we could hire by the hour. We were all a little apprehensive at first because every road user appeared to be an absolute maniac. We ended up hiring bikes for three hours and put Jude in charge of getting us lost, and that's precisely what he did. After half an hour we had the Lonely Planet out trying to work out where the hell we were. Our failed attempts at 'three lefts make a right,' to avoid losing our lives going right, had landed us in the middle of nowhere. We gave up on the Lonely Planet on account of not knowing where we were on its silly little map.

We ended up on a long road to the end of the world where we assumed we could dismount our bikes, cross the road and head back. Along the way, we passed a woman holding her arm out into the road selling something. As I drew closer I realised they were pigeons tied by their legs to a rope she was holding. The pigeons were upside down, wriggling and already plucked. There was nearly an accident as I saw a second and then a third person selling the same thing. I tried to pull my camera out of my waistband-thingy to photograph them. I hate pigeons but to see them like this made my stomach turn. We eventually stopped and I took my picture from afar. Another shocking reminder that I was in a country where things are done very differently.

We eventually decided it was time for a break and found a park not too far away from the mad pigeon salespeople. We bought a cold drink which cost us a dollar each and knew we'd been ripped off, but the smiling salesman wouldn't have understood me calling him a shameless cowboy bastard. We drank, remounted our bikes and headed back the way we'd come, enjoying the ride for the last hour of our bike rental. The roads were just as hazardous, but the skill of the Vietnamese motorcyclist compares to none. We could have fallen into the road and they still would have somehow missed us.

We eventually found the bike place with fifteen minutes to spare and retrieved our ten dollar deposit. I joked to Jude that his arse must have mended to last three hours on the overly pointy saddle, but I don't think he was yet ready to see the funny side.

The downside of Vietnam is that when everything closes, there is nothing to do other than drink and eat, and we weren't drinking because it was a school night. Ordinarily, a 'couple of drinks' on a Sunday is perfectly reasonable. However, to Emily and me a 'couple' had a history of resulting in a hangover and a wet patch. I mentioned the bowling alley but the others weren't interested so Angel and Jude made their way back to the hostel, while Emily and I went to check our email.

I caught up on email and did a search for nursery rhymes. I eventually found a good site that listed the words and lyrics of various children's nursery rhymes and collated them into a document together with my comments. After reading through a lot of different rhymes, it became apparent that all kids nursery rhymes were written by insaniac fucktards on some sort of acid trip.

We got back to the room and discussed the nursery rhymes together. We each chose a poem for our kids to present, mine being the one about the woman swallowing a fly, which is forty lines long and would be a nightmare to teach. I imagined that over time I would change my mind and pick something a little easier that didn't contain any reference to death, but for now my mind was made up. Jude chose the one about the woman who lived in a shoe, Emily chose Old Mother Hubbard, obviously deciding that poverty was a topic that needed to be driven home, and Angel settled on Little Miss Muffet, the little treasure that sits next to spiders. I thought the whole idea was crazy but was outvoted and called a grumpy old bastard.

We began the third week settled into a good routine, and excited to see where the week would take us. My group were super-energetic, and I felt like the kids and I had known each other a lot longer than we had. They were all still as keen as ever, and still great fun to be around. My resolve to adopt each and every one of them hadn't changed.

When we were back at the hostel, I got my first wave of homesickness. I don't know where it came from or what had caused it, but the fact this was the first time I'd been away—which was in itself ridiculous for a twenty-five-year old—was likely a large part of it. I was still enjoying everything that each new day brought, and loved the school life, but I missed my parents and normality—whatever that now was. I was also dying for a proper cup of tea and a bacon sandwich, but I don't think that had a great deal to do with it. After Jude and Angel had gone out, I talked it over with Emily. She admitted to having days like that too, but banished them from her head telling me "they're poison for the mind." The problem with Vietnam, as beautiful and wonderful as it is, is that you are shut off from the rest of the world. Apart from the occasional news clips you see as you pass a television, or the emails you receive from people back home, you know nothing of the outside world. Even the simplest things you take for granted become a chore when you are in another country where your own language is foreign. I'd spent most of my adult life having all the privacy I wanted, whereas here I had little-to-none, and as great as the other three were, there were times I wanted to be alone. I hoped this was a phase and that it would end by the morning. I also hoped that this experience was something that would stand me in good stead for the rest of my life and make me a better person, having taught me so many different things.

I woke up the following morning feeling shitty after a very broken sleep. Jude and Angel had gone down for breakfast, and Emily came and lay down next to me saying nothing—it was what I needed. Her kindness came to an abrupt end at quarter past seven when she told me to get my shit together and get into the shower. As I showered, she dressed and waited for me. I dressed as fast as I could, putting the sadness to the back of my mind. I had a job to do and I couldn't let the kids down. Before we left Emily put her arms around me and told me to be strong. She was right, this would all be over in no time, and I would be back home kicking myself for not manning-the-fuck-up.

We both missed breakfast having just enough time for a quick coffee before we had to climb on the bus. When we arrived at the school and were off the bus Lou put his hand on my shoulder and held me back from the rest.

"Is everything OK Harry?"

"Yes thanks Lou. I just had a bad night's sleep."

"OK," he replied, smiling, "if you need someone to talk to you know where to find me."

"Honestly Lou, I'm fine," I said smiling and appreciating his kind gesture.

"OK Harry, have a good day. But never be too proud to ask for help if you need it. It takes a stronger man to talk about a problem than it does to hide it."

"Thanks Lou. That means a lot to me. Thank you," I said as I walked into the playground to meet the others.

The kids helped me through the rest of the day. It was seeing them, their beaming smiles and their overwhelming zest for life that snapped me out of my self-pity. That afternoon I started teaching them the nursery rhyme as we'd finished the curriculum an hour early. I decided to teach them one line at a time, building on it each day. It was only when I read through it, that I realised they actually do eat all of the animals in the rhyme.

When we were back at the hostel I discussed my nursery rhyme predicament with the others, and they were dumbfounded with how my mind works. In the absence of a vegan nursery rhyme I opted for Rock-a-bye Baby as my less-ridiculous second option.

Jude and Angel went and booked a cycling weekend in Dalat, which Emily and I declined. I see cycling as an activity for those who can't drive, and derive no pleasure from sitting on a seat designed to penetrate you.

CHAPTER FOURTEEN

The rest of the week was spent teaching during the day and relaxing in the evenings. We were all slowly becoming allergic to eggs, having eaten them every morning for three weeks—fried, boiled, scrambled and poached. This week each of us had missed breakfast at least once because of our newly-found aversion to eggs. Unfortunately eggs were our only option and as there were no shops near the school, it was either eggs or eggs.

I made a start on Rock-a-bye Baby which the kids found hysterical. They weren't learning anything from it, merely learning and reciting words that formed a silly nursery rhyme. By Friday I'd taught them enough to recite the first two lines without my help, although I'm sure some of them were miming because there wasn't the usual volume. Occasionally I felt homesick but was managing it a lot better. I'd started my writing in my journal each day, catching up on all the things we'd done since we arrived, writing highlights of things I'd learned at school, where we'd eaten and drank, and everything else I could remember. I also included the personal details that I'd learned from the experience, and the things I wanted to change in my life when I returned home. I found that writing things down made me feel a lot better rather than repeatedly over-analysing them in my head.

Jude and Angel went to Dalat early Friday evening leaving Emily and me alone for the weekend. We immediately made the decision to attempt an all-nighter to see if we could stay out until dawn. We went straight to the Guns & Roses bar with the intention of getting smashed, especially as we were guaranteed a lay-in without Jude being there. Emily swore she was going to murder me at pool and when we walked in to find the place heaving with no pool tables available the blood drained from her face. I think she had been looking forward to proving it hadn't been a one-off. With that idea dead we decided on a pub-crawl all the way along backpacker street. After we'd had a couple of beers in Guns & Roses—still my favourite bar in Ho Chi Minh—we went to a bar called Long Phi. We got a pool table long enough for me to win two games, and then 'winner stays on' saw me annihilated by an Australian hustler called Kevin. We moved on to La Cantina, a cool Mexican bar where Emily got us fajitas and margaritas, which were a bad idea but a good one at the time.

We walked into the Sahara bar further down the street to find a packed house full of fun stuff—pool, darts, table football—and if we became bored with that there were huge TV screens showing sporting cock-ups. We bought beer and went straight over to the table football, where Emily once again embarrassed herself with a shameful performance. When she was losing by about a hundred goals to nil, she demanded we play darts instead. I'm surprised no one was injured the way she was throwing those things.

We ended up on the pool table and set about trying to recreate the previous Sunday evening. I was in better shape than Emily and on the first break she missed the white ball completely, and it was only eleven o'clock. Somehow she still won the first game, after yet another change to the rules, which made it two games to one. After another three games which were taking longer than normal it was four games to two. I begged her to end it there but she was having none of it. We had to play three more games so she could win, but after the third game Emily conceded making it six games to three, and the shameless misery was over.

We went to the bar for another drink and sat down. As we chatted, making fun of everyone in the bar, Emily noticed some guy trying to give her the eye and called him over. At first I found this was a little strange as she was out with me but when he arrived she introduced me as her boyfriend and told him she would appreciate it if he stopped staring at her. He walked away with his tail between his legs, and she leaned over and kissed me a proper, big kiss.

"Oi youuuu, don't start any of that," I slurred, my willpower having disappeared with my sobriety.

"It was to stop him looking at me," she said, winking at me.

"Yeah right."

"You know you love it!" I did. There was something about her, and the way she flirted with me that drove me crazy, plus I enjoyed kissing her. I knew I was heading down that same slippery slope that Emily and booze always take me on. *Once more won't hurt, will it?*

We decided to continue our pub-crawl and made a mental note on the way out that the Sahara bar does all-day full English breakfast. That was tomorrow's hangover cure sorted.

I somehow gave in to Emily's pleading to return to La Cantina for more margaritas, despite knowing they were going to make us ill. After a jug of the frozen green poison followed by nachos followed by a jug of the frozen red poison neither of us were in a good way. The drinks were so strong I was positive my urine would be flammable. I lost a one-dollar bet with the guy using the urinal next to me, destroying my lighter in the process.

We stumbled out of La Cantina at three o'clock, hardly able to walk. We walked in a perfect zig-zag in the general direction of the hostel, and through the darkened residential streets.

"I'm so fucking horny, Harry," Emily slurred. The state she was in, I was surprised any shenanigans were on her mind.

"Stay the fuck away. I will vomit on you." The nausea along with the humid night air convinced me I'd be performing my technicolour rainbow trick again, and I didn't want that to be over Emily.

Her strength took me by surprise as she drove me into the shutters behind me. Her lips were on mine before I could object, with her hands on my shoulders pushing me against the wall. The ferociousness with which she was kissing me was crazy, and the control she maintained was unlike anything I'd experienced before. Her hand moved inside my boxer shorts, and she was like a woman possessed. All I could do was pray for no unwanted detonation. As she wrestled with her own jeans, I was convinced she was going to commit an act of *gross decency* in the street. Suddenly, there was a banging from behind my head and someone shouting.

"What the fuck is that?" I whispered into Emily's ear.

"Shut up!"

The second time the banging was louder, and I felt vibrations in the shutters I was pinned against as they started to open. I launched Emily off me and started to walk faster as the shutters opened. I'm not sure what exactly the Vietnamese screaming was, but can only imagine it translates to something like, "get a fucking room!"

"Look, dawn," Emily said, pointing to the sky, as we turned towards the hostel.

"That's a street lamp!" It wasn't even four o'clock and the sun wasn't due here for a couple of hours yet. What began as an all-nighter with a mission to stay out until dawn had failed.

When we were finally back at the hostel, Emily collapsed against the metal shutters, sliding down them and landing on her arse. I tried to pick her up but being so drunk and giggling like a child, I fell over her. Just as I'd landed Minh was opening the shutters. I tried to lift Emily but she was a dead weight, so I kicked her a couple of times. When the shutters were fully up and Minh had worked out what was going on, he helped me pick her up and dump her into a chair inside. Minh came back with a cup of coffee which I tried to make her drink. As I started to shake her, becoming increasingly worried that she might be dead, she began to come around. Despite her silent protests, I made her drink the coffee, as there was no way I was going to be able to get her up the stairs. Suddenly, she stood up laughing at all the fuss and ran up the stairs leaving Minh and me looking at each other bemused.

I followed her after I'd apologised to Minh once again, and found her vomiting in the bathroom. I sat on my bunk giggling and glad it wasn't me, although the night was still young. By the time I was stripped down to my boxer shorts and a T-shirt she came out of the bathroom looking like death warmed up, brushing her teeth.

"I don't feel well," she slurred as she rinsed out her mouth. "Why did you make me drink all those bloody margaritas?"

"Sorry, I didn't mean to," I said, raising my eyebrows.

When I walked out of the bathroom, Emily was laid out on my bed, with her jeans around her ankles and her T-shirt halfway over her head. As ridiculous as the image was, the black lace underwear looked so sexy against her perfect figure, but the momentary idea of taking advantage of her was quickly pushed aside. I managed to get her clothes the rest of the way off, while she slurred something about being a cheeky man.

"Alcohol is bad you know Harry," she laughed, sitting up. "It's your turn to look after me now!" Her body gave way again, and she fell back to where she'd started. She pulled the cover over herself and turned around to face me. "I threw up," she giggled. Luckily the minty toothpaste had done its job. The giggling was, within seconds, replaced with snoring. Panic over, she wasn't going to molest me after all. I breathed a sigh of relief and closed my eyes as the room began to spin. In all my years as a trainee drinker I still haven't worked out how to stop the spinning but it often means that vomiting is imminent. There were three possible scenarios: The first was to make myself sick, the second was to hope it would go away, the third and worst was that I would wake up and throw up over Emily which, in my defence, would be her fault because she shouldn't have been in my bed in the first place.

I woke up feeling like shit shortly after ten o'clock and Emily was still fast asleep. I was laying on my back with her head on my shoulder, and my arm around her. I lifted the sheet for a cheeky look, and pushed up against my T-shirt clad body was her naked breast. Where did her bra go? Unfortunately because of the angle at which she was laying I couldn't get a proper look, but I kept trying. I tried to close my eyes and go back to sleep but I couldn't stop myself having one last peek. It was wrong. It was very, very wrong but two good wrongs do make a right, contrary to the bullshit cliché. All of a sudden she started to stir. I lowered the sheet back down and pretended I was sleep-fidgeting. She adjusted her head on my shoulder and moved her top leg dangerously close to the action zone. I had this awful fear that the General was going to do something kamikaze like reach over and tap her on the leg, but then I remembered that this was an anatomical impossibility. I lay there with my heart pounding and tried to go back to sleep. So long as she didn't move her leg any further north we were safe. However, if she did, all sorts of wrongness would occur, and the General would likely hurl yoghurt at her again. I eventually fell back to sleep, the hangover from hell overpowering any fight the General could put up. Alcohol and he were lifelong enemies, and on this particular occasion I was thankful the alcohol had won.

I woke up again around midday feeling Emily's leg moving up and down mine. I turned towards her and her face was beaming with a knowing smile. She slowly moved her leg back and forth, and I put my hand underneath the covers to push her leg away.

"Come on Harry, you know you want it," she said smiling, running her hand up my leg.

"We can't," I said, closing my eyes and feeling excitement overwhelm me.

"We might not get the room to ourselves again. Come on!" She wasn't taking no for an answer.

"I shouldn't."

"Come on," she pleaded, "little Harry feels very ready!" She wasn't wrong.

"Get your hands off me you evil temptress!" I did nothing to stop anything she was doing. "And 'little-fucking-who'?" I asked. 'Little' has no place in this conversation.

"For fuck sake Harry, don't make me beg!"

"No. I can't. I won't. It would be wrong."

"Hangovers always make me horny, and we can't let this go to waste, can we?" she said, as she squeezed 'Little Harry' harder.

"Nooooo, stop asking me."

"Pretty please?" *Ahh fuck it. What happens in Vietnam stays in Vietnam!*

The evil temptress had penetrated my extremely robust defence, and I felt compelled to help fix her hangover-induced-horniness. Besides, she had asked very nicely. I rolled her on top of me and threw the sheet out of the way. As she leaned over to kiss me, she forced a very hard Little Harry inside a very soggy Little Emily, and before I could have said "Condom?" I was being ridden like a rodeo bull. The thin walls of the room stood no chance of masking the noise, and each thrust reverberated inside my aching head. Nothing was going to stop this cowgirl short of the bunk beds falling apart, which they were squeak-threatening to do. She was like a woman possessed, and I thankfully broke the one-minute barrier before I exploded inside her. "Congratulations Harry, that's your first time in Vietnam outside of your own underwear. But definitely not your last time inside me!" I swear I could hear angels singing.

We spent the next few hours napping and fooling around some more, and it turned into the best Sunday in the history of all Sundays. Emily was ravenous and way more experienced than me. I'd never met anyone with such an insatiable appetite like her before, and the way she controlled me every single time was mind-blowing. Nevertheless, the time came when we needed to refuel our exhausted bodies.

At four o'clock we arrived at the Sahara bar. The smell of stale alcohol in the bar was nauseating, but we still ordered the full English breakfast. When the breakfasts arrived we both sat looking at them wondering whether or not our bodies would reject them, but forced some down anyway. The bacon was more like sizzled cardboard, the sausages were fucking dreadful, and the eggs were just more eggs. It may well have been called a "full English" but it was as English as a French onion. We left feeling cheated and went back to the hostel.

When we returned we saw Minh who just smiled. Emily apologised at least ten times in the short walk from the door to the stairs. He was probably used to seeing his guests landing themselves in all sorts of trouble. We spent the rest of the day in the room—in our own beds—sleeping and reading. We both had the type of hangover where you have to admit defeat and hibernate until it's worked its way out of the system, although the three litres of water helped to rehydrate our shrivelled organs. By eight o'clock we were feeling a little more human but desperately in need of food. We went back to the place where we'd had the gorgeous green curry, ate that and then went back to bed, hoping Sunday would see us alive and well again.

I woke up at five o'clock. It was too dark to read without switching on a light on and waking Emily, who was happily snoring away even though she doesn't snore. I lay with nothing to do hoping I would fall back to sleep but it didn't happen. I started to think of home again, and of Nicola, and started to feel a little guilty about what had happened with Emily. I started replaying the whole Emily thing in my head, especially the rodeo part, over and over and over and over again, and the guilt seemed to pass. I knew I was being a bit of an insensitive prick, but if anyone saw the duress Emily had put me under they would understand. My thoughts turned to creeping over there and waking her up to a nice surprise. *Fuck, what a magnificent idea. Shut up head you evil bastard. Do it. Shut up.*

I lay there for a few more minutes my head consumed with thoughts of home. I wasn't going to let my head start all this shit again, so I quietly dressed and crept out. Emily's snoring was a good indication I hadn't woken her and she sounded like a tractor as I closed the door behind me. Downstairs, Minh was sitting in his armchair. I wondered if he actually slept in that chair as he always seemed to be in it at whatever time I appeared. I asked him to tell Emily I had gone for a walk if she came down before I returned.

I walked out onto the eerie streets of Ho Chi Minh with the sun still rising and the usual morning bustle of the locals starting their day. I was used to being harassed by cyclos and motorbikes but there were none, just the quiet dusty streets and me. I wandered around breathing in the cool morning air looking at shops and restaurants and noticing things I hadn't seen before. Further along, I looked into the window of the snake wine shop and saw about twenty snakes looking back at me. I cringed at the thought of it. In the bottles with their mouths wide-open and fangs showing made them look even scarier than they had looked in the wild. There were also wines with birds in them. It must have been some weird witch doctor who had discovered this idea for the first time. How would you even come close to thinking of adding a bird or a snake to a cheeky little chardonnay? I send wine back if it has a small piece of cork in it. There'd be hell to pay if I was brought a bottle with a pigeon in it.

I reached the start of backpacker street and stood facing down it, amazed at how boring and dirty it looked during the day with everything closed and no people on the road. I had learned since being in Vietnam that you never see things in their true light until they're stripped back to their core. Take, for example, the room at the school: Four grey concrete walls with a tiny amount of light making them dull, eerie and lifeless. Add fourteen adorable smiling kids and the place comes alive with an energy that makes you forget where you are. I hoped that I would be able to retain these memories when I returned home and not slip straight back into my typically English way of thinking. This trip had taught me a lot about myself and about my life, and I was determined to return home a better person.

I stopped at a coffee shop around the corner from the hostel. I'd completed a huge loop around the surrounding streets, weaving up and down their grid-like layout and had managed to kill an hour consumed with my own little world. I ordered a coffee and sat outside. Another thing I missed about home was fresh milk. The only milk available in Vietnam is the condensed stuff which you pour out of a dusty hole pierced in the top of a can. I was looking forward to the flight home so that I could have a proper half cup of tea with proper milk in a silly little cup.

I got back to the room as Emily was coming out of the shower. I'd remembered the mass at Notre Dame that we'd previously talked about going to and decided today would be a good day to go. However, it started at half past nine and it was quarter to nine.

"Hello stranger, I wondered where you'd gone," she said. She was towel drying her hair loosely wrapped in a towel.

"I went for a walk," I replied unable to keep my eyes from her sexy body. "I woke up at five, and by seven I was going out of my mind. I left you snoring."

"Oh that again," she replied, smiling. "I've told you, I don't snore."

"Do you fancy going to the mass at the Notre Dame?" I asked.

"Do you feel the need to confess the sinful way you got me drunk and took advantage of me Harry?"

"Perhaps," I smiled. The way she was standing there looking me up and down wearing only a towel had me running at multiple sinful thoughts per second.

"I'll come with you if you give me something to confess," she said as she turned her back to me, dropped the towel and leaned over her bed.

Three minutes later, and she had something else to confess. Only a stupid man would refuse a naked Emily, and it was good to finally bend her over her bed rather than just repeatedly visualise it. Plus we were going to church, so it was a good time to get another sin in.

We left at ten past nine for the fifteen-minute walk to Notre Dame with the hustle and bustle of Ho Chi Minh now in full swing. When we arrived it was packed and the only option was to stand against the wall inside the door with the masses of others who were squeezing themselves in behind us. From the surrounding streets you see a beautiful red brick building with stained glass windows and two spires jutting high into the sky—it reminded me of a Walt Disney castle. The inside by contrast is surprisingly plain except for the paintings on the walls of the supporting columns. It's a huge space with seating for probably over five-hundred people, all of them filled on this occasion. At half past nine the music started.

By the end of the hour and a half mass both Emily and I wanted to kill me. Not being Catholic and the whole thing being in French was nothing short of excruciating. We tried to leave early but a wall of people prevented us from making a quiet exit so we were forced to stay. We left feeling exhausted having stood the whole time trying to work out what was going on, but at least it was another thing off the to-do list.

There was one positive though. I asked God to forgive me for all past and future sins with Emily, and I'm almost certain that I heard "OK my child. Sin excessively." coming from somewhere above me, and only God's talk like that, so it must have been him. Game on.

After brunch we decided to have a cyclo tour around the city as we hadn't been on one yet, and we felt too lazy to walk. We spent two hours squashed together in the back of the cyclo in the baking heat with the driver barking the names of places as we passed them. If nothing else it was a good laugh and if it wasn't for the Lonely Planet I'd brought we wouldn't have had any idea of what we were looking at. We had approximately three hundred and twenty near-death experiences as he crossed oncoming traffic without even so much as a hand signal. Motorbikes and cars braked or swerved to avoid us. At fifteen dollars for the two hours—which we later found out was five-times what we should have paid—it was a bit of a waste of money especially as we knew we were being ripped off, but were too scared of our growling driver to argue. It was an easy way to see Ho Chi Minh very quickly but the last time we'd be using one. Still, because of everything we'd seen, we managed to cross another load of things off the to-see list.

When we were safely back on solid ground Emily suggested the bowling alley so we headed there with her banging on about beating me, which inevitably meant she was crap. I hadn't done anything like bowling in about three years, my last experience being a beer and skittles night we had at work.

We arrived and put on the super-cool shoes they force you to wear so everyone looks as daft as each other. We were assigned lane one, which luckily was the furthest away and meant we only had one lot of people to laugh at us. Emily bowled first while I tried to find a ball my fat thumb would fit into. She scored a seven as I found a ball that nearly dislocated my shoulder when I picked it up. I watched a few other people bowl before I did, just to be sure I had the right idea, and then began my run-up.

As I reached the line, I unleashed the ball at such phenomenal speed that it went flying down the 'gutter' missing everything. Emily did a little dance that made her look stupid. Here we go again. She danced up to the line and threw the ball so slowly that even a tortoise would have had time to get out of the way. Strike! She seemed to think that points mattered and the speed of the ball didn't. She danced up, bowled again and scored an eight. I checked the screen above my head which told me she had scored thirty-three to my zero. I decided it was time to unleash 'Hotshot Harry' onto this alley. I charged up to the line, unleashed my propeller-like arm which sent the ball flying down the lane so fast that the two pins it did hit looked like they'd never stand back up again. By the end of the first game Hotshot Harry—playing more like Shitshot Harry—was still in his warming up phase and the final score was one-hundred-and-thirteen to eleven. This was a minor setback but nothing to be too concerned about as there was still plenty of time for me to show her how the game should be played.

Two more games later and it was three games to nil, with the total of my three scores not even match her worst one. I had to win the fourth game to avoid embarrassment so I decided to try and slow down my delivery to see if it made any difference. I slowly paced up to the line and threw the ball at roughly the same speed Emily did. Strike! Now Hotshot Harry was ready to play ball. With my next ball I scored four. I think the ball I was using was a little lumpy. I lost that game one-hundred-and-twenty-two to forty-five. I was improving but knew that it would take another twenty odd games before I got into triple-digits.

At six games to nil I feigned thumb dislocation to halt the humiliation. It was a poor excuse but any further embarrassment could have resulted in her never shutting up ever again. It was six o'clock by the time we left and we walked back to the hostel to see if the other two had returned. As we passed the Sinh Café we popped in to ask them what time they were due, and as it wasn't until nine o'clock, we had something to eat and went back to the room.

I added all the things we'd done during the weekend to my journal, embellishing my sexual prowess in case anyone ever read it. Emily kept asking if she could read my journal, but there was no way I was going to allow that, despite knowing she would love the way I described her.

The other two returned at half past nine, shattered after their long weekend and a long coach journey back. They both sat down on Emily's bunk and told us about Dalat, and the ludicrous amount of cycling they had done. They had both been too frugal with the sunscreen so Jude was very lobster looking and Angel having what she described as a glow. They stayed in a place that, in English, means 'The Crazy House' which they showed us a picture of in the Lonely Planet. The rooms were named after animals, and it looked like something out of a cartoon. They had stayed on the top floor, in the 'Eagle' room, which had two oddly-shaped beds and a big open fire which Jude became fascinated with and 'spent most of the evening burning stuff!' They had arrived very late on Friday night but had luckily made the reservation for two nights. They cycled all over 'super-hilly' Dalat from ten o'clock until four o'clock on Saturday, and then were so tired that they got room-service and went to bed. After Sunday morning breakfast they had been for a short walk before the long return coach journey. We told them about everything we'd done and by the time we'd finished talking it was eleven o'clock. I hadn't realised how much I'd missed them until we were all back in the same room chatting like the friends we'd become.

Our fourth school week began with a crash. The usual annoying alarm went off and as Jude jumped down from his bunk to shower he immediately collapsed into a heap. I heard a crash and then Jude whimpering as he tried to lift himself off the floor. He had forgotten about his six-hour bike ride on Saturday and his leg muscles were fucked. I lay there in hysterics, happy that karma had finally come to get the cock-a-doodle-bastard. With the force with which he had landed he was lucky he didn't smash straight through the floor and land at the breakfast table.

Jude and I went down for breakfast taking the girls' usual orders as we went. I had a new mosquito bite on the end of my nose that was driving me crazy. I'd applied some cream that Angel gave me but it wasn't helping, and I'd probably scratched the end of my nose off anyway. Jude told me that he and Angel had had a fantastic time and that they had discussed continuing this love affair when they returned home. They only lived about fifty miles apart and there was already talk of meeting each other's parents. I made him promise that I would be the best man at their wedding, but he said he was never getting married.

I felt good for having had so much rest over the weekend and was looking forward to school. Other than this past weekend—the best weekend of all—I almost wished the weekends away because I enjoyed being with the kids so much. They were so adorable and I was curious how I would deal with never seeing them again once this was over. We only had fifteen school days left. Somehow I had to desensitise myself to make leaving easier, but I didn't even know where to start. Each and every one of them in their own special way had touched my heart. The younger ones were cute, innocent and affectionate, and the older ones were enthusiastic, playful and had the utmost respect for me. When I closed my eyes I could picture each and every one of them individually with their faces beaming their beautiful smiles at me. It had amazed me how close we'd become without speaking a common language.

Emily and Angel joined us for breakfast with Angel walking like a cowgirl obviously in the same pain post-cycle pain as Jude. Either that, or she'd got some hippy-loving. Angel and Jude were noticeably more affectionate towards each other, which was cute. They made a lovely couple despite looking so scarily alike first thing in the morning.

Lou arrived at his usual time and as always looked pleased to see us. He asked us how our weekend had been, then he and Jude spent a while discussing Dalat. As we arrived at the school Lou turned to us and asked us if we would like to join him and his family for dinner on the Thursday evening before we went home. The way he asked was so sweet and so humbling that we all accepted immediately. He said he would let his wife know we accepted and would pick us up and drop us back.

As usual, each Monday brought renewed vigour to the kids and more adoration from each of us. The way they would walk into the school grounds so full of energy and life never ceased to amaze me. The way they would nearly jump out of their skin shouting "Good Morning Mr Fishy!" beaming their big smiles at me never failed to touch my heart. I had fifteen more school days with them and I was going to make sure I enjoyed every minute.

We led them into their classrooms to begin the day, as we had for the previous three weeks. We were halfway through the course and were starting to see real progress. I paired them off as I did every Monday and asked them to sit and talk using all the English they had learned. I wandered around listening to each pair enjoying the funny things I would hear as I approached. Binh had always been my favourite during these exercises because he would pay no attention to his partner until he noticed me approaching. Then he'd go into verbal overdrive. He was only seven years old and naughty in a good way. Every now and again when we were in the playground he would run up to me grab hold of my leg and force me to walk around with him hanging off it while he laughed his little head off.

We also went through the first two lines of Rock-a-bye Baby that I'd taught them the previous week and which a few of them nearly remembered. I was thankful for choosing that one as I wouldn't have stood a chance teaching the one about swallowing a fly.

As lunchtime approached I finished off the morning's lesson and dismissed them. As Binh passed me he made a buzzing noise as he pointed at my nose and then ran off laughing. As usual I met the others outside the room and we all walked down together to watch the children playing as we ate our sandwiches.

"How do you feel about leaving this little lot behind?" I asked the others.

"Are you going to start on about adopting them again, Harry?" Angel laughed.

"No, nothing like that," I replied, wanting them to take me seriously. "I've become so attached to them that I think it's going to be hard when the time comes to leave them." The others nodded in agreement.

"I know how you feel," Jude replied. "I've thought about it too and tried to work out what's best to do. You can't distance yourself from them because they'll notice. I tried it last week and they went quiet for the whole morning. It's hard to know what to do." He had thought along the same lines as me and had come to the same conclusion. I suggested an idea I'd had about giving them all a stamped addressed envelope so they could write to us if they wanted to. They agreed it was be a good idea as our options were limited and we would discuss it with Lou to see what he recommended.

At the end of the day when Lou dropped us off we asked him to come inside for a coffee. Once inside I explained what we'd discussed at lunchtime. When I'd finished spilling my heart out, and the others had added their own feelings, Lou explained that we were experiencing a very common emotion. He told us that when they first started the project it had been for three months, and volunteers would return home grieving as if they had lost a family member. The previous year they halved the teaching assignments to six weeks to try and combat the issues while still maintaining a worthwhile standard. Anything shorter would be pointless. He admitted that he had no definitive answer and that every individual would deal with it in his or her own way.

The kids would continue with their lives the way people in Vietnam have always done. They would grow up benefiting from and building upon the experiences we had shared with them. The Vietnamese way of life hasn't changed much in decades and nothing we had done would change that. We had to accept that this was just a job and however hard it was to leave them behind they would be better for us having been there. It was something we would feel even if we'd been on assignment in England, and apparently it becomes easier with experience. We would become better people having had this time away, and for the experiences we'd shared. I mentioned the idea of leaving them stamped addressed envelopes. Lou said that it was a good idea and that others had done the same in the past to help them stay connected. He also warned us that the Vietnamese postal system was very slow and that we should not expect anything for at least a month after posting. I went upstairs leaving the others to finish their coffees and lay on my bed with my head a mixture of opposing emotions. One minute I was feeling homesick and the next minute I was worried about going home.

The evening was spent trying to decide what we could do at the weekend so once again we went to the Sinh Café to ask for their advice. They suggested we flew up to Hanoi for the weekend so we could compare the south with the north. Apart from the flying part, it sounded like a great idea, and the Lonely Planet had plenty to do and see in Hanoi. We booked flights leaving seven o'clock on Friday evening and returning at nine o'clock on Sunday night. The whole thing cost us nearly two-hundred dollars but it meant that we would see more of Vietnam than just the south.

By the end of the week I'd taught them the third line of Rock-a-bye Baby and we spent most of Friday afternoon going over them repeatedly so they wouldn't forget it. I was doubled up in laughter at the way they just slotted in a Vietnamese word when they had forgotten the English one hoping I wouldn't notice. Of course my laughing at them only encouraged it more until we were left with something that was more Vietnamese than English. It was such fun listening to them laughing and seeing them so happy that I didn't care if they did exactly that at the recital. It would mean more to me to see them laughing than getting that daft rhyme right. It wasn't as if anyone listening would have a clue what they were saying anyway.

After we'd bid the kids farewell for the weekend we rushed back to meet the four o'clock coach to the airport. We made our way out of Ho Chi Minh listening to Emily read about Hanoi from the Lonely Planet as we excitedly planned some things we wanted to do. The flight was an hour, so we would arrive at Hanoi airport at eight o'clock, which was about another forty minutes away from the city.

CHAPTER FIFTEEN

We got to the airport and checked-in, and with hand luggage only were through to departures within fifteen minutes. I was becoming a little nervous about flying and was even more worried about the fact it was a local plane. Boarding was called shortly after half past six, and we made our way down some stairs onto the tarmac towards a plane half the size of a real one. There were two seats on either side which made me feel a little better as the plane would be lighter. I sat next to Emily with Jude and Angel across from us. I buckled up tightly as the other three watched waiting for me to make a fool of myself again. Jude had told Angel about my routine on the flight from Paris while we were waiting and she couldn't wait to see it. I lied and said I wasn't nervous as I sat taking in deep breaths in an attempt to calm myself.

I was momentarily confused as to why a milk float was pulling the plane backwards, but according to Captain Floppylocks Jude it's not a milk float, it's a truck because planes can't reverse. When the milk float had done its job and we reached the runway the engines started to roar. I sat back and closed my eyes praying, the perpetual fear that the plane's arse would hit the runway and we would all perish in a ball of flames. Our speed increased and we floated into the air. I was pleased with myself for remaining calm during the whole process despite getting cramp in my hands.

There was no tea and biscuits on this flight, nothing at all. The ride was quite bumpy but I remained fixed on my book and tried to ignore it. I knew I hadn't done very well because forty minutes later as we began our descent I'd only managed two pages. As we came into land it became violently shaky and I closed my eyes trying to regain some composure. The plane was rocking from left to right and I noticed the wing was moving way too much. I closed my eyes knowing we were going to be okay and to stop myself observing such frightening things. As we hit the runway the plane felt as if it was tipping to the right and going along on just two wheels. I thought that was the end until the plane suddenly jolted and we crashed down onto all four and skidded down the runway.

"Now tell me that was a bloody normal landing?" I shouted over to Jude.

"No Dude, that was a bad one, I'll give you that." The other two seemed to relax as the plane slowed down.

"We were definitely tipping to the right. I thought we were going to die. I'm getting the bus back," I laughed trying to humour the fear out of myself.

"I might join you," Angel said, as she finally leant forward. She might have been waiting for me to make a fool of myself but I don't think she'd enjoyed that either.

When the plane eventually came to a halt we caught sight of the airport and wondered if we were still in Vietnam, it looked fantastic. A huge building made primarily of glass and looking majestic all lit up. The doors opened and we exited onto the tarmac and into a corridor that led us to baggage collection. Seven minutes from the plane to the arrivals hall. Our quick getaway was scuppered by the fact we had to wait for everyone else before the coach would leave so we sat in arrivals and waited. The last person arrived at ten to nine and we had another forty minutes before we reached the city. As we left the airport and headed towards the city, we couldn't see anything due to the late hour and we spent the entire journey listening to the over-zealous driver playing with his horn.

When we arrived in the city—which has too much spare electricity judging by the number of lights—the coach guide said we would be arriving at the first accommodation. Being somewhat seasoned now we disembarked the coach at the second one primarily because half of the coach emptied into the first. As we climbed off the coach we had to ask the guide where he was talking about because we'd stopped outside a tailor's shop. He pointed into the shop and ushered us in. The checkout doubled as the reception desk—I had wondered why a tailor was still open at such a late hour. We had no choice but to book two double rooms as that was all that remained, and Emily and I were once again sharing. We made our way up to the rooms agreeing to meet back downstairs in fifteen minutes to go for food. Our room was nicely decorated with a double bed in the middle facing a massive chest of drawers with a television on it. At the other side of the room was another door that led to a generously sized bathroom, complete with a bath. I hadn't seen a bath in a month and couldn't wait to be in it. We dumped our stuff on the bed, had a quick wash and went back down to meet the love-birds.

We wandered down the street towards the lake, declining the local cyclo and motorbike drivers. As we reached the end of the road the huge lake revealed itself. According to our research, 'Hoàn Kiếm Lake is a freshwater lake measuring about twelve hectares,' which in layman's terms means its bloody massive and it ain't salty. The moonlit lake looked serene, and the still water mirrored everything around it. An illuminated tower stands in the middle with spotlights that create an orangey-red glow also reflected in the lake's calm water. The downside of the beauty-making lights was the number of mosquito bastards you could see everywhere. We consulted the Lonely Planet for somewhere to eat and decided upon a place called the Kangaroo Café that serves good English grub, and wasn't far away.

We found it with ease, walked in and sat at a table halfway down the restaurant, which doubled as a travel agent. I immediately noticed a T-shirt they sold and had to have one. On the back it had the following:

Toi Khong Muon…
(I don't want…)

* Buu thiep (postcards)
* Xich lo (cyclo)
* Danh giay (shoeshine)
* Keo cao su (chewing gum)
* Xe om (motorbike taxi)

* Xin moi di cho!!!
(Please go away!!!)

It was perfect. These were the things we were offered a thousand times daily, except for the shoeshine. I didn't want to start annoying the locals in Ho Chi Minh with only two weeks left, but it would make a novel memento. I ordered a beer, a cheeseburger and a large T-shirt, which ended up being multiplied by four

We browsed the trips that were available and were disappointed we wouldn't be in Hanoi for longer. There are loads of cool trekking adventures, and weekend trips to different islands for snorkelling, sunbathing, and beach and boat parties.

Massive cheeseburgers and big fat chips arrived, and they looked heavenly. I was so hungry I ordered another one, ignoring the others calling me a pig. I'd lost so much weight since being in Vietnam that the second burger was necessary for health reasons. After having to eat everything on the second plate to avoid 'I told you so' I felt stuffed. When we'd finished we made our way back to the hotel. It was nearly midnight and we were all exhausted after a long week and had planned on being back at the lake by six o'clock to watch the morning exercises.

I set the alarm on my phone for half past five, which is a ridiculous time to wake up. Emily and I got into our double bed, with CNN in the background repeating the usual nonsensical time-fillers in the absence of real news. Emily was instructed to stay-the-fuck-away due to the ungodly hour we had to get up, and we fell asleep with the television still on.

We were no sooner asleep when my annoying phone told us it was time to wake up. I awoke with a start trying to find the shut-up button before it woke someone. We got downstairs at six o'clock to see three of the staff asleep on the floor, and they grumbled something when we asked to be let out. We walked down to the lake with me in a bad mood for having to be awake—even the sun didn't get up this early. As we neared the lake we could hear horribly loud music that sounded like a scratched record being played on an ancient gramophone. When we reached the lake we were amazed by the five hundredish people standing around the lake doing—as Angel informed us—Tai Chi. To me, it looked like a bunch of people pretending they're playing with an invisible beach ball, but I'm apparently 'uneducated'.

The sun slowly started to peak through the buildings, casting a whole new serenity upon the lake with a mist hovering above it, making for some quite breath-taking photos. They did this routine every morning from six o'clock to seven o'clock and then went to work. I'm sure it is a great way to start the day, but surely an extra hour in bed is healthier. They paused midway and formed a large circle facing the back of the person in front, and proceeded to knock the shit out of each other's back with their fists; Or as Jude called it, 'massaging.' After a few minutes of this it was back to the beach ball. At seven o'clock precisely the music stopped and everyone left. I couldn't imagine a bunch of suit-clad workers lining the Thames each morning for those shenanigans, and if they did the back beating part it would end in a mass-brawl.

We wandered around the edge of the lake and were ushered into a coffee shop. We waited for ages for someone to come and take our order, and as I stood to go and buy coffees, the man who had ushered us to our seats ran out and made me sit back down. I asked for four coffees and he shook his head to say no. He explained out of the corner of his mouth that under Communist rule nothing can be served until half past seven. We had no other option but to wait, guessing everywhere else would be the same. At half past seven a loud bell rang out across the lake and within seconds we had four coffees. We had a breakfast of cheese, ham and bread rolls, and then returned to the hotel to shower, agreeing to meet back downstairs at half past nine. With the bath full of hot water and bubbles, I locked myself in the bathroom and lowered myself into the luxurious tub. It was worth the fifteen dollars just for the bath! It was twenty past nine before I reluctantly exited the bath, fingers and toes crinkled from soaking too long.

Our first stop was quite far away, and Jude had the idea of using motorbike taxis as the roads here seemed quieter and better equipped for travel. He had negotiated five dollars per bike with two of us on each, and I'd feared for my life as Emily and I climbed on with our driver having to edge forward to give us enough room. As we set off I held on tight to the back of the bike, squashing Emily between the driver and me. Somehow the bike managed to achieve what felt like Mach-2 as we veered left and right overtaking other road users. I closed my eyes and buried my head into Emily's back to make us more aerodynamic. After a few close calls with other traffic and a few emergency stops for no apparent reason we somehow made it. I climbed off the bike and looked to the sky. Not only had the big man granted me unlimited sins, he was also now looking out for me on the roads.

The Maison Centrale is a prison the Viet Cong used to hold American prisoners of war. The prison felt cold and damp, as we walked around peering through the small windows set into the solid doors of the interrogation rooms. There are tables on which they tied prisoners by their hands and feet to stretch their bodies, and vats they filled with freezing water to put prisoners in, and places where they hung people by their arms or legs for days at a time. Then there were the torture methods using bamboo inserted into places that made me cringe. Yes, one was their arse.

As we climbed some stairs, there were more rooms, each about seven metres square with shackles fixed to the wall, that held up to forty prisoners for weeks and months, secured by their ankles. The rooms would be hard pushed to hold forty people standing let alone lying down. There were pictures of rooms filled with severely malnourished people shackled to the walls overlapping each other on the floor. We followed the stairs back down and were led into a courtyard area with ten-foot-high walls surrounding it, with life-size figures of shackled men carved into them in meticulous detail. In the corner stood a huge wooden guillotine with a two-foot-long sharp blade that—even as a model—felt terrifying and sent a shiver down my spine.

It was a relief to end the hour-long tour. However fascinating the place was it had an air of cruelty and death that I didn't want to think about. It was a stark contrast to what we'd seen in the War Remnants Museum in Ho Chi

Minh which only detailed the 'Americans war crimes,' and showed that the Vietnamese had their share of cruel tactics.

After a delicious lunch of fly-free Pho we were once again back on the two-wheeled death machines. When we made it back to our hotel, the driver talked us into a food walking tour that evening, where we would get to taste the local delicacies. The fact it was a walking tour was of more appeal than his death machine, and we agreed to meet outside our hotel at seven o'clock.

We spent the remainder of the afternoon walking around the Old Quarter, which is a myriad of narrow streets filled with ancient houses and other beautiful scenery. We were acting like proper tourists, frequently stopping to take pictures and ramble through shit souvenir shops. The speciality coffee in Hanoi is 'egg coffee', which in a nutshell, is a cup of misbehaviour. Condensed milk is mixed together with a couple of egg yolks and then mixed with a spoonful of coffee grounds before being topped up with boiling water. I love eggs and I love coffee, but certain things should never ever be combined—coffee and eggs is one such example. I was once again called 'uncultured' and told to shut up. It actually tasted very nice, but I was never going to admit that.

At seven o'clock, Mr Deathtrap was outside waiting with his bike. My protests about this being a 'walking tour' fell on deaf ears, as we made the ten-minute journey to meet our guide. Rosie was one of the cutest little rays of sunshine I have ever met, her smile making me immediately warm to her. She led us around the Old Quarter describing the history behind the many sights we saw. After a half hour we stopped in a cute narrow street at a local restaurant where we sat outside on small blue plastic stools at a blue plastic table. Rosie invited us to try 'bia hoi', Hanoi freshly brewed local beer. Described as 'no-frills' it was scooped from a large bucket into half-pint glasses costing twenty cents each. It didn't take me long to calculate that I could get pissed for the rest of my life, and still have money left for burgers. I was glad I had anti-diarrhoea tablets with me, as beer from a bucket can't be too hygienic. Still, it tasted pretty good and it wasn't long before we were ordering another round. Rosie said the beer has no preservatives, effectively making it healthy so we made a focused effort to increase our hydration in the stifling humidity.

We were brought a selection of 'street food' comprising of barbeque chicken, fried rice and some other deep-fried stuff. We drank and ate enjoying the hustle and bustle of the narrow lane in which we were sat, chatting with locals and fellow tourists. By the time we were ready to move on, the additional beer we'd bought came to less than two dollars, and we agreed to head back to the Bia Hoi Corner when the tour had finished.

We continued down the lane and into another grid of windy tree-lined streets, with Rosie filling us in on the rich history of the fascinating structures we passed. We covered a loop around the Old Quarter and came to our second and final stop back in the Bia Hoi area. This place had even fewer frills than the no-frills place, with stools outside a shop that became a beer joint by night. We sat with the locals—who were cyclo drivers and motorbike drivers—and I was thankful I hadn't worn the T-shirt I'd purchased the night before. More beer was scooped and served, and Rosie crossed the lane to a free-standing cart to get us bánh mì—the famous Vietnamese sandwich. Salad and meat—which I hoped was 'meat' in the traditional sense—stuffed into a baguette and is delicious. The meat is heavily processed, looking something like spam, which at least meant it wasn't rat or dog or any other weird shit.

Rosie left shortly after ten o'clock knowing we had no intention of ending the tour back where it started. What started out as the strangest location to eat and drink—on the street, outside a shop, on stools that felt like they could give-way at any moment—turned out to be a great spot. Laughing and joking with the cyclo and motorbike drivers while the beer disappeared so fast you'd swear it was evaporating. At around eleven o'clock the owner wanted to close up and he brought the bill. I made the decision there and then that I was retiring in Hanoi. I couldn't imagine there are many places on this wonderful planet that four people can get pretty shitfaced for five dollars.

As we walked back to the tailor-cum-hotel, I finally found an ATM and ended up with a wad of Dong so big I couldn't get it into my pocket. My conservative withdrawal of a hundred pounds got me three million Dong, which came in fifty-thousand and one-hundred-thousand notes. It became four separate wads stuffed into four different pockets, leaving me with a bulgy arse and a couple of pocket-rockets—a pick-pocketers dream.

Back in the room and alone once again with Emily, with the mood lighting and lack of sobriety, it was inevitable. We both needed a shower after the sweat-fest of outdoor drinking, and being a third-world country it was our responsibility to be conservative with the water. Why waste water on both of us having separate showers? The fact that I hadn't warned Emily I was going to join her only added to the element of surprise, and when I was greeted with only a raised eyebrow, I knew she wasn't objectionable. I think she appreciated the help as I slowly worked up an incredible lather all over her sexy body, while she faced the wall remaining mostly still.

The original decision to be environmentally-friendly and preserve precious water wasn't helped by the fact we stayed in the shower for nearly thirty-minutes, with more filth than cleaning. We were careful not to waste any more water as I positioned her at the sink, enjoying the view in the mirror as I took charge from behind.

"Where did that come from, Harry Fisher?" She asked as we lay on the bed exhausted. "I didn't realise you had it in you." Neither did I! Perhaps preservatives were historically the issue, and healthy beer-from-a-bucket made me a less-shit lover.

I was brought out of my deep slumber early on Sunday morning to find Emily under the duvet waking me in a slow and controlled manner. Given one wish, it wouldn't be millions of pounds, it would be to wake like this every morning for the rest of my life. Although with millions of pounds, I could probably get this done a few times a day, but that internal debate could wait.

We met Jude and Angel downstairs shortly after eight o'clock, later than anyone had planned, but I was reluctant to get out of bed-heaven to begin with. We wandered out and fell upon a cute little café overlooking the lake for breakfast. We had pastries, baguettes, cheese and ham, and lots of other yummy French stuff, together with a couple of coffees each. The lake setting is very beautiful in Hanoi, and I would have been happy to hang out for hours watching the world go by. However, that earned me the 'boring bastard' badge and I was reminded that we weren't in Hanoi for much longer.

We paid the nominal fee to cross Thê Húc—a red wooden arch bridge meaning 'sunshine bridge'—to Den Ngoc Son island, home of the 'Temple of the Jade Mountain'. The bridge itself is a thing of beauty and the primary reason this is even an attraction, as there isn't much of interest on the little island. The bridge's picturesque reflection in the calm green-tinted water of the lake was the focus of many budding Photographers and plenty of silly people with selfie sticks.

As we wandered around the lake, I was once again taken by Turtle Tower. This structure looked so beautiful illuminated the previous night but not so much during the day. According to my Lonely Planet, it's more than one-hundred-years old, and was rebuilt when something that was two-hundred-years old was destroyed. Legend has it that a hero received a mystical sword from the Dragon King in his underwater palace. A fisherman caught the blade of the sword in his net and the hero found the hilt for the sword up a tree. The sword gave him great power and strength as well as increasing his physical stature when he used it.

After he won the war, he was on the lake in a boat, and a turtle came up and stole the sword and swam away with it, and the sword was never seen again. Turtle Tower stands in honour of the hero—Le Loi—and the magical turtle that is standing guard over it.

"Fucking turtle nicked his sword, whatever next?" The fact that I only took the piss out of that story for twenty minutes shows progress, maturity-wise.

Lunch was another magnificent bacon-cheeseburger overlooking the simply beautiful St. Joseph's Cathedral. It looked like a filthy version of the Notre Dame cathedral in Ho Chi Minh, but it was perhaps the gothic appearance that had me mesmerised. Inside by contrast was so bright and beautiful, with chandeliers above the altar illuminating the intricate detail of the lancet-shaped woodwork and the beautiful stained glass windows. I whispered a quick thank you to the big-man upstairs for the Emily-sin carte blanche, but He didn't acknowledge it. Nevertheless, he would know I'm maximising it because he is all-seeing, and he would appreciate the gesture of visiting him.

For the next couple of hours we continued along the lake back towards the Old Quarter. We browsed the local market with dried fish, fresh herbs and other weird smelling stuff. Then we passed an area where gravestones were being hand-carved, and I did consider getting one for Trev, but it would have been a pain in the arse to get home.

We passed the Bia Hoi area again and reminisced over the previous evening, and then into the traditional street market area of Thanh Ha. Emily regretted leading us down that street, as the sight of a bowl of headless frogs being gutted by hand, bodies still pulsating, was enough to challenge even the strongest stomach.

The chaotic traffic and my protesting stopped us going into Dong Xuan market, so we wandered down the adjacent streets seemingly segregated by trade or product: blacksmith street, toy street, shoe street, ribbon street, and my favourite street that sells only alcohol and cigarettes—or 'Man Street' as it became known.

We decided on an early dinner before heading back to the tailor-cum-hotel for our seven o'clock coach to the airport. We found a Pho restaurant—my recent addiction once I'd realised that the majority of restaurants don't allow flies in their soup—and slurped down a bowl, along with some delicious fresh spring rolls.

The bus collected us at seven o'clock from outside the hotel and we made our way to the airport. The scenery on the way to Hanoi airport was the opposite of the beauty surrounding Saigon, consisting of highways and roads surrounded by concrete buildings. Thankfully the city was near to the airport and was a relatively short drive. We arrived at quarter to eight and checked in as easily as we had before. We made our way through to departures and by half past eight were boarding the plane back to Ho Chi Minh. The seating was the same as on the way: Emily and I across from Jude and Angel, but with Emily in the window seat so I couldn't watch the wings flapping.

After a much calmer flight we landed into the darkness of Ho Chi Minh City airport at ten o'clock and were on the bus back to the city by twenty to eleven. We were exhausted after our long weekend, but glad we'd made the trip. Hanoi is a beautiful place where even without understanding its history, you can't help but notice the cultural differences between the North and the South. We arrived back at the hostel shortly after midnight and went straight to bed looking forward to being back at school the following morning.

Ten more school days to go!

CHAPTER SIXTEEN

Jude managed to beat his personal record by shaving three seconds off it to three-fifty-seven but he was still some way off beating mine. I crawled out of bed deciding to try and beat his record again but gave up once the hot water hit me. I was feeling drained after the long weekend and didn't want to be up yet. Emily and Jude had gone down to breakfast leaving Angel to dress while I showered. When we went down Lou was there drinking coffee with the other two. We mentioned our idea of the nursery rhyme reading, deciding to leave it until now in case we couldn't get the kids to learn them. We said we were planning to do it on the Thursday before going for dinner at his house. He agreed it was a great idea and said he would try and round up some people to come and watch, including the local paper. We made our way to school all the more excited that we had Lou's approval and looking forward to our penultimate week.

In the school playground Jude and I discussed the need to buy a football to make use of the goalposts. The kids slowly started to arrive beaming their perpetual smiles, and running up to us shouting "Good Morning!" before tearing off to chat to their mates. By half past eight, we were back in the familiar setting of the classroom reciting the previous week's work. I knew all too well that I wasn't a real school teacher, but I felt like I was one as I wandered around correcting and complimenting them on their work. I decided that I would look at teacher training options when I got home. It was the first time I'd truly enjoyed working and maybe teaching was my true vocation. It was a welcome change to wake up every morning looking forward to work—something I'd never experienced working on the bloody-fucking helpdesk. We went through the comedy recital of Rock-a-bye Baby with me laughing the whole way through, long past correcting them on the bits they were messing up. What I had now, instead of a group recital, was fourteen individual voices making up their own version, with the occasional English word thrown in for good measure. I decided to leave them to enjoy their own interpretation, laughing their little heads off, and to hell with the correct one. It's bloody daft anyway and their version was far more entertaining.

By the end of the day we had covered everything in the curriculum, and mastered a botched version of Rock-a-bye Baby. My new approach was much easier than trying to teach them the correct words and we were ready for an audience. When we were back at the hostel Jude and I went in search of a football which unfortunately led us back to the Bến Thành market. We made a pact to buy a football and leave immediately, avoiding all rats and livestock. We found a decent quality leather football which we bartered down from fifty dollars to twenty! They do like to try it on with the tourists but it was still good fun getting them down to a reasonably-sensible tourist price. Jude and I paid ten dollars each and said we would leave it behind when we left. We found a field a short walk from the market that seemed to be the place where all the young lovers congregated to snog up against the trees. After half an hour of kicking the football everywhere, except directly at the snoggers, we made our way back to the hostel to meet the girls.

When we arrived back they were both fast asleep so Jude and I crept in and waited, him reading while I added to my journal. I was starting to enjoy writing my journal rather than tediously playing catch-up on the days I'd missed. I was writing a few pages every day detailing what we'd been doing, etc. and putting down how I felt in myself, and in Vietnam. I found it to be of great help when I was having my emotional dips, as I could just deal with my feelings and forget them.

The following day, proudly armed with our football, we made the routine trip to school. Jude and I were like a pair of excitable kids planning our lunchtime footie match with the kids. When they spotted it they wanted to play immediately, and Jude and I were only too happy to oblige. By twenty past eight there were about thirty of us kicking it about when the girls spoiled our fun by confiscating it until lunchtime. We spent the entire morning watching the clock wishing lunch would come so we could get out for a proper kick about. In between we did some English.

We all charged down to the playground when lunchtime arrived after retrieving our ball from spoilsport-Angel. Then we headed for the goalposts and played everyone against everyone. It was carnage and every time Jude or I had the ball the kids came charging at us, and it eventually became everyone against Jude and me. As Jude and I kicked the ball to each other a wall of kids came flying. Before long the ball became irrelevant and the kids just came for us anyway. There was one point where I was trying to pass the ball to Jude and had kids hanging off both my arms and legs, and another around my waist. It ended up with us all toppling over into a big pile onto which the rest of the kids jumped. I had shit all over my face, in my hair, up my arms and all over my jeans and T-shirt— I looked like the tramp that had broken my nose. I spent the afternoon spitting out dust while trying to calm the monsters we had created at lunchtime. They were all proud of themselves for having beaten up Mr Fishy. With hindsight, the football wasn't our smartest idea.

When Lou came to collect us after school he was most amused at the state of Jude and me. Jude—who was just as dirty as me—had the football under his arm, and we looked like we'd been dragged around the playground, which technically we had. For once, the minibus was cleaner than us. However much the football beating damaged our pride and our clothes there was nothing that would stop us from doing it again.

The rest of the week flew by with football being played before school, at lunchtime and at half past two, our new earlier finishing time when we magically completed all the work we had to do. It was proving to be great exercise but was resulting in an awful lot of laundry. What had started life as a joy teaching nice little girls and boys English had become a crazy gang being taught some English in between the football carnage. We still, just about, had control over the classroom and were completing our English work with ease but it had become one big fun group—boys and girls, Emily, Angel—all playing together and having fun. We decided not to go anywhere that weekend, having already spent a fortune and wanting to spend our last full weekend enjoying the remainder of what Ho Chi Minh had to offer.

When the weekend came so did the shocking realisation that in one week this would all be over, and we would have said 'goodbye' to the kids forever. When we got back on Friday I made a list of everything I had to do before I left, the priority being postcards, as despite promising I hadn't posted a single one. I would send a few and blame the postal service. I also made a mental note of things that I mustn't do before leaving, such as getting drunk and ending up in bed with Emily again. We vowed to make it a weekend to remember, starting with Emily's suggestion of a pub-crawl, which came as a surprise following her vomiting dog routine the previous week.

At seven o'clock we made our way to La Cantina for Mexican food and Margaritas. I shuddered at the thought of any more of that frozen tequila-laced devil juice but was outvoted yet again. We arrived and sat at the same table as before and Emily immediately ordered the red poison. We settled on fajitas, ordering two beef and two chicken to share. We were drinking like we'd stole it, and before long it was doing the devil's work. We sat and chatted about each other and our lives back home: what we'd missed the most, what we hadn't missed at all, our families and our jobs, or in Emily's case job hunting. It was good to finally sit and talk about something other than Vietnam and the school, and I realised that we knew very little about each other. I knew nothing of Angel never having had the chance to sit and talk to her. She was thirty-four and had worked for the same solicitors firm since she had completed her exams. Her now ex-husband had left her, and when the divorce came through she quit her job, sold her house and went travelling. She had only arrived back in the UK three weeks before coming away with us, having spent a year in Australia. I told everyone my story: being offered the place on this trip, the fully embellished version of my resignation, bleaching my forehead, having my nose broken by a homeless twat, and all the other good stuff. None of them seemed surprised by any of the events, but were amused by my thematic life. Amazing how my misfortune has caused so much entertainment for so many people. I felt proud.

After our food and three jugs of Margaritas, we decided to move down to the Safari bar to have some fun with the bar games they had. Much to Angel's dismay, we spent the walk there arguing over who had to side with her, with Jude only caving because of her threats of no more sex.

We arrived at the Safari bar and it was jam-packed, with great music and an even better atmosphere. I noticed a girl who was dressed head to toe in leopard skin, who was an accident with a steam-roller away from making the perfect rug. With beers in hand and Jude already admitting defeat we made our way to the pool table and set it up. Angel broke potting the white as Jude stood shaking his head. Emily was next and also potted the white. My demands that the girls sit down was overruled. We were having such a giggle and for the first time I realised that I was going to miss all of them as much as I would miss the kids. Until then I hadn't thought about us going our separate ways once we landed in Heathrow and I told them that we should make a conscious effort to stay in touch with each other. They accused me of becoming a 'soft tart.'

At four games to nil Jude and Angel were making it far too easy for us and conceded defeat. We moved on to table football and it was good to finally play football in a controlled manner, instead of being beaten up by little people in a playground. At three-nil, we decided that Angel wasn't cut out for bar games as she had hardly even hit the ball once. She blamed her 'little men having legs shorter than the others' causing Jude to once again shake his head. When it was about forty-nil they gave up, and Jude became very vocal about boys versus girls at whatever we played next. Emily wasn't impressed.

After boys versus girls pool the girls conceded. After boys versus girls table football the girls conceded. After boys versus girls darts the girls conceded. We decided that the girls should try and outdrink us as that was the only challenge which couldn't be hampered by Angel. They gave it their best shot but in the absence of an impartial judge Jude and I decided they lost that too. We decided to continue our pub-crawl and made our way to Allez Boo for a change of scenery.

None of us managed to walk along the centre of the white line in the road, so by default the girls lost that too. There was a lot left to drink for. We arrived at Allez Boo and ordered more beer. The conversation was becoming silly which is always a good sign and we were laughing at Jude's jokes which was a definite sign that sobriety had passed. At some point we started dancing. My poor form was overshadowed by Jude's hippy routine which drew a lot of unwanted attention from fellow drinkers. He seemed to be able to disappear into his own little world with his eyes closed and head wobbling like it could fall off at any moment. The atmosphere was brilliant and everyone was so friendly. It amazed me that everyone I'd met in Vietnam was so relaxed and friendly. People you'd talk to in bars were interested in you and what you were doing there, and you'd spend ages exchanging stories with complete strangers.

At one o'clock we literally fell out of Allez Boo to move to our next and probably final bar, The Guns & Roses bar. Angel and Emily switched to vodka while Jude and I stuck to beer.

My suggestion of food was met with great relief and suddenly everyone was hungry. We left at quarter to two, and found a mobile kebab van which I initially thought was a mirage. The others warned me not to but once my eyes were locked on there was nothing that would stop me. In retrospect, they were correct. What I ended up with was unworthy of calling itself a kebab, or even calling itself food. The first hair I picked out of it was assumed to be mine, but upon closer inspection it was white and I am fortunate enough to not have any white hair yet. When I found a few more and noticed that they were still attached to the meat, I kicked the kebab into the busy road, narrowly missing a motorbike. I am a naïve and occasionally stupid man, but I know of nothing with human-like hair that belongs on a kebab spit. I never want to know what that shit was, and know beyond any doubt that it was not something you would find in a butcher's in England. If there was ever a time that I have ever eaten dog, cat or rat, that was it.

When we were back at the hostel and chief door banger Emily had done her job, Minh let us in, smiling and now used to our drunkenness. There was to be no vomiting tonight although I was still close to it as a result of the 'kebab' and sleep was only minutes away when we got to our room.

I woke up next to Emily with zero recollection as to how she got there. The sheets were pulled up over our heads and we were completely naked with our legs intertwined. My head was pounding, and my heart joined it. Through my painful eyes, I still felt incredibly turned on by what I was seeing. Emily's perfect body was wrapped around my pathetic little frame. As I was moving the sheet around to get a better view, I realised I was being watched. "Enjoying the view Fisher?" How was I going to talk my way out of this?

"I am actually, but less importantly, how the fuck did we end up like this?" Emily closed her eyes, and her big cheeky smile told me nothing. She lay there moving her leg up and down mine, smiling, her eyes still closed. She leaned in and kissed me. The fact that Jude and Angel were somewhere outside of our man-made tent was of little concern. Our kissing became more passionate and frantic, and our hands were all over each other. "Get on top of me Harry," Emily whispered.

"Get a room you two!" However hard Emily and I believed that the sheet was an invisibility cloak, it wasn't, and Jude had halted the inevitable hangover sex. I sheepishly pulled back the sheet to just below my eyes to find Angel and Jude sat perched on Angel's bed smiling.

"I think we should go to breakfast Jude," was Angel's attempt at masking my embarrassment. "Harry, your boxer shorts are over here in case you were wondering." While the other three found this hilarious, I buried myself back under the sheet and pretended that it was an invisibility cloak.

"Lucky escape Harry," whispered Emily. "But before we leave Vietnam, we need one more night where I can properly get what I want." Her confidence was a crazy turn-on, and I needed her to get what she wanted, whatever the fuck that entailed. *What happens in Vietnam stays in Vietnam!*

"Wait for us," said Emily. And as quickly as she had started it, she ended it.

We walked out together desperate to find food. Jude suggested a Pho restaurant he'd found that Bill Clinton ate at when he visited in the year two-thousand. It was a complete tourist trap, and it wasn't as if Bill would still be there, but it sold Pho, which is the best hangover cure in Vietnam.

The restaurant is next to Bến Thành Market, and by the time we had reached it at tortoise-pace we were starving. We walked into Pho 2000, creatively named after the year Bill was there, and were amused to see how his visit had been milked. There's a big sign on the yellow wall announcing that this was "The noodles of Vietnam" and "Pho for the President". I couldn't wait to see what the toilet had written on it. On the wall was a picture of Bill wearing a suit reading the menu with his mates. No sign of Hillary, perhaps she was in the market next door getting some shoes or a puppy.

The food was average, and the only redeeming quality of the restaurant was the legacy of their famous visitor many years prior. I still managed to inhale two bowls of Pho which helped cure my hangover enough to keep the grim reaper at bay for a while longer.

Jude and I were coerced into joining the girls in the market after lunch so they could get some gifts to bring home. I moaned for the sake of it, and only agreed to go so long as we didn't go near the food area. I didn't want to incur the costs of spraying my Pho all over a stall or three.

As we started navigating the narrow walkways, the heat and humidity made me feel nauseous and the previous night's alcohol was coming out of every pore. I lasted less than ten minutes before I had to evacuate for fear of puking, and sat outside drinking bottles of ice cold water, getting ripped off each time I bought another one.

An hour later, the three time-wasting fools appeared with a shit load of multi-coloured bags full of crap they'd bought. I'd decided no-one was getting anything, intent on playing the charity card to gain their understanding. The truth was that I couldn't be bothered buying needless shit for the sake of it.

We made our way back to the hostel to dump their junk, and to have an afternoon siesta. The previous night's booze was taking its toll on the other three now, and I needed a nap. Angel and Emily decided we were going to go and see the water puppets again that evening, and we bought our tickets on the way back.

At half past three, after a short rest, we made our way over to the Golden Dragon Water Puppet theatre. I was really excited to see the show again, which was in stark contrast to the whinging I'd done the previous time. I'd read about the history of it since we'd booked the tickets, and bored the shit out of the others with every little detail I'd read. Fortunately for Jude and Angel, they weren't subjected to the pointless shoe-shopping beforehand.

We were lucky enough to get great seats again, and from the third row we were close enough to see everything in intricate detail. The lights lowered shortly after half past four and the music started in time with the dragons hovering across the water. I could see the expression on Jude and Angel's face matching exactly how I'd felt when I realised this wasn't going to be a shit waste of time after all.

An hour later we left the darkness of the theatre with the sunlight making us squint as we reached the street outside. Angel and Jude loved the show as much as Emily and I had, and despite the whole performance being in Vietnamese the skill that goes into it is remarkable.

Despite my protest, Angel got a couple of cyclos for a leisurely near-death ride over to Bui Vien Street to find the local Bia Hoi area. The nineteen-seventies looking street sign announcing 'Bui Vien Walking Street' told us we'd arrived, as did the party music. We were man-handled—or woman-handled—by an old lady who was at least three-hundred years old onto red plastic stools, and brought four mugs of beer faster than it could have been scooped. Clearly this is an area where no words are needed, and if you're western you must be in search of immediate beer. The fact that the place we were sat looked like a health hazard in every way possible was of little consequence once the beer was put on the sticky table in front of us.

The first beer was literally forced down in an attempt to combat the fog caused by the previous evening, but the cadence picked up, and before we knew it the shit-talk was back. An array of deep-fried things arrived without being ordered, as did more cigarettes when I ran out. She also brought a plate of crab-things from the shop next door which the others sat whacking with a hammer and smashing with pliers to get tiny morsels of food out of.

Fucking silly carry-on. Not only was the three-hundred-year-old woman psychic, she was also a great salesperson.

With partial drunkenness making another appearance, and even with one-eye covered to ensure my sight wasn't playing tricks on me, the bill came to one-hundred-and-fifty-thousand Dong—about six quid. It was little wonder that she still had to work!

Sunday was spent buried in the Lonely Planet trying to find things we hadn't yet done, which ended up revolving around eating and drinking. The first stop was a café called Sozo for breakfast, where they educate under-privileged kids in the food industry to give them a better opportunity for employment. Once again I was humbled by how wonderful these kids were and how they fully embraced the opportunities they get.

For lunch we went to Huong Lai, which is another restaurant for disadvantaged youths. This building was pretty hard to find with only a dimly-lit sign marking the entrance. It was a more traditional restaurant with mostly local customers, with a couple of tourists dotted among them. The pork and prawn fresh spring rolls, braised pork with pepper, and rice with tofu and vegetables were demolished at speed and worth every Dong.

As we left Huong Lai I got my first opportunity to witness what I learned to be 'tropical' rain. Basically, an ocean gets emptied out of the sky with little or no warning, and everywhere smells like a sewer while getting momentarily drowned. There was nothing we could do while we were walking around soaked through, although I did try and moan myself dry. An hour later and you'd never know it rained at all except for the new ponds created where potholes used to be.

CHAPTER SEVENTEEN

Monday started with a heightened awareness of the fact we only had five school days left. The morning was solemn with all of us washing and dressing in near silence. We had breakfast together before Lou arrived to collect his four unhappy teachers.

"Why are you lot so quiet this morning?" he asked rhetorically.

"We're sad that it's our last week, Lou," Angel replied speaking for all of us.

"I understand. The last week is hard," he replied. "But keep smiling and playing football, the kids are enjoying that. They are also excited about the nursery rhyme reading on Thursday, and I'm expecting a good turn-out. I have two local papers coming to photograph the event too, they love our interaction with Westerners."

Once in class they immediately formed their pairs and had their little chats. I was like a Cheshire cat beaming at how much they had progressed. In the five weeks I'd been teaching them they had picked up everything so well.

When they had finished I immediately began to work on the rhyme, giving myself half an hour so that I could still cover the curriculum before lunch. They started reciting their version which immediately sent me into hysterics, but I did my best not to let them see it as it only encouraged them. I read the proper rhyme out line-by-line praying they would pick it up as quickly as they did everything else. By the time my allocated thirty minutes was up we were only about halfway there. They had at least stopped slotting in Vietnamese guess words.

Lunchtime brought about the usual round-ball carnage with every single pupil and teacher playing in ever-changing teams aiming at the one goal. I decided to go in goal to save being beaten up again, but that didn't stop them. They worked out a tactic whereby whoever had the ball would aim it straight at my crown-jewels. By the end of lunch I was battered, bruised and covered in crap and resigned to being the 'chosen' one they were going to brutalise every day, and I loved it. If I had my way I'd have binned the curriculum and played footie for the remainder of the week.

At the end of the afternoon I once again went through the rhyme and by the time it was three o'clock I could tell they were becoming bored of it. I was hopeful of it being 'alright on the night' on Thursday, but the way I was speed-teaching them had lost its fun.

When Lou dropped us off we went to buy stamps and envelopes for the kids. I also bought some postcards, three for Nicola and three for my parents, which I backdated and scribbled notes on. We spent the rest of the evening addressing envelopes, sticking stamps on them and putting writing paper inside. I realised that I'd finally learned all of their names as I wrote them in the top left-hand corner of each envelope. We went for something to eat choosing a noodle place we'd found near the hostel. We hadn't been very adventurous throughout the trip so vowed to only eat Vietnamese food from hereon in.

Tuesday brought another wave of sadness as we made our way to school and realised that we would be making the trip only three more times. Jude was even more crushed by the fact I managed to shower in three forty-seven which he admitted he would never beat. The kids came as they usually did but instead of playing or chatting with each other they stayed close to us. Whether it was a coincidence or not I'll never know but they had become increasingly clingier, not wanting to leave our side and holding our hands or standing so close that we couldn't move. It was very endearing but it was making it harder as we could detect our own emotions in them.

I tried to make light of it by play fighting with a few of them but they just weren't interested which made me feel like a child battering bastard for punching them in the first place. At half past eight we went through the now simple task of persuading them into the classroom. For the last couple of weeks Jude didn't even have to call them because they just formed their lines at half past eight. When we were in the classroom, silence immediately fell and I struggled to retain focus. Their usual smiles seemed to be strained and the things I was teaching them didn't seem as much fun. I decided to banish the curriculum and move onto Rock-a-bye Baby the old way. Fuck it! As I read the lines they repeated them. So I read them all four lines at once, hoping they'd throw them away and use the make-it-up-as-they-go along tactic. Even that failed as they more or less recited the whole lot word for word. I wanted my monsters back so I could laugh with them but they weren't interested. I replaced a few of the words myself with their names; Rock-a-bye Binh, on Xuan tree Thang, Dung the Hung Lan, the Bich Phuong Chi. This had them in hysterics so I sang it again using different names in different places until I had used all their names. I pointed at them and off they went back to their good old way of making a complete shambles of it. That was the way we were going to do it on Thursday, I was past caring. Oh, and it would contain the word 'pants' too. It was so much better seeing them happy and laughing than sad and disinterested. I had no trouble completing the day's curriculum after that, and each time they looked unhappy we did our nursery rhyme and normality resumed.

"What the hell were you up to in there?" Jude couldn't wait to be out of class and ask me, literally falling over the kids who were in his way.

"Just having a bit of banter with my little mates," I told him smiling, having had my best day yet. My class had become a little unruly towards the end of the day with each new thing they learned having to be hollered back at me followed by over-excitable laughter.

"What was all the laughing about?" he asked.

"You'll find out," I replied, laughing and tapping my nose.

Thursday eventually arrived and started with the usual showering, dressing, breakfast and minibus routine. We were all dressed in our Charity T-shirts looking quite smart. When Lou dropped us off he said he would see us at half past two for the nursery rhyme recital. I was feeling a little apprehensive given I had something unexpected up my sleeve. After a quick knockabout on the football area the kids were in class and we began the day. I was trying hard to forget that this was the penultimate day as every time I did it sent my head into a spin. We completed that morning's work and spent the last hour before lunch going over our nursery rhyme. We always managed the 'Rock-a-bye Baby on the treetop' bit correctly and that was the most important line. They were also doing the last line 'And down will come baby, cradle and all' correctly, looking up to the sky and dropping their heads to the ground as if watching the cradle and the baby smash down. However, the middle two lines had become a free-for-all, with fourteen kids shouting all sorts of illegible bollocks at the top of their voice.

We went to lunch happy and excited at the anticipated reaction, knowing that if nothing else it would be fun. Jude and I played football with them but kept it calm knowing some parents and the newspapers were going to be there and we didn't want to be coated in shit.

We rushed through the afternoon having to be outside and ready to go for half past two, and completed everything in time for one more practice run. It was as good as it was going to get, and we were ready. I went around each of them and tried with moderate success to smarten them up and tuck themselves in. At quarter past two I walked over to Jude's class and called him outside. Emily and Angel came to join us, and we used a variation of coin tosses to work out the running order: Jude was up first, me second, Emily third and Angel last.

We led them downstairs, high fiving them as they passed, and they formed the lines they did each morning. Lou arrived and was surprised by the fiftyish people already there. He had told the kids one morning to tell their parents but didn't expect this many to turn up given the time of day. There were also three photographers that Lou said were from the local papers.

At half past two, Lou was briefed on our order, and he welcomed everyone in Vietnamese. When he finished he gave Jude the nod, and Jude led his class out in front of all the people now totalling about ninety. I felt for Jude as he definitely had the hardest job. My clowns and I were up next and the nervous excitement was tumbling around inside me.

"There was an old woman who lived in a shoe!" Jude's class was amazing, all speaking clearly and in time with him. As the parents stood smiling with cameras flashing all over the place they recited the whole thing perfectly. "And she whipped them all soundly and sent them to bed!" The applause made by such a small group was phenomenal, and as the cameras continued to flash they all took a bow. He had even taught them to bow, the bastard! I felt physically sick as Lou nodded to me and I led my group to the front.

I stood frozen, trying to calm my nerves; Jude's class were a hard act to follow. "Rock-a-bye Baby on the treetop!" The chorus rang out at a nice pace, and everyone was in sync. So far so good. All of a sudden the giggling started and fourteen different voices rhythmically spouted off something that wasn't the rhyme. I saw Lou, Angel, Emily and Jude laughing, and felt my face starting to glowing with embarrassment, with cameras flashing everywhere capturing my 'finest' moment. They looked up to the sky still giggling their little heads off. "And down will come baby, cradle and all," while they followed the fictional cradle-bound baby to an expedient demise. The applause seemed even more deafening as they all stood giggling and making shapes for the cameras going off everywhere. I looked around the crowd and there wasn't a single person who wasn't laughing. Maybe we weren't so bad after all, and it wasn't as if anyone understood a word of it anyway!

"How am I going to top that you fucker?" Emily whispered as she passed me smiling.

"That was fantastic," Jude said, as I walked over to join them, "that explains all the laughter I've heard all week. Where the hell did you get that idea from?"

"I'll tell you later," I smiled as Emily's group was about to start. Lou introduced them as Emily stood ready.

"Old Mother Hubbard!" they began. Emily's class continued with the same perfect prowess as Jude's group, and they too sounded wonderful. Angel was starting to become fidgety and nervous knowing she was next up. I was pleased I was in the middle as first and last are definitely the hardest spots. "So the poor little doggie had none!" The applause continued as the cameras flashed and they too took a bow. Why hadn't anyone let me in on this bowing shit?

Angel was introduced and began on cue, "Little Miss Muffet!" Again, they were all perfectly in time and spoke slowly. I looked into the crowd and saw every single face beaming from seeing their little one perform so well. I was so glad we'd done this because as well as being good fun it must have been a treat for the parents to see their kids perform. I felt honoured as I stood admiring this beautiful group of people, who likely had no idea what any of us were even saying, enjoying the show. "And frightened Miss Muffet away!" The applause was equally as deafening as the kids took a bow and posed for their pictures.

Angel came over to us and we had a group hug. Never in my life had I thought I would be involved in such a wonderful event and we were all so elated it was over. Lou came over with the newspaper men to take a group picture. A shiver ran down my spine as I thought back to the pictures on the wall in Rob King's office. I was going to be in a picture hopefully hanging on a wall being admired by someone standing where I had been less than two months earlier. I was overcome with emotion and pride and felt a solitary tear rolling down my cheek. We stood there with nearly sixty kids and Lou as crowds of people photographed us from every angle. Lou took our cameras and took pictures with them too so that we would have our own copy. It was one of the proudest moments of my life and something I will never forget.

When we'd finished having our pictures taken the kids found their parents and brought them over to meet us. We stood in a line as a queue of people formed to meet us. It was so incredibly humbling that these beautiful people were so eager to shake our hand, smile and thank us. The kids would say our names to their parent or parents beaming their gorgeous smiles, so proud to know us.

It was half past four before the last person left the school grounds. I was so overwhelmed that I turned away from the others to regain my compose, but I needn't have bothered as everyone had separated to have a moment to themselves. Lou gave each of us a big fatherly hug telling us how proud he was, and that sent another kamikaze tear down my cheek.

"And down will come baby, cradle and all!" I shouted as my head fell from the sky in the same crashing motion the kids had done it. Comedy was all I had to lift us out of this. It seemed to work as the others looked at me and shook their heads.

"Where the bloody hell did that come from?" Emily asked as she wiped away her tears.

"No idea," I replied. "I'm just glad I didn't do the one about the woman who swallowed a fly!"

We made our way back to the hostel in the minibus. As he dropped us off Lou said he would be back again at seven o'clock to collect us for dinner, giving us just under two hours. I went straight upstairs and crashed-out on my bed. I was tired and emotional and needed to have a power nap. I think the others did the same but I didn't stay awake long enough to find out.

We put on our nicest clothes (jeans) to look presentable for our dinner. While we were on the journey over Jude asked me how my Rock-a-bye Baby had become so 'different'. I explained that when I first started teaching it the younger ones used to fill in the gaps with Vietnamese words. The more I laughed the more they did it. Then this week I'd tried to do it properly but they got bored, so I'd effectively made a complete bollocks of it by accident. I told them that I hadn't expected theirs to be so polished, and demanded to know why no one had mentioned the bowing thing.

"This is my wife Lauren, and these are our two children, Than and Cara." We arrived at Lou's house and his wife and two children came to meet us at the door. The house is an older wooden structure quite a way out of the City. The living area was very simple and had been set with cushions on the floor with a tablecloth in the middle where we would eat. There were no chairs or furniture apart from a tall chest of drawers where a small television stood. Off the living area was a kitchen, a bathroom, and two bedrooms: one for the children and one for Lou and Lauren. It was quite challenging to squeeze us into the one room but once we were sitting it was nice and cosy. The kids sat staring at us not sure what to think but soon loosened up when I started making faces at them. Lauren brought us a small glass of something and we said "cheers" as we drank it. It was very dry and made my face shrivel a little when I first tasted it, but it wasn't too bad.

"So, how have you found everything?" Lou asked, obviously wanting us to talk for the remainder of the evening. We looked at each other wondering who was going to go first and very soon the conversation was in full-flow. We covered a vast array of topics including the things we'd enjoyed and the few things we hadn't. After about fifteen minutes Lauren called Lou into the kitchen and then the food started to come. With us all sitting around the food Lou told us that they must say grace. We put our hands together and closed our eyes in respect for our hosts while they said a Vietnamese prayer. When they had finished, they removed the lids from the bowls to reveal a feast enough for a village. There was rice, vegetables, noodles and small pieces of meat that I hoped were chicken. We picked up the small bowl set in front of us and helped ourselves to modest portions as our hosts waited for us to finish. We ate in near silence, except for frequently complimenting Lauren on the delicious food.

After a few helpings, I'd had enough. The food was lovely; proper home-cooked food as opposed to the fast-food we'd been living on. There was still enough food to feed us all over again, but no matter how hard he tried Lou couldn't convince us to eat anymore. If the room were any bigger I would have collapsed into a slumber and stayed there.

"I can't believe you travel so far to pick us up and drop us off every day," I said to Lou.

"I travel into Saigon after I drop you off in the mornings and work in a shop from half past eight until half past two. It works out well for collecting you and dropping you back before I go to work in another shop until six o'clock. It's not too bad," he replied. I swear my chin hit the floor.

"So you don't work for the charity then?" Angel asked.

"No. I'm a volunteer like you, but I've been with them for many years." We'd all incorrectly assumed he worked for the charity given he took such a keen interest in our wellbeing.

"Wow," I replied, still in shock. "So have you always worked in Ho Chi Minh?"

"No, I worked for the Americans for five years during the war as a mechanic. They paid me very good money but when they left they discarded us and we got into a lot of trouble with our Government. They took away our National Identity cards which stopped me from working, and they consider us traitors because we didn't side with the Communists. If I am caught working I could face a huge fine or go to jail. That is why I have to keep changing jobs." The man who did such great work for this charity was basically a criminal in his own country. We knew nothing about Lou, the man who had been our friend and looked after us since the day we arrived. We were so wrapped up in ourselves and our experiences that we hadn't even asked about him. It made me feel like a proper narcissistic little shit!

"So, the Americans used you until they left, and then did nothing to protect you." Angel wanted to know more.

"Yes. They promised to look after us but once they left Vietnam they did nothing."

"Bastards!" Angel replied on behalf of all of us.

"They had their reasons," he replied. "Whether they were here or not the same thing would have happened." He had clearly found the ability to forgive and forget. Lou continued talking openly about his experience to his captive audience.

CHAPTER EIGHTEEN

"I'll take you fine people back then," Lou said at ten o'clock as the evening drew to an end. We thanked Lauren and the children for their kindness knowing we were unlikely to see them again. I was in awe of Lou and his life, and what an amazing man he was to be doing charity work for the country that has rejected him. His kindness knows no boundaries and he has the heart of a lion. As he dropped us off we gave him a hug and thanked him for a wonderful evening.

We talked until past midnight, still in shock at the things we didn't know about Lou. It was Jude's idea that we should buy him and his family a gift for everything he had done for us, and for our wonderful dinner, a job that we delegated to the girls.

Our last school day began with faces that would turn milk sour. We'd all been dreading this day for the past few weeks and hoped it would never arrive. As much as I couldn't wait to be home to see my family and Nicola, the thought of leaving Vietnam and the kids hurt my heart. I finished showering feeling the weight of those two opposing worlds on my shoulders. I walked back into the room to find the other three still in bed chatting. I sat on my bunk trying to persuade them to get up, but even calling them "lazy arseholes" didn't work. I started packing my stuff for the day into my rucksack: stamp addressed envelopes, coconut candy, remaining pads and pens, and my camera. I went down for breakfast on my own, and when Lou arrived at twenty past seven there was still no sign of the others.

"Are you OK?" he asked, studying my face.

"I'm feeling kind of nervous," I replied.

"Just don't wish the day away. Whatever is going to happen is going to happen regardless of whether or not you enjoy it." He was right. I had written the day off before it had even begun.

"We're having a long lunch today. England versus Vietnam!" I said to Jude as he arrived and poured himself a coffee. I noticed he had forgotten the football, so I ran back upstairs to find it. I was determined to make today the best day yet. As I walked into the room Emily was sitting on the bed wrapped in her towel crying. I sat down beside her and gave her a hug.

"Listen to me. We have to enjoy every second of today because like it or not it is our last day, and we can be miserable all day or we can have a party." I felt her nodding as she reached up to wipe her eyes. "We're going to have an extended lunch and we'll deal with three o'clock when it comes, OK?"

"OK," she replied as she broke into a smile. "When did you become so wise?" I smiled and decided against telling her that I was repeating what Lou had said.

"Now get your lazy arse up!" I jumped up, grabbed the ball and ran back downstairs. I noticed that Jude was also looking a bit more positive and guessed that Lou had given him the same pep talk.

We boarded the minibus ten minutes later than usual and made our way to school. I tried to lift our spirits planning our big international football match—fifty-something Vietnamese against England's four! When we arrived at the school Lou turned and gave us all the same pep talk he had given me. Emily gave me a look that screamed 'fraud' to which I had no recourse. We climbed out of the bus with Lou agreeing to collect us at half past three so we could have a little longer to say goodbye.

We walked into the playground where a few of the kids were already waiting. I told the others to complete their morning sessions as quickly as they could so we could have a long lunch. At half past eight they were all in their lines for the last time waiting for us to escort them to their classrooms. Once I had settled my lot in class we did a rendition of Rock-a-bye Baby loud enough for the whole school to hear. I knew the others could do with cheering up and I knew that would work. A few moments after we finished I heard "There was an old woman that lived in a shoe" blaring out and started to laugh realising Jude was on to it. "Little Miss Muffet" followed, and then "Old Mother Hubbard." We walked into the corridor and all did Jude's nodding-dog-hippy routine before returning to class.

The rest of the morning was spent speed-learning the remainder of the curriculum which they did with ease. At eleven-thirty we released them into the playground, and Jude and I went down to make some goalposts with piles of stones about thirty-metres away from the proper ones. We would have made them further apart but we might have lost someone down a hole. There were about forty of them choosing to play and we didn't stand a chance from the outset. Jude and I kicked off and I went straight for a shot which missed by a mile. My little mate Binh scored the opener and I was called all the names under the sun for letting a seven-year-old beat me. We spent the next twenty minutes playing like this with them running straight at us when we had the ball, punching us in the stomach or the crown jewels to regain the ball. One little fellow from Jude's class managed to dribble the ball straight through Jude's legs and then pushed through them himself. While it was funny we were being slaughtered. It was carnage because no one knew who was on which team, but we didn't care. At twenty past one after a two hour lunch we had to call the game to an end. None of us wanted to but we knew we had to complete the last part of the curriculum. It was a typically hot day and the sweat and dust combo left us all caked in shit. It was easy to spot the ones who hadn't played because they looked immaculate by comparison.

When we were back in the classroom the sadness hit me again. This was going to be our last session and somehow the kids picked up on my feelings and went deadly quiet. I knew I had to snap out of it as we had about an hour and a half left together. I pulled out the two boxes of coconut candy, which was more than enough for three pieces each, and passed the boxes around. Being the polite and wonderful children they are the first box came back with some left in it as they'd only taken one each. We began the afternoon reviewing what we'd covered, and I paired them off for one final walk around to hear them conversing. They were amazing and I felt so proud at how much we'd achieved.

At twenty past two, I was satisfied that we'd completed everything and brought the lesson to a close. This was when my fear of the uncertain kicked in. I pulled out the envelopes I'd prepared for them and told them what they were for. I said that if they wanted to they could write me a letter and I would reply making us 'pen pals'. One-by-one I called them up to the front of the class to collect them, like some sort of shitty awards presentation. As I handed over the first one to Binh—my little favourite—he grabbed me around the leg, like he always did, and held on not wanting to let go. This was when I felt the first tear falling down my cheek. I looked up trying to stop any more tears falling and to regain composure. I put my hand around his head to return the hug. He walked away and sat down looking sad. My heart ached, but I had to carry on. Most of them gave me a long hug but some of the older lads just shook my hand and said "Thank you Mister Fishy." I would miss being called that. By the time the last one had received his envelope I was desperately fighting back the tears. I walked out of the room and took a few deep breaths. I walked down to Emily's class where she was giving out her envelopes and was pleased to see she was still smiling. I wandered along to Angel's class and saw her much the same as I was. Jude was handing out envelopes and high fiving in his typical carefree manner.

"Harry," Angel shouted, "come and take my class picture, and then I'll do yours?" As I walked towards her she was wiping her eyes. "That was so bloody hard."

"I know," I replied putting my hand on her shoulder. "That's why I had to get out of my room." I took her camera as she walked over and stood behind her class. As they screamed something in Vietnamese I took the picture. As we walked into my class and they saw the camera they were all beaming their beautiful smiles at Angel. I stood behind them and Angel took a few pictures.

"That brings us to the end of our time together. You have been wonderful children and each and every one of you will remain in my heart forever. I will miss you all." I've no idea how much of this they understood, but in my self-pity I felt like saying it anyway. "I wish you all the very best in your lives. Thank you for making Vietnam so wonderfully memorable." And with that, all that was left was the word I hate the most: "Goodbye."

As soon as I finished Binh was around my leg. I pulled him away, knelt down and put my arms around him. He was the one I wanted to take home with me but knew it was illegal. He walked away sobbing as I watched him leave. One-by-one every single child, even the older ones who had shaken my hand, put their arms around me. When the last one left I slid backwards down the wall and sat with my head in my hands feeling quite lonesome. I had spent the last six weeks with these little angels, and they consumed a large part of my heart. Now they were gone and the most I could hope for was a letter. I looked around to see Emily walk into my room sobbing. She came over, sat next to me and we had a little cry. It was only when I saw Lou standing outside the room that I realised it was half past three.

Lou dropped us back at the hostel saying he would be back the following morning at eleven o'clock to take us to the airport. We went up to the room and Emily and I lay on my bed, and Jude and Angel on Angel's. Emily's sobbing was eventually replaced with snoring which was a bizarre, yet welcome transition. I lay there thinking of all the up and down emotions I'd been through, wondering if

I could do something like this again. The six-week experience had been truly amazing and had surely made me a better person, but the pain I was feeling made me question whether or not I could do it again.

Jude and Angel woke around seven o'clock having fallen asleep shortly after we got back. Sleep had evaded me, partly because of Emily's tractor-like noise and face-tickling hair, and because my mind was in overdrive. I was getting excited about going home and returning to some sort of normality, but had no idea what I would do and was still confused as to whether this charity thing was for me or not. I would possibly have to pause the sainthood for a while.

When Emily finally woke she was feeling a little better. I considered beating her to death when she moaned about my shoulder being uncomfortable, but instead dumped her head on the pillow and started to pack my stuff. Apart from what I was wearing that night and for the journey, everything was haphazardly stuffed into my rucksack. When I'd finished packing I wrote my journal, writing pages and pages of the events of the last two days: the recital, dinner with Lou and saying goodbye to the kids. One minute I would be laughing at my own genius and unique humour, and the next feeling sad. It had been a turbulent few days and I wanted to write everything down while it was still fresh in my memory.

We discussed what we could give Lou as a way of saying thank you and settled on putting ten dollars each into an envelope knowing it wasn't a lot to us, but would be to him. We also realised we'd forgotten to leave the football at the school, so Lou would get that too.

Hunger was calling and we decided to treat ourselves to a nice dinner on account of it being our last night, and still having a shit load of Dong to waste. We ambled around the streets taking in the humid evening air for the last time. We passed backpacker street, which had seen plenty of shenanigans in the previous weeks, and the bars that had seen the demise of each of us. I knew I would return to Vietnam one day and imagined myself walking these same streets with Nicola. Or Emily perhaps. My love for Vietnam had grown exponentially with every passing day, and the people, the food, the everything was something I would miss. I looked down at Emily whose arm was linked through mine and was glad she was with me on this trip. Besides all the times the sexy little minx had seduced me against my flailing will she had been a great friend, and someone who I'd really enjoyed spending time with. *What happens in Vietnam stays in Vietnam!* Jude and Angel were also the perfect addition to the group, and despite all of us being quite different, the group dynamic worked perfectly.

It was a pleasantly airy restaurant on the ground floor of The Saigon Hotel that was chosen for its posh look. We knew it wasn't very Vietnamese and was an overpriced tourist trap but it was a fine setting for our last dinner together. We ordered wine and a selection of Vietnamese dishes to share and talked about the trip from start to end: our adventures, the kids, the school and everything else that came up. We discussed whether or not we would do something like this again and how we felt about going back to life as we knew it—nine to five jobs with zero satisfaction. We had a great night filled with laughter, great food and drink and good conversation. We left the restaurant shortly after midnight marginally pissed, having had a bottle of wine each, and slowly walked back to the hostel. We passed the young lovers in the park snogging against the trees where Jude and I had tested the football, passed backpacker street once again, and passed the massage and reflexology place where I got trampled on the day we arrived—so many places and so many fond memories. We sat up talking until after two o'clock, exchanging email addresses, phone numbers and home addresses, promising to stay in touch. Words alone would never be able to describe this trip, and these were the only people who would fully understand the experience.

I woke at six o'clock feeling excited at going home but dreading the journey. I couldn't wait to see Nicola and my parents. I couldn't wait to be back in my own bed in my own house and most of all, I couldn't wait to have a proper cup of tea and a bacon sandwich. When we'd discussed returning to normal life I realised that I didn't have a clue what I was going to do. I knew opportunities like this didn't happen very often, and I wasn't even sure I would be able to afford to do another one. The thought of a new job was nauseating, and banished from my mind.

Up at seven o'clock I went straight into the shower and made the most of it as it would be a long time before the next one. I left the other three lying in bed chatting and went downstairs, bringing my journal so I could continue writing in peace. As usual Minh was there with his morning paper and when I sat down he brought it over to show me the photographs of our recital. There was a half-page with five pictures—one of each class and one of us all together. The one of my group was fantastic and had been taken while the kids were all laughing, and the one of us all together managed to capture every single person smiling. The group picture was fantastic and every single person was smiling. I asked Minh where I could buy a copy of the paper and rushed over to the shop he pointed to. I bought ten copies and rushed back up to the room to show the others. I gave them two copies each, stuffing the other four into my rucksack as we crowded around the paper. The timing was perfect, and we were elated to have copies to take home to show off; a day later and we may never have seen them! I went back downstairs for my second attempt at breakfast and journal writing. Minh brought me some coffee as I sat spilling my heart into my journal one last time. The others eventually arrived one-by-one so I put my journal away and we sat eating eggs, drinking coffee and watching the world pass by. I swore that I would never eat another egg as long as I lived.

At half past ten Lou arrived armed with four copies of the newspaper, and with a big smile he laid one open to show us. He looked so proud and we didn't have the heart to tell him we had already seen it. Minh quickly realised this and smiled as he brought Lou's coffee. Angel handed over the envelope with our collection and when he opened it he was close to tears.

"I can't accept this," he said as he handed the envelope back. "You are all very kind but I can't. I'm sorry."

"Please Lou. We're not taking it back and you've been so good to us," Angel said with a smile. He wiped his moistened eyes, folded the envelope and put it into his pocket.

"You are very good people with such big hearts," he said. If anyone had the big heart it was he. "It has been my pleasure to know you." We each handed over a stamp-addressed envelope asking him to keep in touch.

"If you ever come back to Vietnam you will be guests at my home with my family and me," he said as pocketed the envelopes. I almost considered taking him up on that and staying there.

"That is very kind of you Lou," Jude said. "We also want you to have this." He handed over the battered football with a smile.

"Thank you again," he said inspecting the beaten up old ball.

We sat and chatted with Lou until eleven o'clock arrived. No words were needed as we went upstairs, gathered our belongings and vacated. I took one last look around the room, the overload of visuals messing with my emotions. There were the fun drunken nights, the early morning starts courtesy of Jude's stupid alarm, a bit of slap-and-tickle with Emily and one too many vomiting dog routines. So many great memories in such a tiny space. As much I wanted to get home, part of me wanted to stay and do it all over again. As Lou loaded our stuff onto the minibus it felt like only yesterday he was doing the same at the airport. As much as we'd fit into our six weeks it had passed too quickly. Minh and Linh stood outside and waved us off as we moved from the pavement onto the road. We all sat quietly taking everything in as we slowly left Ho Chi Minh for the last time.

We made our way to the airport in near silence only speaking to point out the weird and wonderful things we saw along the way. When we finally arrived at the airport we exited the minibus, collected our belongings and said our goodbyes to Lou. He gave each of us a big hug as we said our tearful farewell to the man who had become a father figure to us all. We waved him off as he disappeared into the distance.

We queued at the Air France check-in desk for our flight to Paris, looking forward to ridding ourselves of our rucksacks. We managed to book four seats together in the centre aisle and made our way through customs and into the departure area.

At half past two we were called to our boarding gate. Jude and I sat in the middle with Angel and Emily in the aisle seats. Jude offered around the melatonin tablets which I gladly accepted hoping I would sleep the entire journey.

At three o'clock we started to move towards the runway. I made myself comfortable and prepared for the worst part of the journey. As the engines roared we began the slow acceleration bumping along the runway. Whoever tarmacked the bumps into this runway should be taken aside and had the shit kicked out of him! He must have used an elephant as a rolling pin. The shite that goes through one's mind when death is imminent. As I was forced back into my miniature child-sized economy seat the momentary weightless feeling kicked in. 'Please don't let it hit its arse on the ground!' I begged the God I believed in that week. The fear that as an aeroplane poked its nose into the air for take-off its big arse would hit the runway creating an awful mess because of the luggage. I closed my eyes and waited for the explosion. When it didn't happen, I let out a small woohoo which obviously came out a little louder than it had existed in my tiny mind, as I could hear people laughing a few rows ahead. As we headed into the clouds I tried to look out of the toilet-seat-sized window to see the last of Vietnam.

"SSssshhhiiittt!" The drowsy land that the melatonin took me to didn't stop the words forcefully leaving my mouth. However, the fact we'd just fallen from about thirty thousand feet to within inches of the ground in the space of ten seconds more than justified it. Jude being the smart arse that he is reminded me that it was *mild* turbulence, and I reminded him that if he didn't shut up I'd give him a *mild* broken nose! The turbulence continued for another seventeen hours, even though in reality it was probably closer to seventeen seconds. I needed to relax and kept reminding myself that I was safer in the air than on the ground, although the ground was a much more appealing option, even if it meant I had to swim home. Having only ever managed to earn a five-metre swimming badge when I was six, I didn't fancy my chances.

Eventually the plane levelled out and the seat belt light went out. With the hard part over I began to relax and grabbed my book praying for sleep. The coma I'd hoped the melatonin would bring never arrived, and I'd only read fifty-seven pages in six weeks. Just as I made myself comfortable, my child-sized bladder decided to give me a wake-up call. As I stood in the long queue I looked out the window at the tranquil, cotton wool-like clouds. I knew that if I did decide to jump out to test their fluffiness it would end in tears, but the curiosity must be something that even the most seasoned traveller has. The stupid ones at least. I eventually made it into the toilet having to pirouette like a jewellery-box doll between closing the door and setting myself into the peeing position. With my purple-headed warrior tucked safely back where he belongs, I moved to the baffling mission of washing my hands in the dollhouse sink. Why does plane soap have a glue-like consistency which is impossible to remove? To compound the misery, the drizzle that comes out of the sink means that to do it effectively could take up to three hours, and that's if you can figure out a way to keep the bloody-fucking water running for more than five seconds at a time.

I made my way back to my seat whinging to myself about the whole toilet visit wondering at which point in my life I'd become a whinging little bastard. I settled down and put on the in-flight entertainment. Crap. I picked up my book and tried to read it. Crap. The duty-free magazine, a three-day-old Evening Standard and some in-flight crap were also rejected. Everything was crap. I fidgeted and moaned like a three-year-old wanting the flight to be over, and we were only an hour in. "Fuck it, I'm going to test the fluffiness of the clouds. Let me out!" If I had a pound for every time someone told me to stop moaning I'd have been a millionaire before they served the inflight dog food.

Three hours gone, nine to go. I had indigestion from the 'Coq au Vin' I'd eaten. Cock oh what? I'd never tasted cock in my short life, but I'm sure it would have tasted better than that shit.

Five hours gone, seven to go. I'd had a total of thirteen minutes sleep, give or take thirteen minutes. I'd fidgeted away about three-hundred calories and felt thinner. Maybe I could start the trend of in-flight fidgeting instead of that daft shit they show you to do on the video. 'Raise your arms above your head and twist your neck like a fucking meerkat.' What do they think we are, midgets? I tried to do it nearly breaking my own neck and bashing the call button. "Can I help you, sir?" "Eh?" "You pressed the call button." "Oops, sorry, I was trying to prevent deep vein thrombosis."

Six hours. Maybe if I start an in-flight fight they might land the plane early and let me off. Maybe I'll punch the air steward dude with the silly bleached blonde hair. He was beginning to annoy me with his stupid dark roots. The others were starting to annoy me laughing and joking as if this was some sort of fun. I tried telling them to shut up but that met with a chorus of "shut up, Harry." Halfway there. I'm going to go insane.

Six hours and ten minutes gone and I've started on the wine. I'll drink myself to sleep and wake-up nice and fresh at the other end. Blondie bad roots was becoming my friend because he kept serving me wine. His hair was quite nice after all, and there was a nice contrast of bleached and dark co-existing on his pretty little head.

Eight hours gone. Blondie root boy started becoming a bit too familiar and I kept him sweet by flirting with him. Worst-case scenario, I would give him Jude's phone number. The wine was working because Angel said she caught me smiling. I denied it.

Nine hours gone. I offered some Dong to the guy whose newspaper I fell through the middle of, but was brushed off with an upper-class grunt. The altitude sickness was making me slur and I was refused more wine and told I'd be arrested when we landed in Paris if I didn't return to my seat. The visuals of being stuck in a cell with a Frenchman wearing a silly little hat was an unappealing option, so I did as I was told.

Eleven hours gone and I woke with a bit of a headache. Breakfast was being served and my request for a bacon and egg sandwich fell on deaf ears. My luck had definitely run out on this flight. Blondie bad-roots bastard didn't even acknowledge my request for some painkillers for my altitude-sickness.

The seat belt sign came on, and the captain announced that we were forty minutes from landing. I couldn't wait to be back on solid ground and swore I'd never set foot on another plane. I would have to get my Sainthood in Britain, or somewhere I could travel to by boat.

With ten minutes to land I was feeling a bit shitty from my mini-binge and lack of sleep. The trolley dollies were told to be seated as we circled Paris way beneath the clouds. This bit was nearly as bad as take-off as we were flying way too slowly for it to be possible for us to stay in the air. It would be just my luck now to have somehow survived the whole flight only to meet my maker this close to home. The plane started to shake violently as we came in to land and I closed my eyes and held onto the armrests for dear life. I kept my eyes closed until I felt the ground beneath us as we bounced onto the runway and the roar of the engines made a desperate attempt to slow us down before we shot off the other end. I opened my eyes as we were welcomed to Paris and taxied towards the gate. The relief was overwhelming and I knew that unless something ridiculous happened now—such as the pilot accidentally pushing his foot onto the accelerator instead of the brake—we were home and dry.

After a few minutes the plane's engines went off and the quickest-out-of-the-seat bullshit began. The doors eventually opened and the stampede started. I walked off the plane with the nervous anticipation of seeing Nicola again. I'd been so bad at keeping in touch with her while I was away.

We boarded the connecting flight shortly after we'd arrived at the gate, and settled into our seats for the short-hop to Heathrow. My head was starting to clear and I was feeling sad that our adventure was coming to an end. I wondered if we would keep in touch or if it was one of those conversations people have. We'd become so close during our short time together, being in each other's pockets for the past six weeks. I promised that I would stay in touch no matter what and genuinely meant it. Not for the first time that week I was called a 'soft tart'.

My sentiments were soon shelved as the engines started to roar and I went through the motions of praying that the planes arse would make it off the ground. As per usual nothing happened and my pointless fear became other people's amusement. I fell asleep within a few minutes of taking off, finally relaxed and completely knackered.

It was thud of the plane plummeting into Heathrow's tarmac that woke me. I felt so relieved to be home and the journey over. From the minute we'd left Vietnam I just wanted to be home and back in familiar surroundings with familiar cups of tea. I more or less ran off the plane and went straight to the first toilet on the four-hundred-mile hike between plane and luggage. I gave myself a mini sink-shower and felt and looked a lot better. I'd managed to get a pretty good suntan over the previous six weeks and told myself that Nicola would likely start drooling when she set eyes on me. This overly confident bullshit soon disappeared as the nervous excitement set in. I wondered how it would be when I saw Nicola, and if things would still be the same as when I'd left. We had only been together a few days, and as much fun as it had been, we'd been apart for a long time, and I'd been bad at keeping in touch while I was away. The drunken nights with Emily also left me feeling unsure as to how committed I was, but I was fortunate that God had given me a free-pass with Emily, so technically I hadn't done anything wrong, religion-wise.

We said our goodbyes after we'd collected our luggage and vowed to stay in touch. We had a group hug followed by individual hugs, with an especially long one between Emily and me. She and I had become the closest of all and I was going to miss her.

"What happened in Vietnam stays in Vietnam," she whispered as she kissed my cheek and walked away smiling.

As I walked through the trillions of people awaiting their special someone, our eyes met through the crowd. She looked more radiant and beautiful than I remembered, and I thought my heart was going to explode through my chest. The ten metres between us seemed to take an age, and the Hollywood-like slow-motion action as she threw herself at me felt surreal. It was the most amazing feeling as our cheeks touched and we held each other close. Our romantic moment was interrupted by "get out of the way for fuck sake," so we shuffled a few metres to a clearer space and resumed our embrace. Ten minutes must have passed without a word being spoken, which was certainly a first for me.

"Hey you," she whispered in my ear, her warm breath sending a shiver down my spine. That movie-like shit phrase normally grates on me, but this time it just worked.

"Hello gorgeous, I've missed you," and I genuinely meant it. I hadn't realised just how much I'd missed her until that moment. My butterflies soon turned into complete adoration for the person I was holding and I felt as though I belonged in her arms. At the back of my mind, I was curious if she could do the rodeo thing like Emily, but that was just a fleeting moment of weakness, and I was just as curious as to whether she had bacon and fresh milk.

Eventually we decided we couldn't stay in Heathrow forever and made our way towards the car. She told me that my parents had decided against coming as I'd be too overwhelmed, which internally translated into my dad not wanting to miss some documentary that was on the telly.

Nicola drove me back to my house and it was exactly how I'd left it only cleaner. She admitted she had been in the night before tidying for my return and took great pleasure in telling me what a messy bugger I am. I rang my parents to say hello and to let them know I'd arrived back safely, and accepted my mum's dinner invitation for the following evening. My mum, in time-honoured fashion had a good old cry even though she tried to disguise it with one of her 'I've just got a bit of a cold' ploys. Nicola made me a cup of tea and we took it up to bed. I wasn't sure what I wanted more, Nicola or the tea. My total exhaustion made even drinking the tea a chore and within minutes I was asleep.

When I woke up the following morning it was only to hear the rattle of breakfast being brought in. *I will marry you right now.* Nicola had made me the biggest fry-up I'd ever seen. The endless rashers, sausages, mushrooms and beans that covered the plate were hastily disposed of. Oh, and the eggs that I said I'd never eat again were also demolished.

"Anyone would think you hadn't eaten in years the way you murdered that," Nicola laughed as she took the tray away. I felt like I hadn't, and it had been a long time since I'd tasted anything so good. I lay back in bed drinking my tea when moments later Nicola returned wearing nothing but a Brazilian!

For the next hour differently pitched yahoo'ing-like-a-cowboy noises rang through my small house every few minutes. Nicola's inaudible groan was uninspiring and only made me try harder. And thankfully yes, she can do rodeo as well as Emily! And she had bacon and fresh milk.

We spent the rest of the day lounging around the house catching up on my trip and the past six-weeks, and enjoying each other's company. My initial fear that things may have changed was soon forgotten, and things were better than I ever could have imagined.

"So did you meet any nice girls when you were there?" Nicola randomly asked later that afternoon. *What happens in Vietnam stays in Vietnam!*

"Of course not," I replied, deciding my drunken encounters with the evil temptress weren't worth mentioning. "Why would I want anyone else?" The smooth-talking well-delivered lies worked a treat and the conversation thankfully ended there.

Later that afternoon Nicola went back to her place to change for our dinner engagement at my parents'. I'd spoken to my mum a couple of times during the day and I was looking forward to seeing them. On one of the occasions I spoke with her she told me my father was helping her in the kitchen which, although I thought was a joke, turned out to be true. "It must be a special occasion if he's managed to get off his backside." she joked. I realised how much I'd missed everyone, especially my mum, and was looking forward to one of those dinners that only a mother can create.

We settled on taking a cab so we could both have a glass or three of wine and arrived at my parents' house shortly before seven o'clock.

"Did you buy a watch that works, Son?" my mother asked as she opened the door. Bloody typical. The tears were in her eyes before my arms even made their way around her. I thought she was never going to let go. There's something about the feeling of your mother holding you, something so unique that always makes you feel so safe and secure. It felt good and for the first time ever she let go before I did. "Hi Nicola love. I guess you're the reason he's on time."

Nicola laughed, "Hi Alice, how are you? I forgot to bring those brochures, I'll drop them over in the week."

"What brochures?" I enquired whispering so my mum didn't hear.

"Nosey," Nicola smiled. "Just something I told your mum I'd get her last week."

"Last week?" It later transpired that Nicola had been around every week while I was away. "Hi Dad!" I said as I walked over to him.

"Welcome back, Son," he said as he put his arms around me. There were only two times I could remember my father giving me a proper man-hug: the night before I left and this. Was he getting soft in his old age or did he need to hold on to me because his legs were weak? "We've missed you," he said. I could feel the lump in my throat as soon as the words had left his mouth, that heaviness that instantly means tears will follow. He kept hold of me for what seemed like an age, which was handy because it gave me a chance to wipe my eyes. It was the most special moment I could ever remember, and if I could guarantee he'd be like this every time I went away I'd rarely be in England. As he released his grip he held me at arm's length and smiled. At last I could feel my father's pride. I'd spent my life trying to gain his approval and at last I had it. Of course, I could have been wrong, and he could have been checking my face for scars.

We had a lovely chatty family dinner primarily focused on my trip. I told them everything from the second I left until the minute I fell into Nicola's arms at Heathrow, and they couldn't have been more receptive, intrigued and excited. I showed them all the pictures I'd taken on the small screen on my camera, with running commentary from my father about the screen being too small. I always had an uneasiness at my parents' house, primarily because my father never seemed impressed with anything I did. This time it was different and I didn't feel like I was an embarrassment to him. He was different. I was different. It just worked and even when it was late and I started feeling exhausted I still didn't want the evening to end.

CHAPTER NINETEEN

The next few weeks flew by and everything started to return to boringly normal. After only a month it felt like the whole Vietnam trip was a distant memory and I wasn't ready for the memories to disappear. There had been occasional emails exchanges with the others from the trip, and a few pictures that kept the dream alive. Nicola and I were getting closer by the day and spending all of our free time together.

I had my pictures printed and sent them to Rob hoping he'd put one up on the wall next to the ones that had inspired me, and when he called me to tell me he had, I was so proud and so excited.

"Trev, guess what?" I had to call someone.

"No." I'd chosen the wrong someone.

"Rob called me to say he'd put our picture on the wall."

"Who's Rob?"

"From the charity."

"Fuck off."

And this unfortunately became the reaction from all of my friends after I'd bored them rigid with my story. In fact, if I even mentioned anywhere outside of England I was told to fuck off.

I was rapidly running out of money and reluctantly knew I needed to find myself a job. The sainthood would have to go on hold while I found a way to pay the bloody mortgage. After much deliberation, humble-pie eating and a great deal of unnecessary drinking I managed to score myself a six-month contract doing the only thing I knew.

"Hello Helpdesk, Harry speaking."

When Marcus left to join a competitor Trev was apparently the only suitable candidate. How is beyond me as he has the people skills of an ape. It goes to show that it's not what you know, or who you know, it's the bullshit you can talk. Nevertheless, it worked in my favour as Trev got me a six-month contract in my old job at my old desk on a great deal more money, and it was a great deal easier working for Trev than that other fucking idiot.

"I've reset your password to 'welcome'." It felt like I'd never been away, and my head was being bounced off the desk frequently. Lunchtime still revolved around the Builders Arms and its pool table, and the job still seemed to revolve around changing passwords for the multitude of fuckwits that worked there.

"No, it's all lower case. w – e – l – c – o – m – e." My outlook on life had changed but my tolerance for fuckwits hadn't. I knew city life wasn't for me, but the years of being paid so well had made me dependant on the money, and I was left with little choice.

It was slowly but surely driving me mad, and after a couple of months the unexpected happened.

"Harry speaking."

"Harry," came the familiar voice, "it's Rob. How are you?"

"Rob!" I replied rather too excitedly. It was the first phone call I'd received during work hours for weeks where I hadn't wished the caller a slow and painful death. "I'm great, how are you?"

"Fine thanks Harry. What are your thoughts on the Congo?"

"The dance that old people normally do at the end of the night at weddings?" I asked wondering what the fuck a charity dude was ringing me about dancing for.

"That's the conga," Rob laughed. *Fucking idiot.* I quickly typed 'Congo' into Google.

"Oh, sorry. You mean the Democratic Republic," I read straight from the screen, "formerly known as Zaire." I couldn't have made it any more obvious if I'd said 'Wikipedia. The Free Encyclopedia'.

"Yes Harry," Rob laughed. He was a smart man and knew what was going on. "You were quite enamoured with a picture from the Congo on my wall." *The tiny low-roofed classroom with the blond guy and the chalk on the walls.*

"Oh, that Congo! I know nothing about it whatsoever Rob, but you already knew that." I laughed trying to make myself sound less like an idiot. "Why?"

"A spot has come up for a twelve-week mission and I thought you might be interested."

Ahh, fuck.

Printed in Great Britain
by Amazon

74868064R00193